'My name is Templa

SIMON TEMPLAR: a/k/a The Saint, the Happy Highwayman, the Brighter Buccaneer, the Robin Hood of Modern Crime.

DESCRIPTION: Age 31. Height 6 ft., 2 in. Weight 175 lbs. Eyes blue. Hair black, brushed straight back. Complexion tanned. Bullet scar through upper left shoulder; 8 in. scar on right forearm.

SPECIAL CHARACTERISTICS: Always immaculately dressed. Luxurious tastes. Lives in most expensive hotels and is connoisseur of food and wine. Carries firearms and is expert knife thrower. Licensed air pilot. Speaks several languages fluently. Known as "The Saint" from habit of leaving drawing of skeleton figure with halo at scenes of crimes.

By Leslie Charteris

(Parentheses indicate alternate titles)

LESLIE CHARTERIS

ANGELS
OF
DOOM

INTERNATIONAL POLYGONICS, LTD.
NEW YORK CITY

ANGELS OF DOOM

Cover: Copyright © 1989 by Roger Roth.
Library of Congress Card Catalog No. 89-85724
ISBN 1-55882-055-8

Printed and manufactured in the United States
of America.
First IPL printing November 1989.
10 9 8 7 6 5 4 3 2 1

TO
HUGH CLEVELY

CONTENTS

vii

ANGELS OF DOOM

CHAPTER I

HOW SIMON TEMPLAR MET JILL TRE-LAWNEY, AND THERE WERE SKYLARKING AND SONG IN BELGRAVE STREET

THE big car had been sliding through the night like a great black slug with wide, flaming eyes that seared the road and carved a blazing tunnel of light through the darkness under the over-arching trees; and then the eyes were suddenly blinded, and the smooth pace of the slug grew slower and slower until it groped itself to a shadowy standstill under the hedge.

The man who had watched its approach, sitting under a tree, with the glowing end of his cigarette carefully shielded in his cupped hands, stretched silently to his feet. The car had stopped only a few yards from him, as he had expected. He stooped and trod his cigarette into the grass and came down to the road without a sound. There was no sound at all except the murmur of leaves in the night air, for the subdued hiss of the car's eight cylinders had ceased.

Momentarily, inside the car, a match flared up, revealing everything there with a startling clearness.

The rich crimson upholstery, the handful of perfect roses in the crystal bracket, the gleaming silver fittings —those might have been imagined from the exterior.

So also, perhaps, might have been imagined the man with the battered face who wore a chauffeur's livery; or the rather vacantly good-looking man who sat alone in the back, with his light overcoat swept back from his spotless white shirt front, and his silk hat on the seat beside him. Or, perhaps, the girl. . . .

Or perhaps not the girl.

The light of the match focussed the attention upon her particularly, for she was using it to light a cigarette. On the face of it, of course, she was exactly what one would have looked for. On the face of it, she was the kind of girl who goes very well with an expensive car, and there was really no reason why she should not be sitting at the wheel. On the face of it . . .

But there was something about her that put superficial judgments uneasily in the wrong. Tall she must have been, guessed the man who watched her from the shadows, and of a willowy slenderness that still left her a woman. And beautiful she was beyond dispute, with a perfectly natural beauty which yet had in it nothing of the commonplace. Her face was all her own, as was the cornfield gold of her hair. And no artifice known to the deceptions of women could have given her those tawny golden eyes. . . .

"So you're Jill Trelawney!" thought the man in the shadows.

The light was extinguished as he thought it; but he carried every detail of the picture it had shown indelibly photographed on his brain. This was a living

photograph. He had been given mere camera portraits
of her before—some of them were in his pocket at that
moment—but they were pale and insignificant things
beside the memory of the reality, and he wondered
dimly at the impertinence which presumed to try to
capture such a face in dispassionate halftone.

"On the face of it—hell!" thought the man in the
shadows.

But in the car, the man in evening dress said, more
elegantly: "You're an extraordinary woman, Jill.
Every time I see you——"

"You get more maudlin," the girl took him up
calmly. "This is work—not a mothers' meeting."

The man in evening dress grunted querulously.

"I don't see why you have to be so snappy, Jill.
We're all in the same boat——"

"I've yet to sail in a sauceboat, Weald."

The end of her cigarette glowed more brightly as
she inhaled, and darkened again in an uncontested
silence. Then the man with the battered face said,
diffidently: "As long as Templar isn't around——"

"Templar!" The girl's voice cut in on the name like
the crack of a whip. "Templar!" she said scathingly.
"What are you trying to do, Pinky? Scare me? That
man's a bee in your bonnet——"

"The Saint," said the man with the battered face
diffidently, "would be a bee in anybody's bonnet what
was up against him. See?"

If there had been a light, he would have been seen
to be blushing. Mr. Budd always blushed when any-

one spoke to him sharply. It was this weakness that had given him the nickname of "Pinky."

"There's a story——" ventured the man in evening dress; but he got no further.

"Isn't there always a story about any fancy dick?" demanded the girl scornfully. "I suppose you've never heard a story about Henderson—or Peters—or Teal —or Bill Kennedy? Who *is* this man Templar, anyway?"

"Ever seen a man pick up another man fifty pounds above his weight 'n' heave him over a six-foot wall like he was a sack of feathers?" asked Mr. Budd, in his diffident way. "Templar does that as a kind of warming-up exercise for a real fight. Ever seen a man stick a visiting card up edgeways 'n' cut it in half with a knife at fifteen paces? Templar does that standing on his head with his eyes shut. Ever seen a man take all the punishment six hoodlums can hand out to him 'n' come back smiling to qualify the whole half-dozen for an ambulance ride? Templar——"

"Frightened of him, Pinky?" inquired the girl quietly.

Mr. Budd sniffed.

"I been sparring partner—which is the same as saying human punchbag—to some of the best heavyweights what ever stepped into a ring," he answered, "but I always been paid handsome for the hidings I've took. I don't expect the Saint 'ud be ready to pay so much for the pleasure of beating me up. See?"

Mr. Budd did not add that since his sparring-partner

days he had seen service in Chicago with "Blinder" Kellory and other gang leaders almost as notorious—men who shot on sight and asked questions at the inquest. He had acquitted himself with distinction in Kellory's "war" with "Scarface" Al Capone—and he said nothing about that, either. There was a peculiarly impressive quality about his reticence.

"Nobody's gonna say I'm frightened to fight anybody," said Mr. Budd pinkly, "but that don't stop me knowing when I'm gonna be licked. See?"

"If you take my advice, Jill," yapped the man in evening dress, "you'll settle with Templar before he gets the chance to do any mischief. It ought to be easy——"

The man in the shadows shook with a chuckle of pure amusement. It was a warm evening, and all the windows of the car were open. He could hear every word that was said. He was standing so near the car that he could have taken a pace forward, reached out a hand, and touched it. But he took two paces forward.

The girl said, with cool contempt, as though she were dealing with a sulky child: "If it'll make you feel any happier to have him fixed——"

"It would," said Stephen Weald shamelessly. "I know there are always stories, but the stories I've heard about the Saint don't make me happy. He's uncanny. They say——"

The words were strangled in his throat in a kind of sob, so that the other two looked at him quickly,

though they could not have made out his face in the
gloom. But the girl saw, in an instant, what Weald had
seen—the deeper shadow that had blacked out the
grey square of one window.

Then there was something else in the car, something
living, besides themselves. It was strangely eerie, that
transient certainty that something had moved in the
car that belonged to none of them. But it was only an
arm—a swift sure arm that reached through one open
window with a crisp rustle of tweed sleeve which they
all heard clearly in the silence—and a hand that found
a switch and flooded them with light from the panel
bulb over their heads.

"What do they say, Weald?" drawled a voice.

There was a curious tang about that voice. It struck
all of them before they had blinked the darkness out
of their eyes sufficiently to make out its owner, who
now had his head and shoulders inside the car, leaning on his forearms in the window. It was the most
cavalierly insolent voice any of them had ever heard.

It sent Pinky Budd a dull pink, and Stephen Weald a
clammy grey-white.

Jill Trelawney's cheeks went hot with a rising flush
of anger. Perhaps because of her greater sensitiveness,
she appreciated the mocking arrogance of that voice
more than either of the others. It carried every con-
ceivable strength and concentration of insolence and
impudence and biting challenge.

"Well?"

That gentle drawl again. It was amazing what that

voice could do with one simple syllable. It jagged and rawed it with the touch of a high-speed saw, and drawled it out over a bed of hot Saharan sand in a hint of impish laughter.

"Templar!"

Budd dropped the name huskily, and Weald inhaled sibilantly through his teeth. The girl's lip curled.

"You were talking about me," drawled the man in the window.

It was a flat statement. He made it to the girl, ignoring the two men after one sweeping stare. For a fleeting second her voice failed her, and she was furious with herself. Then—

"Mr. Templar, I presume?" she said calmly.

The Saint bowed as profoundly as his position in the window admitted.

"Correct." A flickering little smile cut across his mouth. "Jill Trelawney?"

"*Miss* Trelawney."

"*Miss* Trelawney, of course. For the present. You'll be plain Trelawney to the judge, and in jail you'll just have a number."

It was extraordinary how a spark of hatred could be kindled and fanned to a flame in such an infinitesimal space of time. An instant before he had appeared in that window he had been nothing to her but a name— until then.

And now she was looking at the man through a blaze of anger that had leapt up to white heat within her in a moment. Before that, she had been frankly bored with the fears of Weald and Budd. She had dismissed them, callously. "If it'll make you feel any happier to have him fixed——" It had been completely impersonal. But now . . .

She knew what hate was. There were three men she hated, with everything she did and every breath she took. She would not have believed that there was room in her soul for more hatreds than that, and yet this new hatred seemed momentarily to overshadow all the others.

She was looking fixedly at him, unaware of anything or anyone else, engraving every feature of his appearance on her memory in lines of fire. He must have been tall above the average, she judged from the way he had to stoop to get his head in at the window; and his shoulders fitted uneasily in the aperture, wide as it was. A tall, lean buccaneer of a man, dark of hair and eyebrow, bronzed of skin, with a face incredibly clean-cut and deep-set blue eyes. The way those eyes looked at her was an insult in itself.

"I believe you were proposing to fix me," said the Saint. "Why not? I'm here, if you want me."

He broke the silence without an effort—indeed, you might have said he did not know that there had been a silence.

"If you want a fight," said Budd redly, "I'm here. See?"

"Wait a minute!"

The girl stopped Budd with a hand on his arm as he was fumbling with the door.

"Mr. Templar has his posse within call," she said cynically. "Why ask for trouble?"

The Saint's eyebrows twitched blandly.

"I have no posse. I had a gang once, but it died. Didn't they tell you I was working alone?"

"If they had," said the girl, "I shouldn't believe them. You don't look the kind of man who can bluff without a dozen armed men behind him."

He trembled with a gust of noiseless mirth.

"Quite right. I'm terrified, really!"

The mocking eyes glanced again from Budd to Weald, and back again to the girl. That maddening smile flickered again on the clean-cut lips with a glitter of perfect teeth.

"And are these two of the Lady's maids?"

"Suppose they are?" rapped the girl.

"What a dramatic idea!"

She discovered that the eyes could hold something even more infuriating than insolence, and that was a condescending amusement. A little while before she had been treating Stephen Weald like a fractious child: now she was receiving the same treatment herself.

"I'm glad you like it," she said sweetly.

"You're not," said the Saint cheerfully. "But let that pass. I came to give you a word of advice."

"Thanks very much."

"Not at all."

He pointed with a long brown finger past the girl.

"There's a house up there," he said. "Don't pretend you don't know, because I should hate you to have to tell any unnecessary lies. It belongs to Lord Essenden. My advice to you is—don't go there."

"Really?"

"They're holding a very good dance up at that house," said the Saint sardonically. "I should hate you to spoil it. All the wealth of the county is congregated together. If you could only have seen the jewels——"

She had opened her bag, and there was a white slip of pasteboard in her hand. She held it up so that he could see.

"I think this will admit me."

"Let me see it."

He had taken it from her fingers before she realized what he was doing. And yet he did not appear to have snatched it.

"Quite a good forgery," he remarked—"if it is a forgery. But I could believe you capable of engineering a real invitation, Jill."

"It's quite genuine. And I want it back—please!"

Simon Templar looked down the muzzle of the automatic and seemed to see something humorous there.

He looked perfectly steadily into her eyes, and with perfect deliberation he tore the card into sixteen pieces and let them trickle through his fingers to the floor of the car.

"Your nerves are good, Templar!" she said through her teeth.

He appeared to consider the suggestion quite seriously.

"They've never troubled me. But *that* didn't require nerves. Another time I shall be more careful. This time, you hadn't had long enough to muster up the resolution to shoot. It wants a good bit of resolution to kill your first man in cold blood. But when you've thought it over . . . Yes, I think I shall be careful next time."

"You'd better!" snarled Weald shakily.

The Saint noticed his existence.

"You spoke?"

"I said you'd better be careful—next time!"

"Did you?" drawled the Saint.

He disappeared from the window, but the illusion that he had gone was soon dispelled. The door opened, and Simon Templar stood with one foot on the running board.

"Get out of that car!"

"I'm damned if I will——"

"You're damned, anyway. Come out!"

He reached in, caught Weald by the collar, and jerked him out into the road with one swift heave.

"Stephen Weald, dope trafficker, blackmailer, and confidence man—so much for you!"

The Saint's hand shot out, fastened on one of the ends of Weald's immaculate bow tie, pulled. . . . That would have been enough at any time, the simplest gesture of contemptuous challenge; but the Saint invested it with a superbly assured insolence that had to be seen to be believed. For a moment Weald seemed stupefied. Then he lashed out, white-lipped, with both fists. . . .

The Saint picked him out of the ditch and tumbled him back into the car.

"Next?"

"If you want a fight——" began Budd; and once again the girl stopped him.

"You mustn't annoy Mr. Templar," she said witheringly. "Mr. Templar's a very brave man—with his posse waiting for him up the road."

The Saint raised his eyebrows.

"Still that story?" he protested. "How can I convince you?"

"Don't bother to try," she answered. "But if you'd like to come to 97, Belgrave Street, at three o'clock to-morrow afternoon, we'll be there."

"So shall I," said the Saint cheerfully. "And I give you my word of honour I shall come alone."

He held her eyes for a moment, and then he was gone; but a few seconds later he was back again as the self-starter burred under her foot.

"By the way," he said calmly, "I have to warn you that you'll receive a summons for standing here all this time with your lights out. Sorry, I'm sure."

He stood by the side of the road and watched the lights of the car out of sight. Perhaps he was laughing. Perhaps he was not laughing. Certainly he was amused. For the Saint, in his day, had made many enemies and many friends; yet he could recall no enemy that he had

made for whom he felt such an instinctive friendliness.
That he had gone out of his way to make himself particularly unpleasant to her was his very own business
. . . his very own. Simon Templar had his own weird
ideas of peaceful penetration.

But the smile that came to his lips as he stood there
alone and invisible would have surprised no one more
than Jill Trelawney, if she could have seen it.

He carried in his mind a vivid recollection of tawny
golden eyes darkened with anger, of a golden head
tilted in inimitable defiance, of an implacable hatred
flaming in as lovely a face as he had ever seen. Jill
Trelawney. She should have been some palely savage
Scandinavian goddess, he thought, riding before the
Valkyries with her golden hair wild in the wind.

As it was, she rode before what it pleased his own
sense of humour to call the "Lady's maids"—and that,
he admitted, was a very practical substitute.

2

The first mention of the Angels of Doom had filtered
through the underworld some four or five months
previously. It was no more than a rumour, a whis-
pered story passed from mouth to mouth, of the sort
that an unromantic Criminal Investigation Department
is taught to take with many grains of salt. The mind of
the criminal runs to nicknames; and "Angels of
Doom" was a fairly typical specimen. It was also the
one and only thing about Jill Trelawney which con-

formed to any of the precedents of crime known to New Scotland Yard.

There was a certain Ferdinand Dipper, well known to the police under a variety of names, who made much money by dancing. That is to say, certain strenuous middle-aged ladies paid him a quite reasonable fee for his services as a professional partner, and later found themselves paying him quite unreasonable fees for holding his tongue about the equivocal situations into which they had somehow been engineered. Dipper was clever, and his victims were foolish, and therefore for a long time the community had to suffer him in silence; but one day a woman less foolish than the rest repented of her folly the day after she had given Ferdinand an open check for two thousand pounds, and a detective tapped him on the shoulder as he put his foot on the gangway of the *Maid of Thanet* at Dover. They travelled back to London together by the next train; but the detective, who was human, accepted a cigarette from an exotically beautiful woman who entered their compartment to ask for a match. A porter woke him at Victoria, and a week later Ferdinand sent him a picture postcard and his love from Algeciras. And in due course information trickled in to headquarters through the devious channels by which such information ordinarily arrives.

"The Angels of Doom," said the information.

No crime is ever committed but every member of the underworld knows definitely who did it; but the task of the Criminal Investigation Department is not made any easier by the fact that six different sources of information will point with equal definiteness to six different persons. In this case, however, there was a certain amount of unanimity; but the C.I.D., who had never heard of the Angels of Doom before, shrugged their shoulders and wondered how Ferdinand had worked it.

Three weeks later, George Gallon, motor bandit, shot a policeman in Regent Street in the course of the getaway from a smash-and-grab raid at three o'clock of a stormy morning, and successfully disappeared. But about Gallon the police had certain information up their sleeves, and three armed men went cautiously to a little cottage on the Yorkshire moors to take him while he slept. The next day, a letter signed with the name of the Angels of Doom came to Scotland Yard and told a story, and the three men were found and released. But Gallon was not found; and the tale of the three men, that the room in which they found him must have been saturated with some odourless soporific gas, made the commissioner's lip curl. Nor was he amused when Gallon wrote later from some obscure South American republic to say that he was quite well, thanks.

More than three months passed, during which the name of the Angels of Doom grew more menacing every week, and so it came about that amongst the extensive and really rather prosaic and monotonous files of the Records Office at Scotland Yard there arrived one dossier of a totally different type from its companions. The outside cover was labelled in a commonplace manner enough, like all the other dossiers, with a simple name; and this name was Jill Trelawney. Inside, however, was to be found a very large section occupying nearly three hundred closely written pages, under a subheading which was anything but commonplace. Indeed, that subheading must have caused many searchings of heart to the staid member of the clerical department who had had to type it out, and must similarly have bothered the man responsible for the cross-indexing of the records, when he had had to print it neatly on one of his respectable little cards for the files. For that subheading was "The Angels of Doom," which Records Office must have felt was a heading far more suitable for inclusion in a library of sensational fiction than for a collection of data dealing solely with sober fact.

How Simon Templar came upon the scene was another matter—but really quite a simple one. For the Saint could never resist anything like that. He read of the early exploits of the Angels of Doom in the rare newspapers that he took the trouble to peruse, and was interested. Later, he heard further facts about Jill Trelawney from Chief Inspector Teal himself, and was even more interested. And the day came when he inveigled Chief Inspector Teal into accepting an invitation to lunch; and when the detective had been suitably mellowed by a menu selected with the Saint's infallible instinct for luxurious living, the Saint said, casually: "By the way, Claud Eustace, do you happen to remember that I was once invited to join the Special Branch?"

And Chief Inspector Teal removed the eight-inch cigar from his face and blinked—suspiciously.

"I remember," he said.

"And you remember my answer?"

"Not word for word, but——"

"I refused."

Teal nodded.

"I've thought, since, that perhaps that was one of the kindest things you ever did for me," he said.

The Saint smiled.

"Then I want you to take a deep breath and hold on to your socks, Claud Eustace, old okapi," he murmured, and the detective looked up.

"You want to try it?"

Simon nodded.

"Just lately," he said, "I've been feeling an awful urge towards that little den of yours on the Embankment. I believe I was really born to be a policeman. As the scourge of ungodliness, I should be ten times more deadly with an official position. And there's one particular case on hand at the moment which is only waiting for a bloke like me to knock the hell out of it. Teal, wouldn't you like to call me 'Sir'?"

"I should hate it," said Teal.

But there were others in Scotland Yard who thought differently.

For it had long since been agreed, among the heads of that gloomy organization of salaried kill-joys which exists for the purposes of causing traffic jams, suppressing riotous living and friendly wassail, and discouraging the noble sport of soaking the ungodly on the boko, that something had got to be done about the Saint. The only point which up to that time had never been quite unanimously agreed on was what exactly was to be done.

The days had been when, to quote one flippant commentary, Chief Inspector Teal would have given ten years' salary for the privilege of leading the Saint gently by the arm into the nearest police station, and a number of gentlemen in the underworld would have given ten years' liberty for the pleasure of transporting the Saint to the top of the chute of a blast furnace and quietly back-heeling him into the stew. These things may be read in other volumes of the Saint Saga. But somehow the Saint had continued to go his pleasantly piratical way unscathed, to the rage and terror of the underworld and the despair of Chief Inspector Teal—buccaneer in the suits of Savile Row, amused, cool, debonair, with hell-for-leather blue eyes and a Saintly smile. . . .

And then, all at once, as it seemed, he had finished his work, and that should have been that. "The tumult and the shouting dies, the sinners and the Saints depart," as the Saint himself so beautifully put it. All adventures come to an end. But Jill Trelawney . . .

"Jill Trelawney," said the Saint dreamily, "is a new interest. I tell you, Teal, I was going to take the longest holiday of my life. But since Jill Trelawney is still

at large, and your bunch of flat-footed nit-wits hasn't
been able to do anything about it . . ."

And after considerable elaboration of his point, the
Saint was permitted to say much the same thing to
the commissioner; but this interview was briefer.

"You can try," said the chief. "There are some
photographs and her dossier. We pulled her in last
week, after the Angels wrecked the raid on Harp's
dope joint——"

"And she showed up with a copper-bottomed alibi
you could have sailed through a Pacific hurricane,"
drawled the Saint. "Yeah?"

"Get her," snapped the chief.

"Three weeks," drawled the Saint laconically, and
walked out of Scotland Yard warbling a verse of the
comedy song hit of the season—written by himself.

> "*I*
> *Am the guy*
> *Who killed Capone——*"

As he passed the startled doorkeeper, he got a
superb yodelling effect into the end of that last line.

And that was exactly thirty-six hours before he met
Jill Trelawney for the first time.

And precisely at three o'clock on the afternoon after
he had first met her, Simon Templar walked down Belgrave Street, indisputably the most astonishingly immaculate and elegant policeman that ever walked down
Belgrave Street, was admitted to No. 97, was shown
up the stairs, walked into the drawing room. If pos-

sible, he was more dark and cavalier and impudent by daylight than he had been by night. Weald and the girl were there.

"Good-afternoon," said the Saint.

His voice stoked the conventional greeting with an infinity of mocking arrogance. He was amused, in his cheerful way. He judged that the rankling thoughts of the intervening night and morning would not have improved their affection for him, and he was amused.

"Nice day," he drawled.

"We hardly expected you," said the girl.

"Your error," said the Saint comfortably.

He tossed his hat into a chair and glanced back at the door which had just closed behind him.

"I don't like your line in butlers," he said. "I suppose you know that Frederick Wells has a very eccentric record. Aren't you ever afraid he might disappear with the silver?"

"Wells is an excellent servant."

"Fine! And how's Pinky?"

"Budd is out at the moment. He'll be right back."

"Fine again!" The mocking blue eyes absorbed Stephen Weald from the feet upwards. "And what position does this freak hold in the establishment? Pantry boy?"

Weald gnawed his lip and said nothing. There was a cross of sticking plaster over the bruised cut in his chin to remind him that a man like Simon Templar is apt to confuse physical violence with abstract repartee. Stephen Weald felt cautious.

"Mr. Weald is a friend of mine," said the girl, "and I'd be obliged if you'd refrain from insulting him in my house."

"Anything to oblige," said the Saint affably. "I apologize."

And he contrived to make a second insult of the apology.

The girl had to call up all her resources of self-control to preserve an outward calm. Inwardly she felt all the fury that the Saint had aroused the night before boiling up afresh.

"I wonder," she said, with a strained evenness, "why nobody's ever murdered you, Simon Templar?"

"People have tried," the Saint said mildly. "It's never quite succeeded, somehow. But there's still hope."

He seemed to enjoy the thought. It was quite clear that his detestableness was no unfortunate trick of manner. It was too offensively deliberate. He had brought discourtesy in all its branches to a fine art, and he ladled out his masterpieces with no uncertain enthusiasm.

"How are the Angels this afternoon?" he inquired.

"They are"—she waved a vague hand—"here and there."

"Nice for them. May I sit down?"

"I think——"

"Thanks." He sat down. "But don't let me stop you thinking."

She took a cigarette from the box beside her and

fitted it into a long amber holder. Weald supplied a match.

"You forgot to ask me if I minded," said the Saint reproachfully. "Where are your manners, Jill?"

She turned in her chair—a movement far more abrupt than she meant it to be.

"If the police have to pester me," she said, "I should have appreciated their consideration if they'd sent a gentleman to do it."

"Sorry," said Simon. "Our gentlemen are all out pestering ladies. The chief thought I'd be good enough for you. Backchat. However, I'll pass on your complaint when I get back."

"*If* you get back."

"This afternoon," said the Saint. "And I shan't worry if he takes me off the job. Man-size criminals are my mark, and footling around with silly little girls like you is just squandering my unique qualities as a detective. More backchat."

Weald butted in, from the other side of the room:

"Jill, why do you waste time——"

"It amuses her," said the Saint. "When she's finished amusing herself, she'll tell us why my time's being wasted here at all. I didn't fall through a trapdoor in the hall, I wasn't electrocuted when I touched the banister rail, no mechanical gadget shot out of the wall and hit me over the head when I trod on the thirteenth stair, I wasn't shot by a spring gun on the way up. Where's your ingenuity?"

"Saint——"

"Of course, your father was English. Did you get your accent from him or from the talkies?"

He was enjoying himself. She was forced to the exasperating realization that he was playing with her, as if he were making a game of the encounter for his own secret satisfaction. At the least sign of resentment she gave, he registered the scoring of a point to himself as unmistakably as if he had chalked it up on a board.

"By the way," Simon said, "you really must stop annoying Essenden. He came in to see us the other day, and he was most upset. Remember that his nerves aren't as strong as mine. If you murdered him, for instance, I couldn't promise you that he wouldn't be really seriously annoyed."

"Whether I'm responsible for any shocks that Essenden's had, or not," said the girl calmly, "is still waiting to be proved."

"I don't expect it will wait very long," said the Saint comfortably. "You amateur crooks are never very clever."

Jill Trelawney took from her bag a tiny mirror and a gold-cased lipstick. She attended to the shaping of her mouth unconcernedly.

"Templar, you gave me your word of honour you would come alone to-day."

"Fancy that! And did you believe it?"

"I was prepared to."

"Child," said the Saint, "you amaze me."

He stood up and walked to the window in long jerky strides.

From there he beckoned her, looking down to the street from behind the curtains.

"Come here."

She came, after a pause, with a bored languidness; but it was impossible to make him show the least impatience.

"See there!"

He pointed down with a challenging forefinger.

"See and hear that man singing 'Rose in the Bud' at the harmonium? He's just waiting for me to come out and tell him he can go home. And you see the man farther up with the ice-cream cart? He's standing by. And the man selling newspapers on this side? More of the posse. You credited me with the darn thing, so I thought I'd live up to it. There's ten of 'em spread around this block now!"

"I'm sorry. I thought even your word of honour might be worth something. But now——"

"You'll know better next time, won't you?" Little flinty jags of amusement twinkled in his eyes. "What was the joke I was supposed to buy? Pinky Budd waiting downstairs in the hall with a handful of Angels? Or just a button you press up here that starts off the trapdoor and the electric banister rail and the mechanical gadget in the thirteenth stair?"

She faced him, flaming now without the slightest attempt at concealment, suddenly transformed into a beautiful tigress.

"You think you're clever—Saint!"

"I'm darn sure of it," murmured the Saint, modestly.

"You think——"

"Often and brilliantly. I kicked up the rug before I stepped on it, and saw the edge of the trap. I'm always suspicious of iron banister rails on indoor staircases. And the thirteenth stair gave an inch under my weight, so I ducked. But nothing happened. Rather lucky for you the things weren't working—in the circumstances —isn't it?"

It was bewildering to think that the girl, according to official records, was only twenty-two. Simon Templar treated her like a petulant child because it pleased him to do so. But in that moment he recognized her anger as a grown reality with nothing childish in it. That he chose to keep the recognition to himself was nobody's business.

"No one will stop you going back to your posse, Templar."

"I didn't think anyone would."

He glanced at his watch.

"They'll be expecting me in another five minutes. I only came because I didn't want to disappoint you— and because I thought you might have something interesting to say."

"I've nothing more to—*say*."

"But lots of things to do?"

"Possibly."

That extraordinarily mocking smile bared his teeth. "If only," he murmured softly—"if only your father could hear those sweet words fall from your gentle lips!"

"You'll leave my father out of it——"

"You'd like me to, wouldn't you? But that won't make me do it."

There was a renewed hardness in her eyes that had no right to be there.

"My father was framed," she said in a low voice.

"There was a proper inquiry. An assistant commissioner of police isn't dismissed in disgrace for nothing. And is that an excuse for anything *you* do, anyway?"

"It satisfies me."

Her voice held a depth of passion that for a moment turned even Simon Templar into a sober listener. She had never flinched from his sardonically bantering stare, and now she met it more defiantly than ever. She went on, in that low, passionate voice: "The shock killed him. You know it could have been nothing else but that. And he died denying the charge——"

"So you think you've a right to take vengeance on the department for him?"

"They condemned him for a thing he'd never done. And the mud sticks to me as well, still, a year after his death. So I'll give them something to condemn me for."

The Saint looked at her.

"And what about that boy over in the States?" he asked quietly, and saw her start.

"What do you know about him?" she asked.

The Saint shrugged.

"It's surprising what a lot of odd things I know," he

answered. "I think we may talk some more on that subject one day—Jill. Some day when you've forgotten this nonsense, and the Angels of Doom have grown their tails."

For a span of silence he held her eyes steadily—the big golden eyes which, he knew by his own instinct, were made for such gentle things as the softness into which he had betrayed them for a moment. And then that instant's light died out of them again, and the tawny hardness returned. She laughed a little.

"I'll go back when the slate's clean," she said; and so the Saint slipped lightly back into the rôle he had chosen to play.

"You missed your vocation," he said sweetly. "You ought to have been writing detective stories. Vengeance —and the Angels of Doom! Joke!"

He swung round in his smooth sweeping way and picked his hat out of the chair. Weald seemed about to say something, and, meeting the Saint's suddenly direct and interrogative gaze, refrained. Simon looked at the girl again.

"I'm leaving," he said. "We shall meet again. Quite soon. I promised to get you in three weeks, and two and a half days of it have gone. But I'll do it, don't you worry!"

"I'm not worrying, Templar. And next time you give me your word of honour——"

"Be suspicious of everything I say," Simon advised. "I have moments of extreme cunning, as you'll get to know. Good-afternoon, sweetheart."

He went out, leaving the door open, and walked

down the stairs. He saw Pinky Budd standing in the
hall with six men drawn up impassively behind him;
but it would have taken more than that, at any time, to
make Simon Templar's steps falter.

The girl spoke from the top of the stairs.

"Mr. Templar is leaving, Pinky. His men are waiting for him outside."

"Now that," said the Saint, "is tough luck on you—
isn't it, Pinky?"

He walked straight for the door, and the guard
stood aside without a word to give him gangway. Only
Budd stood his ground, and Simon halted in front of
him.

"Getting in my way, Pinky?"

Budd looked at him with narrowed, glittering eyes.
They were of a height as they stood, but Budd would
have been a couple of inches taller if he had straightened his huge hunched shoulders. His long arms hung
loosely at his sides, and the ham-like fists at the end of
them were clenched.

"Nope, I'm not getting in your way. But I'll come
'n' find you again soon, Templar. See?"

"Do."

The Saint's hand came flat in the middle of Budd's
chest and overbalanced him out of the road. And
Simon Templar went through to the door.

A few strides up the street he stopped and laid half
a crown on a harmonium.

"Do you know a song called 'A Farewell'?" he
asked.

"Yes, sir," said the serenader.

"Play it for me," said the Saint. "And miss out the middle verse."

He went on towards Buckingham Palace Road as soon as he had heard the introductory bars moaned out on the machine; and his departure was watched by vengeful eyes from the drawing-room window.

"You let him get clean away," snivelled Weald. "We had him——"

"Don't be an imbecile!" snapped the girl. "He only came to see if he could tempt us into doing anything foolish. And if we had, he'd have been tickled to death. And I just asked him to come so I could get to know a little more about him, for future reference. He's——"

"What's that bull with the organ singing?"

They listened. The words of the unmelodious performance came clearly to their ears. The troubadour, startled by the magnitude of the Saint's largesse, was putting his heart into the job.

*"Maaaye fairest chiiild-da, I have no gift to giiive
    theeee;
  No lark-ka could pipe-pa to skies sow dull
    and gra-a-ay;
 Yet-ta,.ere I gow, one lesson I can leeeave theeee
    For every da-a-ay. . . ."*

"I saw Templar speak to him——"

"Shut up, you fool!"

"Be gooood-da, sweet maaid, and-da let who
      can-na be cle-evah;
      Do nowble things, not-ta dream them, awl
      daaay lawng . . ."

The telephone bell screamed.

"See who it is, Weald. No, give it to me."

She took the instrument out of his hands. There was no need to ask who was the owner of the silkily endearing voice that came over the wire.

"Hullo!"

"Yes, Mr. Templar?"

"Please don't let the Angels pester the innocent gentleman with the criminal voice. He doesn't know me from Adam, and probably never will. I warned you I had moments of extreme cunning, didn't I?"

She hung up the receiver thoughtfully, ignoring Weald's splutter of questions.

The musician below, a man inspired, was repeating the last verse with increased fervour—perhaps as a consolation to himself for having been deprived of the middle one.

"Bee goooooda-da, sweet maaid-da, and-da let
      whoo caan-na be cle-e-e-ev-ah. . . ."

The girl stood by the window, and something like a smile touched her lips.

"A humorist!" she said.

Then the smile was gone altogether.

"Second round to Simon Templar," she said softly. "And now, I think, we start!"

CHAPTER II

IF IT had been possible to prepare a place-time chart of the activities of the Angels of Doom, it would have shown, during the eighteen hours following Simon Templar's departure from the house in Belgrave Street, a distinct concentration of interest in the region of Upper Berkeley Mews, where the Saint had converted a couple of garages, with the rooms above, into the most ingeniously comfortable fortress in London. Also, like other concentrations of the Angels of Doom, it appeared to be conducted with considerable labour and expense for no prospect of immediate profit.

It may be suggested that the district of Mayfair was an eccentric situation for the home of a policeman; but Simon Templar thanked God he wasn't a real policeman. In fact, he must have been the weirdest kind of policeman that ever claimed to be attached to Scotland Yard. But attached he indisputably was, and could claim his official salutes from some of the men who would once have given their ears to arrest him.

"Thus are the mighty fallen, and the weapons of walloping perished," he said to Teal at another lunch, with a kind of wicked wistfulness; and the detective sighed, and kept his misgivings to himself. For the Saint, in his new disguise of a respectable citizen, seemed much too good to be true—much too good. . . . Teal had an uneasy feeling that no bad man who had suddenly reformed would have been quite so overpoweringly sanctimonious about it. All that he had ever seen of the Saint, all that he had ever known of him, made Chief Inspector Teal feel like a performing elephant dancing a hornpipe over a thin glass dome in the presence of this inexplicable virtue. And in his mountainously bovine way Chief Inspector Teal watched the Saint enforcing the law by strictly legal methods, and wondered. . . .

Not that anyone's mystification would have worried Simon Templar in the least. If he had thought about it at all, he would have been impishly amused, in his serenely contented fashion. As it was, he went on with his life, and the job he had taken on, with a sublime disregard for the feelings and opinions of the world at large, seeming to be distressed only by the lack of an adequate supply of victims for his exaggerated sense of humour.

One thing, however, could disturb his tranquillity, and that was to have business troubles intruded upon the hours which he had allotted to himself for rest or recreation. At midnight of the day after his visit to Belgrave Street, for instance, when he was sitting up

in bed, happily engaged in polishing the opening lines
of a new song dealing with the shortcomings of the
latest Honours List, and a bullet smacked through the
window behind him and chipped a lump out of a perfectly good ceiling, he was distinctly bored.

With a sigh he climbed out and pulled on his dressing gown. One glance at the line between the star-
shaped split in the window and the scar in the plaster
was enough to show that the shot had come in at a
wide angle. The Saint sighed again. Perhaps his esti-
mate of himself had been wrong. It seemed that there
was something else which annoyed him even more than
to be interrupted after business hours—and that was
to be taken for a fool.

He glanced round the room and selected a battered
pickelhaube—relic of a grimmer warfare than that.
Then he switched off the light. Returning to the window, he knelt down so that he was below the level of
the sill, and raised the lower sash. On one side of this
opening he displayed the *pickelhaube,* looped over the
back of a chair which he edged into position with his
foot, and awaited developments with a kindly interest.

The mews was deserted, and there were no pedes-
trians visible at the entrance in Berkeley Square at
that moment, but he could pick out the shadowy bulk
of a big saloon car parked in the cul-de-sac of the mews
itself, and the second shot from it impinged accurately
upon the *pickelhaube* with a noise like that of a dull
gong.

Neither of the shots from outside had been accom-

panied by a report, but Simon Templar, since acquiring
the right to be as noisy as he pleased, had ceased to
be of such a retiring disposition. He emptied his automatic without stealth, and crammed in a fresh magazine as he raced down the stairs.

His servant met him in the hall.

"Count ten, and then open the front door—but lie
flat on the ground when you do it!' snapped the Saint,
and vanished into the sitting room without explaining
how this feat of contortion was to be performed.

He was edging back the window curtains when the
door began to open.

He had no fear for the man who was opening it, for
there were so few flies on Orace that even a short-
sighted man would have had no excuse for mistaking
him for a Chilean mule. Neither had he any fear of
the agile gunman who was upsetting his evening. Either
the car was an ordinary car, in which case the gunman
was winged if Simon Templar had ever learnt anything about the art of shooting up automobiles; or the
car was an extraordinary car, lined throughout with
half-inch nickel steel, in which case the gunman was
probably not winged. And, either way, if it came to
a fight . . .

"Joke!" murmured the Saint, and lowered his head
again quickly.

Ordinary guns he was prepared for, and ready to
take on any time. Not that he particularly fancied
himself with guns, but he reckoned he could just about
pull his weight in most kinds of rough stuff. But there

was another kind of gun before tackling which Simon
Templar always paused to take a deep breath and
recite rapidly the verse from the hymn which contains
a line about shelters from the stormy blast; and it was
undoubtedly a specimen of that kind of gun which was
spluttering a horizontal hailstorm of lead sufficiently
close to his direction to be appreciably unpleasant.

Taking the breath, and postponing the recitation to
a later date, Simon put up his head again; and as he
did so the fire ceased, and the car picked up speed with
a rush and swooped round into the emptiness of Berkeley Square.

The Saint, standing at the corner of the mews and
trying to draw a bead on one of the departing tires as
the car turned into Mount Street, was briskly arrested.

"Don't be a bigger fool than you can help," he
snarled; and the constable, recognizing him, released
him with a stammered apology.

"It was a car, sir——"

"You amaze me," said the Saint, in awe. "I thought
it was a team of racing camels. Get the number down
in your book."

The policeman obeyed; and Simon, with a shrug,
turned and shouldered his way back to the house
through the nucleus of a gaping crowd.

He found Orace dabbing an ear with a stained handkerchief.

"Hurt?"

"Nossir—just a splinter er wood. They were firin'
low."

"It's more painful through the stomach," said the Saint enigmatically, and went on upstairs.

The pursuit of the car from which the machine gun had been fired wasn't Simon Templar's business. It could be carried on just as effectively by the regulars—or just as ineffectively, for the number plates were certain to have been changed. But it made the Saint think.

When the assistant commissioner called in later for the story, however, Simon showed no signs of perturbation.

"It was Budd's idea, of course. He's seen service in Chicago. But machine guns in the streets of London are nothing new on me—I've had it happen before. There's no blamed originality in this racket, that's the trouble."

"They seem to think you're important."

"There's certainly some personal bias against me," admitted the Saint innocently. "I was expecting a demonstration—I had further words with Jill Trelawney yesterday. Cigarette?"

"Thanks."

The commissioner helped himself. He was a grizzled, hard-featured man who had worked his way up from the very bottom of the ladder, and he had all the taciturn abruptness common to men who have risen in the world by nothing but a relentless devotion to the ambition of rising in the world.

"How did she strike you?"

"She didn't," said the Saint perversely. "I think she

would have, though, but for the low cunning with which I made my escape. She's a sweet child."

"Charming," agreed the commissioner ironically. "So gentle! Such endearing ways!"

"Ever meet her?"

"No. I knew her father, of course."

Simon grinned.

"He never made any friendly advance towards me," he murmured. "But of course there was some prejudice against me at the time. Tell me that story again— from the inside."

Cullis settled himself.

"The inside is that Trelawney swore all along that he'd been framed," he said. "It's not such an inside, anyway, because he told exactly the same tale at the inquiry. After all, that was the only defense open to him: he was caught so red-handed that no one could have thought out any other explanation except that he was guilty."

"The story?"

"Police plans were leaking out; raids falling flat regularly. Something had to be done. The chief commissioner took a chance on myself and another superintendent—we had the longest service records—and arranged for us to lead a surprise raid on a Thursday night. On Thursday morning he let it get round the Yard that the raid was to take place on Saturday. We raided on Thursday without any fuss, roped in a gang that had slipped us twice before, and kept everyone on the premises—including the men who made the raid, and they were officially supposed to be on leave. Therefore there was nobody left at the Yard, except the chief, who knew that the raid was over. We had one man sitting over the telephone and another over the letter box. First post on Friday morning, a letter came in. Just one word, typewritten: *Saturday.* It was on official paper, with the heading cut off, and the experts put it under the microscope and traced it to the typewriter in Trelawney's office."

"Which anyone might have used."

"It was postmarked Windsor. Trelawney went down to Windsor for a consultation on Thursday afternoon—and he went alone."

"Flimsy," said the Saint. "An accomplice might have posted it."

Cullis nodded.

"I know it wasn't any good by itself. But it was a clue. Nobody saw the letter but the chief and myself. We watched Trelawney ourselves. We were after Waldstein then. He was always slippery, and at that time we reckoned he was vanishing an average of one girl a week through the Pan-European Concert Agency, which was one of his most profitable incarnations. But he was clever, and he never appeared in person, and there was never a line of evidence. Then I had the inspiration. I suggested to the chief that he go to Trelawney with the story that one of Waldstein's men had squealed. He saw the point, and agreed. He told the tale to Trelawney, as he'd naturally have told him anything else in the way of business that he was pleased about. Waldstein was in Paris, and the chief said that the Sûreté had arranged to intercept any letters, telegrams, or telephone calls addressed to him, so that no one could warn him, and one of our men was going over to arrest him the next morning. And the next morning, bright and early, Trelawney chartered a special aëroplane and set off for Paris."

"No!"

"He did. The chief and I, having been waiting for just that, chased him in a faster aëroplane, and trailed him all the way from Le Bourget to Waldstein's hotel. Then, when we'd heard him ask for Waldstein at the office, the chief tapped him on the shoulder."

"And?"

"He'd got his story pat. Gosh, I've never met such a nerve! He just blinked a bit when he first saw the chief and me, but from then on he never batted an eyelid. We went into a private room, and the chief told him the game was up.

" 'What game?' asked Trelawney.

" 'What are you doing here?' asks the chief.

" 'What you told me to do,' says Trelawney.

" 'I never told you to come here,' says the chief.

"The chief says Trelawney went a bit white then, but I never noticed it. Anyway, Trelawney's story was that he'd been called up by the chief early that morning and told to go over and attend to Waldstein himself, as there was some difficulty with the French police, and Waldstein was likely to get away during the argument. We asked him why he hadn't gone to the Quai d'Orsay first, to present his papers, and he said the chief had told him to get Waldstein first and argue afterwards."

"Well?"

Cullis shrugged.

"After that, it was all over."

"Don't see it," said the Saint. "If Trelawney was guilty, why should he tell that story to the very man who would know at once that it wasn't true?"

"Brains," said the assistant commissioner. "He'd thought out the possibility of being caught, and he'd got his defense ready—a frame-up. That story was the best he could have told. It prepared his ground for when we opened his safe deposit and found, among others, banknotes that were traced to Waldstein."

"How did he account for those?"

"He couldn't."

"And afterwards?"

"The chief decided not to make a public scandal of it. For one thing, it would have been difficult to get a conviction, even on that evidence, because we couldn't bring Waldstein into it. Waldstein, in the eyes of the ignorant world, was a perfectly respectable citizen and is the same to this day. So there wasn't any lawful reason why he shouldn't have given Trelawney money. Still, Trelawney was asked for his resignation, and he died a month afterwards. I don't like thinking about that part of it—it isn't pleasant to think that I was indirectly responsible, even if he was a grafter."

Simon reached for an ashtray.

"And yet," he said, "it seems rather a fluke. Why should Waldstein have been the right bait? And why should Trelawney have walked into the trap so easily?"

Cullis shrugged again.

"Waldstein was the sort of man who might have been the right bait. We took a chance. If it had failed, we'd have had to think of something else. But if Waldstein was the right bait, Trelawney was bound to walk into the trap. If a man takes graft, he can't let his clients down; if he does, they can squeal on him. Waldstein being in Paris put Trelawney in a tight corner, but he had to take his chance. He didn't know how big a chance it was. Ordinarily, you see, he might easily have got away with it. But he didn't know that there was already some sort of evidence against him; he didn't know he was being followed; and he couldn't have guessed that there could be enough suspicion to lead to the opening of his safe deposit."

"Had he any particular enemies?"

"No more than the average successful policeman."

"No name you can remember hearing him mention?"

Cullis tugged at an iron-grey moustache.

"Heavens! I don't know!"

"No one of the name of—Essenden?"

It was a shot in the dark, but it creased two additional wrinkles into the assistant commissioner's lined forehead.

"What made you think of that?" he asked.

"I didn't," said the Saint. "It just fell out of the blue. But Jill was on her way to Essenden's when I first met her, and that was the first time the Angels have been seen out *before* an arrest. Get me?"

"But they were there to cover Dyson. Surely it's reasonable for them to have realized that it's easier to prevent a man being arrested than to get him away after the arrest?"

Simon nodded.

"I know. Still, I'm keeping an open mind."

He continued in communion with his open mind for some time after the commissioner had left—and went to bed with the mind, if possible, more open than before.

Perhaps Sir Francis Trelawney had been framed. Perhaps he had not been framed. If he had been framed, it had been brilliantly done. If he had not been framed . . . Well, it was quite natural that a girl like Jill Trelawney, as he estimated her, might refuse to believe it. And, either way, if you looked at it from the standpoint of a law-abiding citizen and an incipient policeman to boot, the rights and wrongs of the Trelawney case made no difference to the rights and wrongs of Jill.

Within the past five months, a complete dozen of valuable prisoners had been rescued from under the very arms of the law, long as those arms were traditionally reputed to be; and the manner of their rescue, in every case, betrayed such an exhaustive knowledge of police methods and routine that at times a complete reorganization of the Criminal Investigation Department's system seemed to be the only possible alternative to impotent surrender. And this, as is the way of such things, accurately coincided with one of those waves of police unpopularity and hysterical newspaper criticism which make commissioners and superintendents acidulated and old before their time. Clearly, it could not go on. The newspapers said so, and therefore it must have been so. And the Saint understood quite calmly and contentedly that, after the manner in which the Saint had made his début as a law-abiding citizen, either the Angels of Doom or Simon Templar had got to come to a sudden and sticky end.

Completely comprehending this salient fact, the Saint drank his breakfast coffee black the next morning, and sent the milk bottle from outside his front door to an analyst. He had the report by lunchtime.

"At least," he told Cullis, "I'm collecting the makings of a case against the Angels."

"There was nothing against them before," assented the commissioner sarcastically.

Simon shook his head.

"There wasn't. Assaulting the police, obstructing the police—I tell you, in spite of everything, you could only have got them on minor charges. But attempted murder——"

"Or even real murder," said Cullis cheerfully.

2

"Slinky" Dyson had squealed. Simon Templar had to admit that nothing but that happy windfall had enabled him to step so promptly upon the tail of the Angels of Doom. Slinky was pulled in for suspicious loitering one evening, and when they searched him they found on his person a compact leather wallet containing tools which were held to be house-breaking implements within the meaning of the Act. Simon happened to be in Marlborough Street police station at the time, and witnessed the discovery.

"I was waiting for a friend," said Slinky. "Honest I was."

"Honest you may have was," said the inspector heavily. "But you grew out of that years ago."

Shortly after Slinky had been locked up, he asked to speak to the inspector again, and the inspector thought the squeal sufficiently promising to fetch Teal in to hear it. And then Teal sent in the Saint.

"I told you I was waiting for a friend," said Slinky, "and that's gospel. But if you'd pulled me to-morrow . . . I was going down to take a look at Lord Essenden's party. I had a tip from the Angels. You'll find the letter in my room—I put it in the Bible on the shelf over the bed. They said I was to take what I liked, how I liked, and they'd see I made a good getaway. Now, you ain't told me why I'm here, but I know. There's been a scream. I don't know why they should want to shop me, but there's been a scream. . . . An'

I'd take it as a favour, sir, if you'd tell me who was the screamer."

"I don't know," said the Saint truthfully. "Maybe you talk in your sleep."

They found the letter as Slinky had said they would find it, and it was short and to the point.

And the Saint, acting upon it, went to Lord Essenden's party unknown to Lord Essenden, and thus met Jill Trelawney and Stephen Weald and Pinky Budd; and what followed we know.

After the jokes of the machine gun and the milk, the Saint saw Slinky Dyson again, and was able to give some unhelpful information to that puzzled man.

"There was no scream," he said. "That is official. It was just your bad luck, Slinky."

Dyson scratched his head.

"I'll believe you, Mr. Templar. It was bad luck all right. But you'll remember my squeak, sir?"

"You were remanded for a week, weren't you?"

"Yes, Mr. Templar."

"If we let you out, will you take a job?"

"What sort of job?" asked Slinky suspiciously.

"Oh, not work," said the Saint soothingly. "I wouldn't dream of asking you to do that."

Slinky relaxed.

"I'll hear about it, Mr. Templar."

"How much do you want for a black eye?"

Slinky stared.

"Beg pardon, Mr. Templar?"

"You heard me."

The man shifted his eyes nervously, and giggled. "Wh-what?"

"I didn't ask you to give an imitation of a consumptive Wyandotte laying a bad egg," said the Saint patiently. "I asked you how much you wanted for a black eye."

"You want to give me a black eye, Mr. Templar?"

"Very much indeed."

"What for?"

"Five pounds."

"What for after that?"

"Do you know how to get in touch with the Angels?"

Slinky shook his head.

"Never mind that," said the Saint. "I guess they'll hear about it, if you carry it round and talk a lot about how I gave it to you—without mentioning the five pounds. Tell the world how I beat you up and tried to make you howl on the Angels, and how you're going to get even with me one day. The Angels don't like me, and they'd be glad to find a man who hates me as much as you're going to. If we're lucky, you'll find yourself enlisted in the gang in less than no time. Then you keep me posted."

"You mean," said Slinky, "you want me to be your nose?"

"That's the idea."

Dyson sighed.

"I've never been a nose," he said solemnly. "No, Mr. Templar, it can't be done."

"You will be paid," said the Saint deliberately,

"twenty pounds' cash for every genuine piece of news you send in about what the Angels are going to do next and how they're going to do it."

Slinky closed his eyes sanctimoniously.

"My conscience," he said, "wouldn't allow me to do a thing like that, Mr. Templar."

"You'll remember," the Saint reminded him persuasively, "that I could get you sent down for six months' hard right now."

Dyson blinked.

"If it wasn't for my principles," he said sadly, "I'd be very happy to oblige you, Mr. Templar."

Eventually, when he found that the Saint had no intention of raising his price, except in the matter of ten pounds instead of five for the black eye, he managed to choke down his conscience and accept. Simon arranged for him to be brought before the magistrate again the next morning, when he would be released, and started back to Scotland Yard in a taxi. But on the way he had an idea.

"The machine gun," he reflected, "was Pinky's voluntary. Weald would have thought of the prussic acid in the milk. We're still waiting for Jill's contribution —and it might be very cunning to meet it halfway."

The inspiration, duly considered, appealed to him; and he gave fresh instructions to the driver.

The door of the house in Belgrave Street was a long time opening in response to his peal on the bell. Perhaps to make up for this, it was very quick in starting to shut again as soon as Frederick Wells had recognized the caller. But Simon Templar was more than ordinarily skilful at thrusting himself in where he was not wanted.

"Not good enough, Freddie," he drawled regretfully, and closed the door himself—from the inside.

The butler glowered.

"Miss Trelawney is out," he said.

"You lie, Ferdinand," said the Saint pleasantly, and went on up the stairs.

He really had no idea whether the butler was lying or not, but he gave him the benefit of the doubt. As it happened, this generous impulse was justified, for Jill Trelawney opened the door of the sitting room just as Simon put his hand on the knob.

"Hullo," said the Saint amiably.

His eyes flickered with an offensively secret mirth, and he caught the answering blaze from hers before she veiled them in a frozen inscrutability.

"Lovely day, Jill," remarked the Saint, very amiably.

She relaxed wearily against the jamb.

"My—sainted—aunt! Have you got away from your keeper again?"

"Looks like it," said the Saint apologetically. "Yes, I will stay to tea, thanks. Ring down to the kitchen and tell them not to mix arsenic with the sugar, because I don't take sugar. And it's no use putting strychnine in the milk, because I don't take milk. Just tell 'em to shovel the whole bag of tricks in the teapot."

He walked calmly past her into the room, and sat

down in the best chair. As an afterthought, he removed his hat.

The girl followed him in.

"Is your posse outside again?"

"I wonder?" said the Saint. "Why don't you go out and ask? You don't know where you are just now, do you? One time I tell you I haven't a posse, and I haven't. Another time I tell you I have a posse and I haven't. Now suppose I tell you I haven't a posse you'll know I have, won't you?"

She shrugged and took a cigarette from a silver box. Then she offered the box to him.

"Have one?"

"Not with you, darling."

"Did I hear you say 'No, thanks'?"

"Er—no, I don't think so," said the Saint seriously. "Did you?"

With the smoke trickling through her lips the girl looked at him.

"Have you come on business this time?" she inquired. "Or is this just another part of the official persecution?"

"Partly on business, partly on pleasure," said Simon, unabashed. "Which will you have first?"

"The business, please,"

"It's a pleasure," said the Saint accommodatingly. "I've come to do you a good turn, Jill."

"Is that so?"

"Yes, that is so. Oh, yeah? Yeah. Ses you? Ses me. In fact, yes. . . . I want to warn you. A dark man is going to cross your path. Beware of him. His name is Slinky Dyson."

The name roused no more response than a flicker of her eyelids.

"What about him?"

"He is a police spy," said the Saint solemnly. "I have been able to buy him over. In return for a cash reward he is going to try to join your gang and give me all the information about you that he can get hold of. So, whatever happens, don't be taken in by him."

She read with glittering eyes the dancing devil of amusement behind his expressionlessness.

"Is this another of your funny stories?"

"It is." The Saint sighed. "In fact, it's one of my best. Do you know, Jill, I'm afraid you're going to get in a devil of a muddle about me, aren't you? First the business of the posse, then this. Now, do you think I'm telling you the truth in the hope that you will think I'm bluffing and fall into the trap, or do you think I'm inventing the yarn to keep you away from a man I don't want you to have? I can't help thinking that some of these questions are going to make life very difficult for you for the next few days."

She tapped her cigarette delicately on the edge of an ashtray.

"Is that all you came to say?" she asked patiently.

"Not quite," said the Saint, in that tone of gentle mockery that would have been like sandpaper rasped across the nerves of anyone less self-possessed. "I just wanted to ask one thing—about your father."

She faced him.

"Haven't I told you," she said dangerously, "to leave my father out of this?"

"I know," said the Saint. "And I've told you that I shall bring anyone into it whom I choose to bring in. So we know where we are. And now listen to this. I've been making some inquiries about your father, and I've come on a name which interests me. It may mean something to you. The name is—Waldstein."

She stared at him narrowly.

"Well?"

The monosyllable dropped like a flake of hot metal.

"I thought you might be after him," said the Saint. "Do you mind telling me if I'm right?"

Slowly she nodded.

"You're quite right—Templar!"

The Saint beamed.

"That's one of the most sensible things I've heard you say," he remarked. "In fact, if you concentrated your attention on Waldstein you'd be doing yourself and everyone else much more good than you're doing at present. If your father was framed, Waldstein knows all about it. I'll tell you that. But what good you expect to do by simply making yourself a nuisance to the police force in general is more than my logical mind can see."

She pointed to the table.

"I suppose you've seen the papers?"

"We have. All about the inefficiency of the police. Of course, everybody doesn't know that I'm in charge of the situation. But does it give you the satisfaction you want?"

"It gives me some satisfaction."

"We are also amused," said Simon. "The chiefs of the C. I. D. meet together twice a day to roar with laughter over it. . . . And I think that's all for to-day. I'll see you again soon. If you like, I'll drop you a line to say when I'm coming, so that you can arrange to be out."

"Perhaps," she said silkily, "you will not be in a position to come again. So you might save the stamp."

"That's all right," said the Saint easily. "I shouldn't have stamped the letter."

He stood up and picked up his hat, which he brushed carefully with his sleeve. She made no move to delay him.

At the door he turned for his parting shot.

"Just for information," he said, "is there going to be any trouble about my leaving this time?"

"No," she said quietly. "Not just now."

He smiled.

"Something else arranged, I suppose. Not machine guns, I hope. And no more poisoned milk. I don't want you to let yourself down by repeating yourself too often, you know."

"You won't be in suspense for long," she said.

"I'm glad to hear it," said the Saint, with intense earnestness. "Well, bye-bye, old dear."

He strolled down the stairs, humming a little tune.

No one attempted to stop him. The hall was de-

serted. He let himself out and sauntered down Belgrave Street, swinging his stick.

As a bluffing interview it had not borne the fruit he
had hoped for. Since their first encounters, the girl
had recovered a great deal of the poise and self-control
that his studied impudence had at first been able to
flurry her into losing. On that occasion she had given
nothing away of importance—only that she had an
interest in Waldstein. This was perhaps the one interest that Simon Templar shared with her whole-
heartedly.

CHAPTER III

HOW SIMON TEMPLAR MADE A SLIGHT ERROR,
AND PINKY BUDD MADE A BIG ONE

Two days later, Simon Templar went unostentatiously to a certain public house in Aldgate. He was not noticed, for he had made some subtle alterations to his appearance and bearing. One man, however, recognized him, and they moved over to a quiet corner of the bar.

"Have they been in touch with you again?" was the Saint's immediate question.

Mr. Dyson nodded.

His right eye was still disfigured by a swollen black-and-blue bruise. Mr. Dyson, thinking it over subsequently, had decided that ten pounds was an inadequate compensation for the injury, but it was too late to re-open that discussion.

"They sent for me yesterday," he said. "I went at once, and they gave me a very good welcome."

"Did you drink it?" asked the Saint interestedly.

"They've definitely taken me on."

"And the news?"

"It was like this . . ."

Simon listened to a long recital which told him nothing at all of any value, and departed a pound poorer than he had been when he came. It was the highest value he could place upon Mr. Dyson's first budget of information, and Slinky's aggrieved pleading made no impression upon the Saint at all.

He got back to the Yard to hear some real news.

"Your Angels have been out again while you weren't watching them," said Cullis, as soon as the Saint had answered his summons. "Essenden was beaten up last night."

"Badly?"

"Not very. The servants were still about, and Essenden was able to let off a yell which fetched them around in a bunch. The man got away. It seems that Essenden found him in his bedroom when he went upstairs about eleven o'clock. He tried to tackle the man, and got the worst of the fight. The burglar was using a cosh."

"And who did the good work?"

"Probably your friend Slinky. I've put a warrant out for him, anyway."

"Then take it back," said the Saint. "Slinky never used a cosh in his life. Besides, I happen to know that he didn't do it."

"I suppose he told you so?"

"He didn't—that's why I believe him. Have you had the report from Records on the general features of the show?"

"I've given them the details. The report should be through any minute now."

The report, as a matter of fact, was brought up a few minutes later. The Saint ran through the list of names submitted as possible authors of the crime, and selected one without much hesitation.

"Harry Donnell's the man."

"At Essenden's?" interjected Cullis skeptically. "Harry Donnell works the Midlands. Besides, his gang don't go in for ordinary burglary."

"Who said it was an ordinary burglary?" asked the Saint. "I tell you Harry Donnell's the man on that list who'd be most pleased to take on an easy job of bashing like that. I could probably tell your Records Office a few things they didn't know about Harry—you seem to forget that I used to know everything there was to know about the various birds in his line of business. I'm going to pull him in. Before I go I'm going to tell Jill Trelawney that I'm going to do it. I'll go round and see her now. She'll probably try to fix me for some sticky end this time. But that's a minor detail. Having failed in that she'll try to get on the phone to Donnell and warn him—I expect he went back to Birmingham this morning. You'll arrange for the exchange operator to tell her that the line to Birmingham is out of order. Then, if I know anything about Jill Trelawney, she'll set out to try to beat me to Birmingham herself. She's got to keep up her reputation for rescues, especially when the man to be rescued is wanted for doing a job for her. . . ."

He outlined his plan in more detail.

It was one which had come into his head on the spur of the moment, but the more he examined it the better it seemed to be. There was no evidence against Jill

Trelawney on any of the scores which were at present held against her, and the Saint would have been bored stiff to spend his time sifting over ancient history in the hope of building up a live case out of dead material. Besides—which was far more important—that procedure wouldn't have fitted in at all with the real ambition that the story of the Angels of Doom had brought into his young life. And to set Jill Trelawney racing into Birmingham to the rescue of Harry Donnell struck him as being a much more entertaining way of spending the day.

In spite of the two attempts which had already been made on his life, he bore the girl no malice. Far from it. The Saint was used to that kind of thing. In fact, he had already found more amusement in the pursuit of Jill Trelawney than he had anticipated when he first set forth to make her acquaintance, and he was now preparing to find some more—but this, however, he did not confide to the commissioner.

They talked for a while longer, and the Saint left certain definite instructions to be passed on to the appropriate quarter. And then, as the Saint rose to go, the commissioner was moved to revert to a thought suggested by the original subject of the interview.

"Isn't it curious," said the commissioner, "that only the other night you should have been asking whether there might be a reason for the Angels to have a feud with Essenden?"

"Isn't it a scream?" agreed the Saint.

He set off for Belgrave Street in one of his moods of Saintly optimism.

It struck him that he was spending a great deal of his time in Belgrave Street. This would be his third visit that week.

He had no illusions about the possible outcome of it—the gun with which he had provided himself before leaving testified to that. A man cannot make himself as consistently unpopular as, for his own inscrutable reasons, it had in this case pleased the Saint to make himself, without there growing up, sooner or later, a state of tension in which something has to break. The thing broken should, of course, have been Simon Templar, but up to that time the thing broken had somehow failed to be Simon Templar. But this time . . .

In the three days since his last visit life had been allowed to deal peacefully with him. He had used the milk from outside his front door with a sublime confidence in its purity, and had not been disappointed. He had walked in and out of the house without any fear of being again enfiladed by machine-gun fire; and in that again his judgment had proved to be right. On the other hand, he had treated letters and parcels delivered to him, and taxis which offered themselves for his hire, with considerable suspicion. He had as yet found no justification for this carefulness, but he realized that the calm could only be the herald of a storm. Possibly this third visit to Belgrave Street would precipitate the storm. He was prepared for it to do so.

He was kept waiting outside for some time before his summons was answered. He did not stand at the top of the stairs, however, while he was waiting, in a position where sudden death might reach him through the letter box, but placed himself on the pavement behind the shelter of one of the pillars of the portico. From behind this, with one eye looking round it, he was able to see the slight movement of a curtain in a ground-floor window as someone looked out to discover who the visitor was. Simon allowed his face to be seen, and then withdrew into cover until the door opened. Then he entered quickly.

"Miss Trelawney is expecting you," said Wells as he closed the door.

The Saint glanced searchingly round the hall and up the stairs as far as he could see. There was no one else about.

He smiled seraphically.

"You're getting quite truthful in your old age, Freddie," he remarked, and went up the stairs.

The girl met him on the landing.

"I got your message to say you were coming."

"I hope it gave you a thrill," said the Saint earnestly.

He looked past her into the sitting room.

"Are you staying to tea again?" she asked sweetly.

"Before I've finished," said Simon, "I expect you'll be wanting me to stay the week."

"Come in."

"Thanks. I will. Aren't we getting polite?"

He went through.

In the sitting room he found Weald and Budd, as he had expected to find them, though they had not been exposed to the field of view which he had from the landing through the open door.

"Hullo, Weald! And are you looking for Wald-stein, too?"

Weald's sallow face went a shade paler, but he did not answer at once. The Saint's mocking gaze shifted to Budd.

"Been doing any more fighting lately, Pinky? I heard that some tough guy beat up a couple of little boys in Shoreditch the other night, and I thought of you at once."

Pinky's fists clenched.

"If you're looking for trouble, Templar," he said pinkly, "I'm waiting for you, see?"

"I know that," said the Saint offensively. "I could hear you breathing as I came up the stairs."

He heard the door close behind him, and turned to face the girl again.

It was a careless move, but he had not been expecting the hostilities to be reopened quite so quickly. The fact that the mere presence of his own charming personality might be considered by anyone else as a hostile movement in itself had escaped him. In these circumstances there is, by convention, a certain amount of warbling and woofling before any active unpleasantness is displayed. Simon Templar had always found this so—it took a certain amount of time for his enemies to get over the confident effrontery of his own bearing, and, in these days, their ingrained respect for the law which he was temporarily representing—before they nerved themselves to action. But this was not his first visit to Belgrave Street, nor their first sight of him, and they might have been expected to show enough intelligence to fortify themselves against his coming beforehand. Simon, however, had not expected it. It was the first slip he had made with the Angels of Doom.

He felt the sharp pressure in his back, and knew what it was without having to turn and look. Even then he did not turn.

Without batting an eyelid he said what he had come to say, exactly as if he had noticed nothing amiss whatever.

"I've still some more news to give you, Jill."

There was a certain mockery in the eyes that returned his gaze.

"Do you still want to give it?"

"Why, yes," said the Saint innocently. "Why not?"

Weald spoke behind him.

"We're listening, Templar. Don't move too suddenly, because I might think you were going to put up a fight."

The Saint turned slowly and glanced down at the gun in Weald's hand.

"Oh, that! Wonderful how science helps you boys all along the line. And a silencer, too. Do you know, I always thought those things were only used in stories written for little boys?"

"It's good enough for me."

"I couldn't think of anything that wouldn't be too good for you," said the Saint. "Except, perhaps, a really mutinous sewer." Then he turned round again. "Do you know a man named Donnell, Jill?"

"Very well."

"Then you'd better go ring him up and tell him good-bye. He's going to Dartmoor for a long holiday, and he mightn't remember you when he comes out."

She laughed.

"The police in Birmingham have been saying things like that about Harry Donnell for the last two years, and they've never taken him."

"Possibly," said the Saint in his modest way. "But this time the police of Birmingham aren't concerned."

"Then who's going to take him?"

Simon smoothed his hair.

"I am."

Pinky Budd chuckled throatily.

"Not 'arf, you ain't!"

"Not 'arf, I ain't," agreed the Saint courteously.

"May I ask," said the girl, "how you think you're going to Birmingham?"

"By train."

"After you leave here?"

"After I leave here."

"D'you think you're leaving?" interjected Weald.

"I'm sure of it," said the Saint calmly. "Slinky Dyson will let me out. He's an old friend of mine."

The girl opened the door. Dyson was outside.

"Here's your friend the Saint," she said.

"Hullo, Slinky," said the Saint. "How's the eye?"
Dyson slouched into the room.

"Search him," ordered Weald.

Dyson obeyed, doing the job with ungentle hands.
Simon made no resistance. In the circumstances that
would only have been a mediocre way of committing
suicide.

"How true you run to type, Jill!" he murmured.
"This is just what I was expecting. And now, of course,
you'll tell me that I'm going to be kept here as your
prisoner until you choose to let me go. Or are you
going to lock me in the cellar and leave the hose running? That was tried once. Or perhaps you're going
to ask me to join your gang. That'd be quite original."

"Sit down," snapped Weald.

Simon sat down as if he had been meaning to do so
all the time.

Jill Trelawney was at the telephone. The Saint observed her out of the corner of his eye while he selected and lighted a cigarette from his case. He waited
quite patiently while she tried to make the call, but he
feigned surprise when she failed.

"That really upsets me," he said. "Now you'll have
to go to Birmingham yourself. I hate to think I'm putting you to so much inconvenience."

He saw Budd busying himself with some loose rope,
and when the ex-prize fighter came over with the obvi-

ous intention of binding him, the Saint put his hands behind him without being told to. Weald was talking to the girl.

"Do you really mean to go to Birmingham?"

"Yes. It's the only thing to do. I can't get in touch with Donnell by telephone, and it wouldn't be safe to send a wire."

"And suppose it's a trap?"

"You can suppose it's what you like. The Saint's clever. But I think I've got the hang of him now. It's just a repetition of that posse joke. He's come to tell us that he's going to get Donnell just because he thinks we won't believe it. And if he does get Donnell, Donnell will squeal. If you've got cold feet you can stay here. But I'm going. Budd can go with me if you don't like it. He'll be more use than you, anyway."

"I'll go with you."

"Have it your own way."

She came back to watch Budd putting the finishing touches to the Saint's roping.

"You'll be pleased to hear," she said, "that for once I'm going to believe you."

"So I heard," said the Saint. "Hope you have a nice journey. Will you leave Dyson to look after me? I'm sure he'd treat me very kindly."

She shook her head.

"Budd," she said, "will be even kinder."

It was a blow at the very foundations of the scheme which the Saint had built up, but not a muscle of his face betrayed his feelings.

He spoke to her as if there were no one else in the room, holding her eyes in spite of herself with that mocking stare of his.

"Jill Trelawney," he said, "you're a fool. If there were degrees in pure, undiluted imbecility I should give you first prize. You're going to Birmingham with Weald. When you get there you're going to walk into a pile of trouble. Weald will be as much use to you as a tin tombstone. Not that the thought worries me, but I'm just telling you now, and I'd like you to remember it afterwards. Before to-night you're going to wish you'd been born with some sort of imitation of a brain. That's all. I shall see you again in Birmingham—don't worry."

She smiled, with a lift of her eyebrows.

"Aren't you thoughtful for me, Simon Templar?"

"We don't mind doing these things for old customers," said the Saint benignly.

He was still looking at her. The bantering gaze of his blue eyes from under the lazily drooping eyelids, the faint smile, the hint of a lilt of laughter in his voice —these things could rarely have been more airily perfect in their mockery.

"And while you're on your way," said the Saint, "you might have time to remember that I never asked you to become a customer. You're making the most blind paralytic fool of yourself that ever a woman made of anything that God had given her such a long start on! But that's your own idea, isn't it? Now go ahead and prove it's right. Go to Birmingham, take that diseased blot of a Stephen Weald with you——

Weald stepped forward.

"What did you say, Templar?"

"I said 'diseased blot of a Stephen Weald,'" said the Saint pleasantly. "Any objection?"

"I have," said Weald. "This——"

He struck the Saint three times in the face with his fist.

". . . and this—for the first time I met you."

Simon sat like a rock.

"You've found some courage since then," he remarked, in a voice of steel and granite. "Been taking pink pills or something?"

Then the girl stepped between them.

"That'll do," she said curtly. "Weald, go and get your coat. Pinky, you and Dyson can carry Templar downstairs."

"So it's to be the cellar and the hose pipe, is it?" drawled the Saint, unimpressed.

"Just the cellar, for the present," she answered coolly. "I'll decide what else is to be done with you when I come back."

"*If.* If you come back," said the Saint indulgently.

2

Simon lay in the cellar where he had been carelessly dropped, and meditated his position by the light of the single dusty globe which provided the sole illumination in the place. Having dropped him there, Budd and

Dyson departed, but the hope that they might have gone for good, thereby leaving him to try all the tricks of escape he knew upon the ropes with which he had been tied, was soon dispelled. They returned in a few moments, Budd carrying a table and Dyson a couple of chairs. Then they closed the door and sat down.

Clearly, the watch was intended to be a close one. Budd took a pack of greasy cards from his pocket, and the two men settled down to a game.

Cautiously, as well as he could without attracting attention, the Saint tested his bonds. The process did not take him long. His expert tests soon proved that the roping had been done by a practised hand. It remained, therefore, to depend on the loyalty of Slinky Dyson. And how much was that worth? In an interval in the game he caught Dyson's eye. Slinky's expression did not change, but Simon found something reassuring in that unpromising fact.

For a quarter of an hour the game continued, and then Slinky wiped his mouth with a soiled handkerchief.

"This is a thirsty job," he complained.

"Ain't it?" agreed Budd. "Would you like a drink?"

"Not 'arf. Is there anything?"

Budd nodded.

"I'll see if I can find something. You keep your eyes skinned for Templar, see?"

"You bet I will."

Budd rose and went out, leaving the door open, and

Simon listened without speaking as the sound of the man's heavy footsteps faded up the stairs.

A moment later he found Dyson beside him.

"I don't want to hustle you," said the Saint easily, "but if you've nothing else to do at the moment——"

Dyson swallowed.

"If Budd comes back and catches me at this I'm a goner," he said.

He had opened a murderous-looking jackknife, and Simon felt the ropes loosen about his arms and legs as Dyson slashed clumsily at them. Then, beyond the sound of Dyson's laboured breathing, he heard Budd coming back. Slinky gave a little grunt of panic.

"You'll see I'm all right, Mr. Templar, won't you?"

"Sure," said the Saint.

He stood up and swiftly untwisted the loose cords that held him and dropped them on the floor.

Pinky Budd saw him standing up free beside the table, and very carefully he put down the tray he was carrying.

"So that's the idea!" breathed Budd.

"It is," said the Saint gently. "And now we're going to have a fight, aren't we?"

Dyson was still holding the murderous jackknife, but the Saint pushed him smoothly aside.

"You can put that away," he said. "This is a vegetarian party. Fairly vegetarian, anyway. I'm going to give Pinky beans, and—— Oh, don't go yet, Pinky!"

Budd had made a dive for the door. The key was still in the lock, and if he had brought off the manœuvre

he might have been able to get outside and lock the
door behind him. But the Saint was a shade quicker.
The table was between him and Budd, but he hurled
it aside as if it had been made of cardboard, and
caught Budd's hand as it went to the lock.

Budd dropped the key with a scream of pain. He
tried to kick, but Simon dodged neatly.

Then he pushed Budd away so that the man went
reeling across the room, and the Saint picked up the
key and put it in his trouser pocket. Then he slipped
off his coat.

"And now, Pinky Budd, we have this fight, don't
we?"

But Budd was coming on without any encouragement. He was on his toes, too. The fighting game had
not dealt lightly with Pinky's face, but he had all the
science and experience that he had won at the cost of
his disfigurements.

He led off with a sledge-hammer left that would
have ended the fight then and there if it had connected.
But it did not connect. Simon ducked and landed a
left-right beat to the body that made Budd grunt. Then
the Saint was away again, sparring, and he also was
on his toes.

Moreover, he was between Budd and the door, and
he meant to stay there. Budd had asked for the fight,
and he was going to get it. Budd might have been
glad of the chance, or he might have wanted to get out
of it, but he wasn't having the choice, anyway. Simon
Templar was seeing to that. But to a certain extent

that tactical necessity of keeping between Budd and the door was going to cramp his style. He appreciated the disadvantage in a fight which wasn't going to be an easy fight at any moment. But it couldn't be helped.

Budd's next lead was another left, but it was a feint. The Saint divined that and changed his guard. But he was a little slow in divining that the right cross which came over after the left was a second feint, and the half-arm jolt to the short ribs which followed it caught him unprepared and drove him back gasping against the wall.

Budd came in like a tiger, left and right, and Simon dropped to one knee.

He straightened up with a raking uppercut that must have ricked Budd's neck as though a horse had kicked him under the chin. That blow would have been the end of the average man for some time to come. But Budd had been trained in a tougher school. He fell into a clinch that the Saint, still rib-bound from the smashing blow he had taken, was not quick enough to avoid. There Budd's weight told. There was no referee to give them the break-away, and the professional was free to use every dirty trick of holding and heading and heeling for which a clinch gives openings. But the Saint also knew a few of those himself, and he broke the clinch eventually with a blow that would certainly have got him disqualified in any official contest. As he stepped out he swung up a pendulum left which should have caught Budd under the jaw. Pinky got his head back quickly enough, but not quite far enough, and the blow snicked up his nose.

It maddened him, but it also blinded him. No man, however tough, can have his nose snicked up in that particular way without having his vision momentarily fogged. And before Budd could see what was happening the Saint had sent in a pile-driving right-hander to the heart. Then he turned on his toes and followed through with a left to the solar plexus that had every ounce of his weight behind it, and Budd went smashing down as if a steam hammer had hit him.

Simon picked up his coat.

"We ought to be just in time to get that train, Slinky," he remarked, and then he turned round to find that Slinky Dyson had already gone.

With a shrug the Saint went out, locking the door behind him.

A taxi took him to Paddington, and he arrived outside the platform barrier just as the guard was blowing his whistle.

He had no ticket, but such minor difficulties were never allowed to stand in Simon Templar's way. Nor was the ticket collector. Simon picked him up and sat him on a convenient luggage trolley, and raced down the platform as the train was gathering way. He opened the door of the first convenient carriage and swung into it. Looking back through the window, he saw the chase of porters tailing off breathlessly. They might telephone to Birmingham and prepare a reception for him there, but that would not take long to deal with.

Then he turned to inspect the other occupants of the carriage, whose flabbergasted comments had been audible behind him as he looked back out of the window; but the first person he noticed was not a man in the carriage. It was a man who happened to be passing down the corridor.

The Saint strode over a barricade of legs, odd luggage, and a bird cage, and went down the corridor in the man's wake. Coming up sufficiently close behind him, he trod heavily on the man's heels; and Stephen Weald turned with an oath.

"What the——"

The exclamation died suddenly, and Weald's face went grey as he recognized the offender.

Simon's lips twitched into a little smile of sprightly merriment.

"So we're all going to Birmingham together!"

Then, with a surprising abruptness, he turned away into the nearest carriage, where he had already perceived a vacant seat, and composed himself to the enjoyment of a cigarette.

Weald passed on.

A little farther down the corridor was the compartment in which he and the girl had found places. She looked up as he showed in the doorway, and he gave her an imperceptible signal. She came out to join him in the corridor.

"What is it?"

"Let's go to the dining car," said Weald. "We shan't be overheard there."

He led the way, and no more was said until they were securely ensconced and tea had been ordered.

"Well, what is it, Weald?"

"The Saint's on the train! I've just seen him."

She stopped in the act of fitting a cigarette into a holder.

"The Saint? You're dreaming."

He shook his head. The hand with which he offered her a match was shaking.

"I tell you I saw him. He spoke to me. He's in a compartment three divisions back from ours. I don't know how he got away, but he's done it."

The girl's eyes narrowed.

"It's that man Dyson. Heavens, Templar's clever! You were listening when he warned me about Dyson, weren't you? And we took it just the way the Saint meant us to take it. Dyson's done the double-cross."

"And Pinky——?"

"Pinky's a back number."

The girl admitted the fact grimly. She was calm about it.

"Why do you think the Saint is in this, Jill?"

"Who knows why the Saint does anything? You've read the stories in the newspapers—he was pardoned, and now he seems to be working right in with the police. . . . But you're right. This isn't like any ordinary racket of the Saint's."

"What are we going to do?" asked Weald tremblingly.

"I'll tell you in a minute," she said. "Keep quiet, and don't bother me."

She drew at her cigarette, looking out of the window at the darkening scenery. It was some time before she looked at Weald again.

Then she said:

"We go on, of course!"

Weald's mouth fell open.

"But Templar's on the train. I'm not being funny——"

"Neither am I. The Saint's expecting to scare us off Donnell, but we aren't going to be scared. If he's on the train, we haven't a way out, anyway. The only thing for us to do is to go on. We may be able to deal with him at Donnell's, but we can't here, that's certain. The train's packed, and we'd never get away with it."

"He'll have a posse at Donnell's."

She laughed, a hard little laugh.

"That posse's another of the Saint's fairy tales. I don't believe a man like that would dream of using one. He's got too darn good an opinion of himself. Don't you see that it amuses him to go about alone like this and get away with it? He gets twice as much kudos for the job as he would if he went round with a bodyguard. But this time he isn't going to get away with it. That's my answer. If you know anything better I'll hear it."

Weald said nothing. The train ran on.

He avoided her eyes. Picking up his cup to drink mechanically, he spilt tea over the tablecloth. But that might have been the jolting of the train. He hoped she would think it was. He knew she was watching him.

What little colour there could be in his face had not come back since he saw the Saint, for Stephen Weald had seen the jaws of destruction yawning at him at the same time.

It had all happened so quietly and gently up to that point that he had never seen the danger until it was upon him. There had been nothing concrete in the mere knowledge that the Saint was after the Angels of Doom, imposing as the Saint's reputation was. And though each of Simon Templar's visits to Belgrave Street had been both an insult and a threat, none of them had been sufficiently terrifying to rouse an alarm which could not be dissipated with a drink after he had left. And now it seemed as if all that had changed as suddenly as if a charge of dynamite had been detonated under the whole situation. And all through such a simple thing. Before that there had been no evidence against any of them. But now there was. Simon Templar had been held up and bound and locked in a cellar, and now he was free to tell the tale, with Dyson's evidence to support it.

That might well be the beginning of the end. Weald had always had a wholesome respect for the tenacity of the police when once they got hold of a solid bone to chew. Throughout his career he had made a point of keeping away from any material contact with them. As long as they were working in the dark against him he could feel safe, but once they could make any definite accusation, and thus get a hold on him, there was no knowing where it might end.

But in Jill Trelawney there was no sign of weakening.

"We can still pull through," she said.

Weald's thin fingers twitched his tie nervously.

"How can you say that after what we know now?"

"We're not dead yet. In your way, you're right, of course. We've tripped over about the most ridiculous little thing that we could have tripped over, and if we aren't careful we'll go stumbling over the edge of the precipice. But I'm not giving an imitation of a jelly in an earthquake."

"Nor am I," said Weald angrily.

The mocking contempt remained in her eyes, and he knew that he was not believed.

With a certain grim concession to her sense of humour she remembered the Saint's warning before they left Belgrave Street. The Saint had certainly been right. In the circumstances, Weald was likely to be very much less use than a tin tombstone. She saw the way he put a hand to cover the twitching of his weak mouth, and realized that Stephen Weald was going to pieces rapidly.

CHAPTER IV

HOW JILL TRELAWNEY TOLD A LIE, AND SIMON TEMPLAR SPOKE NOTHING BUT THE TRUTH

HARRY DONNELL lived in a house in a mean street on the outskirts of Birmingham. It was a curious house, but as soon as he had seen it he knew that few other houses could have fulfilled his requirements so completely, for he had always boasted that if necessary he would resist arrest to the death.

This house had grown up, somehow, in the very inside of a block. Being completely surrounded by the other houses of the block necessarily deprived its rooms of most of the light of day, but Donnell could not see this as a disadvantage. The same fact made the house very difficult to attack, and this to his mind was compensation enough. In fact, the building could only be approached directly through a straight and narrow alleyway between two of the outer houses.

He rarely stirred out of doors except on business, preferring to sleep and drink and smoke at home, and amuse himself with his own inscrutable and animal meditations. He was at home when Jill Trelawney and Stephen Weald arrived, and went down to open the door to them himself when he recognized the signal on the bell which showed that the visitors were friendly.

"Good-afternoon, Miss Trelawney," he said politely, for Harry Donnell prided himself on his accomplishments as a·ladies' man. Her manner, however, cut short any courtesies.

"The Saint's after you," she said bluntly. "Where can we talk?"

He looked at her, and then led the way upstairs without a word.

They went up two flights of dingy, creaking stairs, for the first and ground floors were devoted to the sleeping accommodations of his gang. On the second floor he opened a door and showed them into a big, bare room, of which the principal articles of furniture appeared to consist of a rough deal table and a case of whisky. This room, like most of the others in the house, was lighted only by a small and dirty window which admitted hardly any light, and the gloom was made gloomier by the fog of stale tobacco smoke which hung in the air.

Donnell closed the door behind them.

"Did you say the Saint?"

"I did. Do you know him?"

Donnell drew back his lips from a row of black and broken teeth.

"I met him—once."

"You look like meeting him again," said the girl shortly.

Donnell was not immediately impressed. He took a

pipe from his pocket and began to fill it from a tin on the table.

"What do you mean?"

"He's after you for that show at Essenden's. He came and told me that he was going to take you himself. We shut him up in the cellar and came to warn you ourselves. But he got away somehow and caught the same train as we did. Weald saw him. We didn't see him again at the other end, but he can't be far behind. In fact, I know how far behind he is. He knows I'm coming here and he's hanging just far enough behind to get me into the trap as well. He's after me, too."

Donnell looked from her to Weald.

"Is this a joke?" he demanded.

And Weald's face told him it was not a joke. He turned to the girl again.

"Why didn't you get me on the telephone?" he asked harshly. "Isn't that what it's here for?"

"The exchange told me that the trunk line was out of order," said Jill quietly. "And don't talk to me like that. I don't like it."

Donnell faced her cold gaze three seconds and then dropped his eyes.

"No offense," he muttered.

"Forget it," said the girl briskly. "We've got about three or four minutes, I should say, before Templar turns up. I'd like him to have a welcome. He'll be alone—I'm certain of that. What can you do about it?"

"There are half a dozen of the boys downstairs."

"Can you stop him getting in?"

Donnell grinned.

"I could stop an army," he bragged.

"Can you stop the Saint?"

"Haven't you seen round this house?" asked Donnell. "I've had it ready for years, just for something like this. I'll take you round, if you like, and you can see for yourself."

Jill tightened the belt of her coat.

"I'll look round on my own, if you don't mind," she said. "I know what to look for, and it probably isn't what you'd show me. Give Weald a drink while I'm gone—I guess he needs it."

She went out, and Donnell picked up a bottle and a glass. He poured out four good fingers of the spirit, and Weald grabbed it and drank it neat. Then he turned to Donnell; the fire-water had steadied him up a bit—in a way.

"You believe it isn't a joke?" he said.

Donnell nodded.

"Yes, I believe it now."

"I'm up against it," panted Weald flabbily. "I'm up against it much more than you are. They can only get you for a bashing, but they can get me for a lot more."

"Ever beat up a 'tec?"

"More than that. I can't tell you. They might . . . Donnell, you've got to get us out of this!"

Donnell's eyebrows came down.

"What do you mean, get you out of it? What about me?"

Weald clutched his arm.

"You don't understand. I've got to get away. I've got to take the girl with me. Is there any back way out of this—any bolt hole you've prepared? I've got money——"

Donnell thrust him roughly into a chair and pushed the whisky bottle towards him. Weald helped himself greedily to another half-glassful.

"Now you're talking," said Donnell. "How much?"

Weald dragged a note case from his pocket. It bulged. Donnell's eyes fastened on it hungrily.

"A thousand, Donnell. It's all I can spare. I've got to leave myself some money to get clear."

"Let's see it."

Feverishly Weald counted out the notes with shaking fingers and put them on the table. Donnell moistened his thumb and counted them deliberately. Then he put them in his pocket.

"That cupboard behind you," he said. "The back of it's a sliding door. You'll find some stairs. Go right down. There's a tunnel under the block and the street, and it comes up in the cellar of a house on the other side."

"But you've got to hold Templar up."

Donnell struck his chest with a huge fist.

"Me? I'll hold the Saint up. I don't run away from anyone—but you can clear out when you want to. You'd be more trouble than use, anyway."

Weald swallowed the taunt without a protest.

"All right. As soon as the girl comes back you get out and say you're going to warn your gang. I'll look after the rest."

Donnell sat down heavily on a truckle bed in one corner. He took a massive revolver from his pocket, spilled the cartridges into his hand, and squinted up the barrel. He spun the cylinder with his fingers, tested the hammer action to his satisfaction, and reloaded the gun methodically.

"What's the idea?" he asked laconically. "You sweet on her?"

Weald nodded, with the bottle in his hand.

"That's not the half of it. I've been wanting her for months. I thought I'd do it gradually, working with her and making her like me. But there isn't time for any more fooling about. If the police are going to get me I'm going to get her first. I don't care if it's the last thing I do. Donnell—on the train—she was sneering at me!"

"Anyone would," said Donnell unemotionally. "A white-livered rat like you!"

Weald wiped his mouth. The whisky was going to his head.

"I'm not a white-livered rat, Donnell!" he blustered.

"You're a white-livered rat and a yellow cur at the same time," said Donnell without heat, testing the sights of his Colt on the whisky bottle.

Weald lurched towards him.

"Donnell, you take that back!"

"Don't be a blasted nuisance," said Donnell impatiently.

He took Weald's shoulder in a huge hand and pushed him away. Then Jill Trelawney came into the room.

"I've seen all I want to see," she said. "Donnell, will you go down and rouse up the boys?"

"I was just going to, Miss Trelawney," said Donnell heavily.

He went to the door and leered, behind her back, at Weald. Then he went out, and Weald heard him clumping heavily down the stairs.

"I didn't say you were to drink a whole bottle," remarked Jill, surveying Weald's unsteady balance.

"You don't understand, Jill. I've been finding a way out."

He walked rockily to the cupboard that Donnell had indicated and dragged open the doors. After some fumbling he was able to open the sliding door at the back, and then he found a switch. The light showed a flight of steps leading down into a damp and musty darkness.

"Our way out!" declaimed Weald grandiosely.

"Very interesting," said the girl, "but we don't happen to be going that way."

He stared.

"Not going that way?"

"How the Angels of Doom would miss you!" she said caustically. "Without you they'd be absolutely helpless. The great brain, always clear and alert in times of crisis."

"Jill!"

"Oh, be quiet!" Her sarcasm turned to contempt suddenly. "When you're sober you're futile, and when you're drunk you maunder. I don't know which is worse. Now pull yourself together. Donnell is ready to do his part, and his boys are with him, but he's looking to you and me to pull him through. The Angels have never failed yet, and they can't fail now."

"But, Jill——"

"And a little less of the 'Jill,' " she cut in icily. "This place can stand a siege for a week, and we can still get out that way if we have to. But I'm going to let Templar in—right in—and there's going to be no mistake about him this time."

He swayed towards her.

"And I say we're going out this way—now!" he shouted. "I've had about enough of being ordered about by you, and being snubbed, and treated like a child. Now you're going to do what I say, for a change. Come on!"

She regarded him with a calculating eye.

"About one more drink," she said, "and you'd be dead drunk. On the whole, I think I'd prefer that to your present state."

"Oh, you would, would you?"

The resentment which Weald had been afraid to let loose before Donnell he had no need to control now. He grasped her shoulders with clumsy hands.

"That's the sort of talk I'm not standing from you any longer," he said shrilly. "You're going to stop it, right now, do you see? From now on I'm going to give the orders and you're going to obey them. I love you!"

"You're mad," she said coldly. But for the first time in her life a little imp of fear plucked at her heart.

He thrust his face down close to hers. She could smell the drink on his breath.

"I'm not mad. I've been mad before, but I'm sensible now. I want to take you away—out of here—out of England—out into the world! I'm going to give you jewels, and beautiful clothes. And you're going to love me, and there's going to be no one else. You're going to forget all this nonsense about your father. You're not going to think about it any more. It's going to be just you and me, Jill! Lovely Jill——"

She flung him off so that he went reeling back against the wall and almost fell. Then she jerked from her bag the little automatic she always carried, but he leapt at her like a tiger and tore it out of her hands.

"No, Jill, that's not the way. Not like that. Like this."

His arms went round her. She fought him back desperately, but he was too strong for her. Once she was almost able to tear herself away, but he blundered after her, still clutching her sleeve, and caught her again. His lips were trying to find her mouth.

Suddenly she went limp in his arms. It was the only thing she could do at that moment—to pretend to faint, and thus give herself a chance to catch him off his guard. And for a space Stephen Weald looked down at her stupidly. Then, with a sudden resolution, he swung her off her feet and carried her through the open cupboard.

Hampered by his burden, he could only feel his way down step by step. The direct light above was soon lost, and the stairs grew darker and darker. He went on. Then another light dawned below, and grew more powerful as he proceeded farther downwards; at last the bulb which gave the light was on the level of his eyes. He went down beneath it, and presently found himself on level stone.

A corridor stretched away before him, lighted at long intervals by electric bulbs. He went on down it and felt a faint breath of fresh air on his face. Presently the tunnel forked. Donnell had not told him about that. He hesitated, and then plunged into the right-hand branch. In a few yards it took a turn, and a door faced him. He got it open and went into darkness. Groping round, he found a switch, and when he had clicked it over he discovered that he was in a dead end —the tunnel did not go on, but stopped in the room into which he had opened the door.

There was a tattered carpet on the floor, and a table and a chair on the carpet. In one corner was a couch, in another were a pile of tinned foods and a beaker of water.

He should have turned back and tried the left-hand branch of the tunnel, but he was not an athletic man, and the effort of carrying even such a light weight as the girl for that distance had taxed his untrained muscles severely. He put her down on the couch and straightened up, mopping his streaming brow and breathing heavily.

His back was towards her when she opened her eyes, but she saw the bulge of the gun in his coat pocket. She raised herself cautiously and put out her hand. Her fingers were actually sliding into his pocket when he turned and saw her.

"Not that either, you little devil!" he snarled.

He caught her wrist and wrenched it away from the gun she had almost succeeded in grasping.

"You'd like to shoot me, wouldn't you?" he said thickly. "But you're not going to have the chance. You're going to love me. You're going to love me in spite of everything—even if I *am* Waldstein!"

She shrank away from him with wide eyes.

"Yes, even if I *am* Waldstein," he babbled. "Even if I did help to break your father. He was an officious nuisance. But you're quite different. You're going to settle with me in my way, Jill!"

2

There had been another man on the train to Birmingham, whom Simon Templar had not seen. He did not meet him until he had disembarked and was hailing a taxi; and, seeing him, the Saint was not pleased.

But this was the kind of displeasure about which Simon Templar never let on, and it was the assistant commissioner who stared.

"Good Lord, Templar, how did you get here?"

"I came on a tricycle," said the Saint gravely. "Did you use a motor-scooter?"

"I got your message——"

"What message?"

Cullis tugged at his moustache.

"Dyson rang up to say you were caught at Belgrave Street. He said he was to tell me that you wanted to be left there, and I was to come to Birmingham and take Donnell."

The Saint looked at him thoughtfully.

"Is this another of the old Trelawney touches of humour?" he murmured. "I never sent you that message. What's more, I'll swear Dyson never sent it, either. He was never out of my sight from the time I was stuck up in Belgrave Street until a few seconds before I left. Someone's been pulling your leg!"

He bent his eyes on the commissioner's nether limbs as if he really entertained a morbid hope that he would find one of them longer than the other.

Cullis pushed his hat back from his forehead.

"Just what's the idea?"

"There's some funny scheme behind it," said the Saint, with the air of a man announcing an epoch-making discovery, "and we've yet to learn what it is. However, since you're here, you can be of some use. Beetle round to the local police and make what arrangements you like. They can surround the block and be ready to take over Donnell when I bring him out. That'll save me some time."

"You're going in alone?"

"I'm afraid I've got to go in alone," said the Saint sadly. "You see, this is my nurse's afternoon off. . . . See you at a dairy later, old pomegranate."

He tapped Cullis encouragingly in the stomach, climbed into the taxi, and closed the door, leaving the commissioner standing there with a blank look on his face.

He did not drive directly up to the mouth of the alleyway which admitted to the front door of Donnell's fortress. That would have been too blatant even for Simon Templar. Besides, reckless as he might be, he did not believe in suicide, and the long, straight alleyway which he would have to traverse if he approached in the ordinary way would leave even the worst of marksmen very little chance of missing him. And the Saint had no interest in any funeral festivities in which he could not occupy a vertical position.

He drove instead to a tobacconist's shop round the corner, and there he discharged the taxi. He went in and bought a packet of cigarettes, and then he showed his police identity card.

"Do you live in the rooms over here, or do they belong to someone else?"

"No, sir. I live there."

"I'll go right up," said the Saint. "Don't bother to show me the way. You stay right here and carry on business as usual. I shan't come back by this route, so don't wait up late for me."

He went through the shop and up the stairs.

From a window on the landing of the first floor he was able to survey the battleground.

It was unpromising. Donnell's house formed, as has been explained, a kind of island site in the centre of the block, separated by a matter of about fourteen feet from the houses that surrounded it. The four pairs of walls which surrounded the square canyon thus formed were bare of any convenience for passing between them except the solid ground at the bottom. And that was certain to be watched and covered from the windows of Donnell's house. From the window where he looked out, Simon Templar might, if he had been that kind of a lunatic, have considered the possibility of running a plank across to the window opposite and entering the house that way. It is interesting to record that he was not that kind of lunatic—he had, amongst other weaknesses, a distinct urge towards being buried in one piece, when his time came.

There was, however, one other solution.

He went on up the stairs. On the third floor the stairs came to an end, but above his head were a trapdoor and a swinging ladder. He pulled the ladder down and mounted it.

He found himself in a kind of attic, lumbered with boxes and odds and ends of broken furniture. It had one cobwebbed window, barely wide enough for a man to squeeze through; but Simon squeezed through it and emerged on the leads. At that point, from where he stood with his heels in the gutter, leaning back against the tiles of the roof with a sixty-foot drop in front of him, the flat roof of Donnell's house, with a high embrasured wall running round it and a kind of penthouse in the centre, was about six feet below him, and still fourteen feet away. But it was in the convenient position of not being overlooked by any of the windows from which his attack was likely to be watched for.

The Saint bent his knees and braced himself. He tested the strength of the gutter, found it firm, and without further hesitation launched himself into space.

He cleared the wall and landed on the flat concrete of Donnell's roof, stumbling forward and saving himself with his hands.

Then he picked himself up and released the safety catch of his automatic.

He circumnavigated the penthouse warily. It was square and solidly built, with narrow barred windows, and had obviously been designed as a point of vantage from which any attempt to reach the house over the roofs could be repelled. On that occasion, however, the possibility seemed to have been overlooked, for no shots came from it to greet him.

He worked his way round it and came to a massive door faced with iron. There was no handle on the outside, and the Saint tried to open it without success.

He gave up the task after a few seconds, and went and looked over the wall down the face of the building.

There was a window directly below him, about six feet down, at the point where he had chanced to look over. He climbed up on the wall and looked down at it, considering the lie of the land.

The wall was about five feet high. Lowering himself over it, he was able to rest his toes on a ledge about three inches wide which ran round the outside. Then he had to stoop quickly and allow himself to fall literally into space, catching at the ledge with his fingers as he did so. For one hair-raising second he had the awful sensation of hurtling downwards to certain death; but Simon Templar's nerves were like ice, and he knew the strength of his hands. His hooked fingers on the ledge brought him up with a jerk at the full stretch of his arms, and he hung there for a few seconds while he recovered his breath. His feet were then, he judged, at the level of the centre of the window which he had made his objective. And then he had to let go his hold again and drop another couple of feet down the side of the building, landing on his toes on the out-jutting sill and clutching at the window frame to recover his balance. He did so.

Then, stooping a little, he was able to pull down the upper sash as quietly as it could be done, and climb down into the room.

There was no one there. He had not seriously expected that there would be, for the attention of the garrison would naturally be concentrated on the ways by which he might more ordinarily have been expected to attempt to enter. Certainly if there had been anyone in the room it would have meant the end of Simon Templar's useful career, for he could hardly have made any active resistance against being pushed off his unstable foothold into space. But there had been no one there to do it.

He crossed the room cautiously in the semidarkness, placing his feet with infinite precautions against making a noise which might be heard by anyone in a room below, and thus gained the door. The door was ajar. He opened it a little farther, slowly and with respect for its creaking hinges, and crept out onto the narrow landing.

The stairs faced him. He went down them like a cat, keeping close to the wall, where he would be least likely to make a loose board creak. In that way he came down to the second floor, and there the choice of four doors was open to him. He selected one at random, turned the knob silently, and entered with a rush that was swift and sudden without being noisy.

There was no one there. He saw that in his first lightning glance round. Then, reassured upon that point, his interest was taken by the sight of the open cupboard that seemed to lead through to a lighted flight of stairs.

This was not quite what he had expected—he had not credited Donnell with the provision of any such melodramatic devices as concealed doors and secret passages. And the look of things seemed to indicate that someone had recently passed that way in a hurry —and in such a hurry that he had forgotten to disguise his retreat by closing the cupboard doors behind him.

The Saint went quickly through to the hidden stairway, his gun in his hand.

He listened there and heard nothing. And then he went down into the darkness, and came at length upon the tunnel which Weald had found.

He could see no one ahead, and his steps quickened. Presently he came to the fork at which Weald had hesitated. As he paused there irresolute, his eye fell on something that sparkled on the stone flags. He bent and picked it up. It was a small drop earring.

And he was putting it in his pocket when he heard a muffled cry come faintly down the branch on his right. The Saint broke into a run.

Stephen Weald, with his back to the door, and so intent upon the object of his madness that he could notice nothing else, did not hear the Saint's entrance; and, indeed, he knew nothing whatever of the Saint's arrival until two steely hands took him by the scruff of the neck and literally bounced him off his feet.

Then he turned and saw the Saint, and his right hand dived for his pocket. But Simon was much too quick. His fist crashed up under Weald's jaw and dropped him in his tracks.

He turned to find the girl beside him.

"Did you hear what he said—that he was Waldstein?"

The Saint nodded.

"I did," he said, and bent and seized Weald by the collar and jerked him half upright. Then he got his arms under the man's limp body and hoisted him up in a lump, as he might have picked up a child.

"Where are you going?"

The girl's voice checked him on his way to the door, and Simon glanced back over his shoulder.

"I'm going to collect Donnell and fill the party," he said. "We policemen have our jobs to hold down. D'you mind?"

Then he went on his way. He seemed totally unconscious of having performed any personal service for the girl, and he utterly ignored the sequel to the situation into which a hackneyed convention might pardonably have lured any other man. That sublimely bland indifference would have been as good as a blow between the eyes to anyone but Jill Trelawney. He went on up the stairs carrying Weald. He heard the girl following behind him; but she did not speak, and Simon appeared to take no notice of her presence.

And thus he stepped through the open cupboard, and found Harry Donnell waiting for him on the other side of a Colt.

Simon stood quite still.

Then——

"It's all right, Donnell," spoke the girl. "I've got him covered."

She was standing behind the Saint, so that Simon and his burden practically hid her. Donnell could not see the gun with which she was supposed to be covering the Saint, for her hand was behind Simon's back, but Donnell believed, and lowered his own gun.

The Saint felt only the gentle and significant pressure of the girl's open hand in the small of his back, and understood.

"Go on," said Jill Trelawney.

Simon advanced obediently.

The movement brought him right up to Harry Donnell, who stood with his revolver lowered to the full length of a loose arm. There was only the width of Weald's body between them.

Simon relaxed his hold suddenly and dropped Weald unceremoniously to the floor; and then he hit Donnell accurately on the point of the jaw.

Donnell went down, and the Saint was on him in a flash, wrenching the revolver out of his hand.

And then, as the Saint rose again, he laughed—a laugh of sheer delight.

"You know, Jill, the only real trouble about this game of ours is that it's too darned easy," he said; and there was a new note in his voice which she had never heard before, that made her look at him in a strange puzzlement and surprise.

3

But still for a moment the Saint seemed egotistically oblivious of every angle on the situation except his own. The gun he had taken covered Harry Donnell,

who was crawling dazedly up to his feet; and the Saint
had backed away to the table and was propping himself against it. His cigarette case clicked open, and a
cigarette flicked into his mouth; his lighter flared, and
a cloud of smoke drifted up through the gloom; he
had his own private satisfaction. And Jill Trelawney
said: "I suppose I ought to thank you . . ."

The Saint tilted his head.

"Why?" he inquired blankly.

"You know why."

Simon shrugged—an elaborate shrug.

"I hope it will be a lesson to you," he said solemnly.
"You must be more careful about the company you
keep. Oh, and thanks for helping me to get Harry,"
said the Saint incidentally. "What made you do that?"

She looked at him.

"I thought it might go a little way towards settling
the debt."

"So that we could start fighting again—all square?
. . . Yes, I should think we can call it quits."

"I suppose you'd like to take my gun?"

"Please."

She was fumbling in her bag, and the Saint was not
watching her. He was smoking his cigarette and beam-
ing with an infuriating smugness at Harry Donnell.
About two seconds ago, his own weird intuition had
raised an eyelid and wrinkled a thin hairline of clairvoyant light across his brain; and he knew exactly what
was going to happen. There was just one little thing
left that had to happen before the adventure took the

twist that it had always been destined to take. And the Saint was not bothered about it at all, for he had his immoral views on these matters of private business. He had taken no further notice of Weald since he had dropped him to the floor. He had not even troubled to search Weald's pockets. And when he turned his head at the sound of the shot, he saw the automatic half-out of Weald's pocket, and the man lying still, and turned again to smile at another gun.

"Don't move," said Jill Trelawney quietly, and the Saint shook his head.

"Jill, you really mustn't commit murder in the presence of respectable policemen. If it happens again——"

"Never mind that," said the girl curtly.

"Oh, but I do," said the Saint. "May I smoke, or would you prefer to dance?"

The girl leaned against the wall, one hand on her hip, and the shining little nickelled automatic in the other.

"Your nerves are good, Simon Templar," she remarked coolly.

"I can say the same for yours."

She regarded him with a certain grim amusement.

"I suppose," she said, "it wouldn't be any use pleading that I shot Weald to save trouble? You can see that he was drawing when I fired. And saving the life of a valuable detective. . . . Would it be any use?"

"Not much, I'm afraid," answered the Saint, in the same tone. "You see, I've got a gun myself, and there

wasn't really any call for you to butt in. You just had
to say 'Oi!'—and I would have done the work. Besides, Harry would just love to be a witness for the
Crown—wouldn't you, Harry?"

He saw the venomous darkening of Donnell's eyes,
and laughed.

"I'm sure you would, Harry—being the four-flush-
ing skunk you are."

He had not moved from the table, and his right
hand, holding Donnell's revolver, still rested loosely
on his knee.

"You aren't going to be troublesome, Templar?"
asked the girl gently, and Simon shrugged.

"You don't get me, Jill. Personally, I'm never troublesome." He held her eyes. "Others may be," he said.

The silence after he spoke was significant; and the
girl listened on. And she also heard, outside, the sound
of heavy hurrying footsteps on the stairs.

"Excuse me," said the Saint.

He stepped quickly to the door, and turned the key
in the lock. Then he picked the table up and jammed
it into the defense for ballast, with one edge under the
handle of the door and the other slanting into the
floor.

"That'll hold Donnell's boys for three or four minutes," he said.

She smiled.

"While I slip out through the tunnel?"

"While we slip out through the tunnel."

He saw the perplexity that narrowed her eyes, the

hesitant parting of her lips, but he saw these things only in a sidelong glimpse as he crossed to the side of Harry Donnell. And he saw the vindictive resignation that twisted Donnell's mouth, and laughed.

"Sorry to trouble you again," said the Saint.

His fist shot up like the hoof of a plunging cayuse. But this time the Saint had had one essential fraction of a second more in which to meditate his manœuvre —and that made all the difference in the world. And this time Donnell went down and stayed down in a peaceful sleep.

"Which is O. K.," drawled the Saint, after one professional glance at the sleeper.

He turned briskly.

"Are you all set for the fade-away, Jill? Want to powder your nose or anything first?"

She was still staring at him. The new atmosphere that had crept into his personality from the moment of his first swipe at Donnell's jaw had grown up like the strengthening light of an incredible dawn, and the intervening interlude had merely provided circumstances to shape its course without altering its temper in the least. And the gun that she had been levelling at him half the time had made no difference at all.

"Aren't you going to try to arrest me?" she asked, with a faint rasp of contempt laid like the thinnest veneer on the bewildering beginnings of preposterous understanding that lay beneath.

And Simon Templar smiled at her.

"Arrest you for ferreting out and bumping off the

bloke I've been wanting to get at myself for years?
Jill, darling, you have some odd ideas about me! . . .
But there really is a posse around this time—they're
waiting at the other end of that there rat's hole, with
the assistant commissioner himself in command, and
you wouldn't have a hope in hell of getting through
alone. D'you mind if I take over the artillery a moment?"

He detached the automatic from her unresisting
hand, dropped it into his pocket, and swept her
smoothly through the open door of the dummy cupboard. It was all done so calmly and quietly, with such
an effortless ease of mastery, that all the strength
seemed to ebb out of her. It was impossible to resist
or even question him: she suffered herself to be steered
down the stairs without a word.

"On the other hand," said the Saint, as if there had
been no interruption between that remark and the con-
clusion of his last speech, "you'll have to consider
yourself temporarily under arrest, otherwise there
might be a spot of trouble which we shouldn't be in a
position to deal with effectively."

She made no answer. In the same bewildered silence
she found herself at the junction of the two forks in
the tunnel; they took the left-hand fork this time, and
went on for about a hundred yards before the light of
the last electric bulb was lost behind them and they
found themselves in darkness. She heard the crackle
of the Saint's lighter, and saw another flight of steps
on the right.

"Up here."

He took her arm and swung her round the turning and up the stairs. At the top, what appeared to be a blank wall faced them; the Saint's lighter went out as they reached it, and she heard him fumbling with something in the dark. Then a crack of light sprang into existence before her, widening rapidly, and she felt fresh air on her face as the Saint's figure silhouetted itself in the gap.

"Easy all," came the Saint's imperturbable accents; and she followed him through the opening to find the assistant commissioner putting away his gun.

They had stepped into a poorly furnished parlour; besides Cullis there were a couple of plain-clothes detectives and four uniformed policemen crowded into it.

"The first capture," said the Saint, taking the girl's arm again. "I laid out Donnell and Weald, but I couldn't bring them along with me. You'll find them in the house, if you get there quick enough—the rest of Donnell's boys were chipping bits out of the door when we left."

Cullis nodded; and the uniformed men filed through the opening in the wall. The plain-clothes men hesitated, but the Saint signalled them on.

"I'll take Trelawney myself—my share of this job is over."

As the detectives disappeared, the Saint opened the door and led Jill Trelawney out into a small bare hall.

Cullis followed. Outside, a taxi was waiting and Simon pushed the girl in.

Then he turned back to the commissioner.

"You might find it entertaining to take a toddle up that tunnel yourself," he said. "There's something amusing in the room at the other end which the boys should be discovering about now. Oh, and you might give my love to Claud Eustace next time you see him. Tell him I always was the greatest detective of you all—the joke should make him scream."

Cullis nodded.

"Are you taking her to the station?"

"I am," said the Saint truthfully, and closed the door.

And then the Saint settled back and lighted another cigarette as the taxi drew away from the curb.

"We've just time to catch the next train to town with eighty seconds to spare," he remarked; and the girl turned to him with the nearest thing to a straight-forward smile that he had seen on her lips yet.

"And after that?"

"I know a place near London where the train slows up to a walking pace. We can step off there, and the synthetic sleuths who will be infesting Paddington by the time the train gets in can wait for us as long as they like."

She met his eyes steadily.

"You mean that?"

"But of course!" said the Saint. "And you can ask me anything else you want to know. This is the end of my career as a policeman. I never thought the hell of a lot of the job, anyhow. I suppose you're wondering why?"

She nodded.

"I suppose I am."

"Well, I butted into this party more or less by way of a joke. A joke and a promise, Jill, which I may tell you about one day. Or maybe I won't. Whether you were right or wrong had nothing to do with it at all; but from what the late lamented Weald was saying when I crashed his sheik stuff it seems you're right, and that really has got something to do with the flowers that bloom in the spring."

There was another silence. She accepted a cigarette from his case, and a light.

Presently she said: "And after we leave the train?"

"Somewhere in this wide world," said the Saint, "there's a bloke by the name of Essenden. He is going to Paris to-morrow, and so are we."

CHAPTER V

Now, once upon a time Lord Essenden had fired a revolver at Simon Templar with intent to qualify him for a pair of wings and a white nightie. Simon bore Lord Essenden no malice for that, for the Saint was a philosopher, and he was philosophically ready to admit that on that occasion he had been in the act of forcing open Lord Essenden's desk with a burglarious instrument, to wit, a jemmy; so that Lord Essenden might philosophically be held to have been within his rights. Besides, the bullet had missed him by a yard.

No, Simon Templar's interest in Essenden, and particularly in Essenden's trips to Paris, had always been commonplace and practical. Simon, having once upon a time watched and pried into Lord Essenden's affairs conscientiously and devotedly for some months, knew that Essenden, on his return from every visit he paid to Paris (and these visits were more frequent than the visits of a respectably married peer should rightly have been), was wont to pay large numbers of French francs into his bank in London. And the Saint, who had been younger than he was at this time, knew that Englishmen who are able to pay large numbers of

French francs into their London banks when they return from a short visit to Paris are curiosities; and collecting curiosities was the Saint's vocation.

So Simon Templar and Jill Trelawney went to Paris
and stayed two days at the Crillon in the Place de la
Concorde, which they chose because Lord Essenden
chose it. Also, during those two days the Saint held
no conversation with Lord Essenden beyond once beg-
ging his pardon for treading on his toes in the lift.

It was during the forty-ninth hour of their residence
at the Crillon that Simon learnt that Essenden was
leaving by the early train next morning.

His room was on the same floor as Essenden's. He
retired to it when Essenden retired, bidding the peer
an affable good-night in the corridor, for that night
the Saint had met Essenden in the bar and relaxed his
aloofness. In fact, they had drunk whisky together.
This without any reference to their previous encounter.
On that occasion the Saint had been masked; and now,
meeting Essenden in more propitious circumstances,
he had no wish to rake up a stale quarrel.

So they drank whisky together, which was a dangerous thing for anyone to do with Simon Templar;
and retired at the same hour. Simon undressed, put on
pajamas and a dressing gown, gave Essenden an hour
and a half in which to feel the full and final benefit of
the whisky. Then he sauntered down the corridor to
Essenden's room, knocked, received no answer, sauntered in, and found the peer sleeping peacefully. Essenden had not even troubled to undress. The Saint

regarded him sadly, covered him tenderly with the quilt, and went out again some minutes later, closing the door behind him.

And that was really all that happened on that trip to Paris which is of importance for the purposes of this chronicle; for on the next day Lord Essenden duly went back to London, and he went with a tale of woe that took him straight to an old acquaintance.

Mr. Assistant Commissioner Cullis, of Scotland Yard, disliked having to interview casual callers. Whenever it was possible he evaded the job. To secure an appointment to see him was, to a private individual, a virtual impossibility. Cullis would decide that the affair in question was either so unimportant that it could be adequately dealt with by a subordinate, or so important that it could only be adequately coped with by the chief commissioner, for he was by nature a retiring man. In this retirement he was helped by his rank; in the days when he had been a more humble superintendent, it had not been so easy to avoid personal contact with the general public.

To this rule, however, there were certain exceptions, of which Lord Essenden was one.

Lord Essenden could obtain audience with Mr. Assistant Commissioner Cullis at almost any hour; for Essenden was an important man, and had occupied a seat on more than one royal commission. Indeed, it was largely due to Essenden that Mr. Cullis held his present appointment. Essenden could not be denied. And so, when Essenden came to Scotland Yard that evening, demanding converse with Mr. Cullis, on a day when Mr. Cullis was feeling more than usually unfriendly towards the whole wide world, he was received at once, when a prime minister might have been turned away unsatisfied.

He came in, a fussy little man with a melancholy moustache, and said, without preface: "Cullis, the Angels of Doom are back."

He had spoken before he saw Teal, who was also present, stolidly macerating chicle beside the commissioner's desk.

"What Angels of Doom?" asked Cullis sourly.

Essenden frowned.

"Who is this gentleman, Cullis?" he inquired. He appeared to hesitate over the word "gentleman."

"Chief Inspector Teal, who has taken charge of the case."

Cullis performed the necessary introduction briefly, and Essenden fidgeted into a chair without offering to shake hands.

"What angels of what doom?" repeated Cullis.

"Don't be difficult," said Essenden pettishly. "You know what I mean. Jill Trelawney's gang——"

"There never has been a gang," said Cullis. "Trelawney and Weald and Pinky Budd were the only Angels of Doom. Three people can't be called a gang."

"There were others——"

"To do the dirty work. But they weren't anything."

Essenden drummed his finger tips on the desk in an irritating tattoo.

"You know what I mean," he repeated. "Jill Trelawney's back, then—if you like that better. And so is the Saint."

"Where?"

"I came back from Paris yesterday——"

"And I went to Brixton last night," said Cullis annoyingly. "We do travel about, don't we? But what's that got to do with it?"

"The Saint was in Paris—and Trelawney was with him."

"That's better. You actually saw them?"

"Not exactly——"

Cullis bit the end off a cigar with appalling restraint.

"Either you saw her or you didn't," he said. "Or do you mean you were drunk?"

"I'd had a few drinks," Essenden admitted. "Fellow I met in the bar. He must have been the Saint—I can see it all now. I'm certain I drank more than whisky. Anyway, I can only remember getting back to my room, and then—I simply passed out. The next thing I knew was that the valet was bringing in my breakfast, and I was lying on the bed fully dressed. I don't know what the man must have thought."

"I do," said Cullis.

"Anyhow," said Essenden, "they'd taken a couple of hundred thousand francs off me—and a notebook and wallet as well, which were far more important."

Cullis sat up abruptly.

"What's that mean?" he demanded.

"It was all written up in code, of course——"

"What was written up in code?"

"Some accounts—and some addresses. Nothing to do with anything in England, though."

The assistant commissioner leaned back again.

"Someone's certainly interested in you," he remarked.

"I've told you that before," said Essenden peevishly. "But you never do anything about it."

"I've offered you police protection."

"I've had police protection, and one of your men was on guard outside my house the night I found a man breaking open my desk. That's all your police protection is worth!"

Cullis tugged at his moustache.

"Still," he said, "there's nothing to connect the Saint with that burglary, any more than there's anything to connect either him or Trelawney with your—er—accident in Paris."

Essenden fumbled in his pocket and produced a sheet of paper. He laid it on the desk beneath Cullis's eyes.

"What about that?" he asked.

Cullis looked at a little drawing that was already familiar to him—a childish sketch of a little skeleton man with a symbolical halo woven round his head. But beside this figure there was another such as neither Cullis nor Teal had ever seen before in that context— a figure that wore a skirt and had no halo. And under these drawings were three words: *"April the First."*

"What about that?" asked Essenden again.

Teal raised his sleepy eyes to the calendar on the wall.

"A week next Friday," he said. "Are you superstitious?"

Essenden was pardonably annoyed.

"If you're supposed to be in charge of this case, Mr. Teal," he said testily, "I don't think much of the way you do your job. Is this the way you train your men to work, Cullis?"

"I didn't train him," said Cullis patiently. "April the first is All Fools' Day, isn't it?"

"I don't see the joke."

"It may be explained to you," said Cullis.

He stood up with a businesslike air, meaning that, so far as he was concerned, the interview had served its purpose. As a matter of fact, this story was a mere variation on a theme which Cullis was already finding wearisome. He had heard too much in a similar strain of late to be impressed by this repetition, although he was far from underestimating its significance. But he could not discuss that with Essenden, for there was something about Lord Essenden which sometimes made Cullis think seriously of murder.

"Let me know any developments," he said with curt finality.

Lord Essenden, it should be understood, though important enough to be able to secure interviews with the assistant commissioner, was not important enough to be able to dictate the course which any interview should take, and this fact was always a thorn in Essenden's vanity.

"You treat it all very lightly," he complained weakly. "I do think you might make some sort of effort, Cullis."

"Every policeman in England is looking for Simon Templar and Jill Trelawney," said the assistant commissioner. "If and when we find them they will be arrested and tried. We can't do more than that. Write down your story and give it to Sergeant Berryman downstairs on your way out, and we'll see that it's added to the dossier. Good-evening."

"I tell you, Cullis, I'm scared——"

Cullis nodded.

"They certainly seem to have it in for you," he said. "I wonder why? Good-evening!"

Essenden felt his hand vigorously shaken, and then he found himself in the stone corridor outside, blinking at a closed door.

He went downstairs and wrote out his formal report, as he had been directed, but with a querulous lack of restraint which spoilt the product as a literary effort. Then he drove to his club and dined and wined himself well before he returned to his waiting car and directed a cold and sleepy chauffeur to take him home.

"Home" was on the borders of Oxfordshire, for Essenden preferred to live away from the social life of London. Lady Essenden had objections to this misanthropy, of which Lord Essenden took no notice. In his way, he was almost as retiring a character as Mr. Cullis.

Through all that drive home, Lord Essenden sat uncomfortably upright in one corner of his car, sucking the knob of his umbrella and pondering unpleasant thoughts.

It was after midnight when he arrived, and the footman who opened the door informed him that Lady Essenden had gone to bed with a headache two hours earlier.

Essenden nodded and handed over his hat and coat. In exchange, he received one solitary letter, and the handwriting on the envelope was so familiar that he carried it to his study to open behind a locked door. The letter contained in the envelope was not so surprising to him as it would have been a month before:

Have a look at the safe behind the dummy row in your bookcase.

And underneath were the replicas of the two drawings that he had seen before.

Essenden struck a match and watched the paper curl and blacken in an ashtray. Then, with a perfectly impassive fatalism, he went to the bookcase and slid back the panel which on one shelf replaced a row of books. He had no anxiety about any of the papers there, for since the first burglary he had transferred every important document in his house to a safer place.

He opened the safe and looked at the notebook he had lost in Paris.

Thoughtfully he flicked through the pages.

Every entry had been decoded, and the interpretation written neatly in between the lines.

Essenden studied the book for some minutes; and then he dropped it into his pocket and began to pace the room with short bustling strides.

The notebook had not been in the safe when he arrived back from Paris that afternoon. He knew that, for he had deposited some correspondence there before he left again to interview the commissioner. And yet, to be delivered that night, the letter which told him to look in the safe must have been posted early that morning. And early that morning Jill Trelawney and the Saint were in Paris—and the letter was postmarked in London. There was something terrifying about the ruthless assurance which emerged from the linking of those two facts.

A gentle knock on the door almost made Essenden jump out of his skin.

"Would there be anything else to-night, my lord?" inquired the footman, tactfully.

"A large brandy and soda, Falcon."

"Very good, my lord."

In a few moments the tray was brought in.

"Thank you, Falcon."

"I have cut some sandwiches for you, my lord."

"Thank you."

"Is there nothing else, my lord?"

Essenden picked up his glass and looked at it under the light.

"Have there been any callers to-day?"

"No, my lord. But the young man you sent down from London to inspect your typewriter came about six o'clock."

Essenden nodded slowly.

He dismissed the servant, and when the door had closed again, he went to another bookcase and extracted a couple of dusty volumes. Reaching into the cavity behind the other books, he brought out an automatic pistol and a box of cartridges. The books he replaced. Carrying the gun over to the table, he first carefully tested the action and then loaded the magazine, bringing the first cartridge into the chamber and then thumbing in the safety catch.

With the gun in his pocket he experienced a slight feeling of relief.

But for hours afterwards he sat in the study, staring at the embers of the dying fire, sipping brandy and smoking cigarette after cigarette, till the fire died altogether, and he began to shiver as the room grew colder. And thus, alone, through those hours, he pondered fact upon fact, and formed and reviewed and discarded plan after plan, until at last he had shaped an idea with which his weary brain could at the moment find no fault.

It was a wild and desperate scheme, the kind of scheme which a man only forms after a sleepless night fortified with too many cigarettes and too much strong drink taken alone and in fear; but it was the only answer he could find to his problem. He was quite calm and decided about that. When at last he dragged himself to bed, he was more calm and cold and decided than he had ever been before in all his life, was Lord Essenden, that fussy and peevish little man.

2

Simon Templar picked up the sheet of paper on which he had been working spasmodically during the return from Paris, and cleared his throat.

"We understand," he said, "that the following lines have been awarded the Dumbbell Prize for Literature:

"The King sits in the silent town,
Sipping his China tea:
'And where shall I find a fearless knight
To bear a sword for me?

'The beasts are leagued about my gates,
The vultures seek the slain,
Till a perfect knight shall rise and ride
To find the Grail again.'

Then up and spake a Minister,
Sat at the King's right knee:
'Basil de Bathmat Dilswipe Boil
Has a splendid pedigree.

'His brother is Baron de Bathmat Boil,
Who owns the Daily Squeal,
And everybody knows he is
Impeccably genteel.'

'Has he been with my men-at-arms,
    Has he borne scars for me,
That I should take this Basil Boil
    Among my chivalry?'

'Sire, in a war some years ago
    You called him to the fray,
And he would have served you loyally,
    But his conscience bade him nay.

'And they took him before the judges,
    Because he did rebel,
And he lay a year in prison
    To save his soul from hell.'

'Then what have I for a portent,
    What bring you me for a sign,
That I should take this coistril
    To be a knight of mine?'

'Sire, we are bringing in a bill
    Which the Daily Squeal could foil,
And it might be wise to wheedle
    Baron de Bathmat Boil,

Then the King rose up in anger
    And seared them with his gaze:
'You have taken the wine and the laughter,
    The pride and the grace of days;

'The last fair woman is faded,
   And the last man dead for shame,
But a dog from the gutter shall serve me
   Before this man you name.'

They heard, and did not answer;
   They heard, and did not bend;
And he saw their frozen stillness
   And knew it was the end.

Basil de Bathmat Dilswipe Boil
   They brought upon a day,
And the King gave him the accolade
   And turned his face away,

And saw beyond his windows
   The tattered flags unfurled;
And on his brow was a crown of iron
   And the weariness of the world."

"What's that supposed to be?" asked the girl blankly.

"If you don't recognize poetry when you hear it," said the Saint severely, "you are beyond salvation. But I'll admit it's rather an amorphous product—my feelings got too strong for gentle satire as I went along. If you saw a paper the other day, you'll notice that a sometime pacifist has recently received a knighthood. A violent atheist will probably be the next Archbishop of Canterbury, and a confirmed teetotaller is going to be the chairman of the next Liquor Commission. After which I shall put my head in a gas oven."

Jill Trelawney selected two lumps of sugar from a silver bowl.

"Something seems to have upset you," she remarked.

"The bleary organization of this wall-eyed world is always upsetting me. It would upset anyone who hadn't been spavined from birth."

"But apart from that?"

"Apart from that," said Simon Templar luxuriously, "I feel that life is very good just now. I have about a hundred thousand francs in my pocket, waiting to be translated into English as soon as the banks open in the morning. I have had a drive in the country. I have discovered that, if all else fails, I can always earn an honest living as an inspector of typewriters. I have bathed, changed, and refreshed myself from my toils and travels with a trio of truly superb kippers cooked with a dexterity that might have made me famous as a chef. My latest poetic masterpiece gives me great satisfaction. And finally, I have your charming company. What more could any man ask?"

He sat at ease in the comfortable little flat near Sloane Square, which he had established long ago as a reserve base against the day when a hue and cry might make his home in Upper Berkeley Mews too hot to hold him. A cup of coffee stood in front of him and a cigarette was between his fingers; and, across the table, he looked into the golden eyes of Jill Trelawney, and made his speech.

"But, Jill," he protested, "there is a far-away look about you. Is it indigestion or love?"

She smiled abstractedly.

"I'm thinking about Essenden," she said.

"So it's love," said the Saint.

"I'm wondering——"

"Seriously, why? In the last twenty-four hours we've devoted ourselves entirely to Essenden. Personally, I'm ready to give the subject a rest. We've done our stuff, for the moment. The egg, so to speak, is on hatch. The worm is on the hook. All we can do now, for a while, is to sit tight and wait."

"Do you think he'll rise?"

"I've told you," said the Saint extravagantly, "he'll rise like a loaf overloaded with young and vigorous yeast. He'll rise so high that pheasants and red herrings won't be in the same street with him. When he's finished rising, he'll have such an altitude that he'll have to climb a ladder to take his shoes off. That's what I say. Take it from me, Jill."

The girl stirred her coffee reflectively.

"All the same," she said, "like all fishing, it's a gamble."

"Not with that fish and that bait, it isn't," answered the Saint. "It's a cinch. Look here. We put the wind up his lordship. We fan into his pants a vertical draught strong enough to lift him through his hat. There's no error about that. So what can he do? He must either (a) sit tight and get ready to face the music, (b) go out and get run over by a bus, or (c) prepare a counter-attack. Well, he's not likely to do (*a*). If he does (*b*), we're saved a lot of trouble and hard work. If he does (*c*)——"

"Yes," said the girl. "If he does (*c*)——"

"He plays right into our hand. He comes out of balk. And once he's in play, we can make our break. Burn it——!"

Simon put out his cigarette and leaned forward.

"This isn't like you, Jill," he said. "It isn't like anything I've ever heard about you; and it certainly isn't a bit like the form you were showing this time last week. Don't tell me your nerve's going soft in the small of the back, because I shan't believe you."

"But what's he likely to do?"

Simon shrugged.

"Heaven knows," he said. "I tell you, our job is just to stand around the landscape and wait. And who cares?"

Jill Trelawney lighted a cigarette and smiled.

"You're right, Simon Templar," she said. "I'm getting morbid. I'm starting to get the idea that things have been just a bit too easy for me—all along. You know how much I've got away with already, and you ought to know that nobody ever gets away with the whole works for ever."

"I do," said the Saint cheerfully.

She nodded absently. For a moment the tawny eyes looked right through him. It was extraordinarily humiliating, and at the same time provocative, that feeling which the eyes gave him for an instant—that, for a moment, he was not there at all, or she was not there at all. Although she heard him, she was quite alone with what she was thinking.

And then she saw him again.

"Do you know, you're the last partner I ever thought I should have," she said; and the Saint inhaled gently.

"I shouldn't be surprised."

"And yet . . . you remember when you reminded me of that boy of mine back in the States?" The golden eyes absorbed his smile. "That was a mean crack. . . . I suppose I deserved it."

"You did."

"It made a difference."

Simon raised his eyebrows; but the mockery was without malice.

"After which," he murmured, "you shot Stephen Weald."

"Wouldn't you have done the same?"

"I should. Exactly the same. And that's the point. You might have left it to me, but I stood aside because I figured he was your onion. . . . Which was half-witted, if you come to think of it, because if we'd kept him we could have made him squeal. But who am I to spoil sport?"

"I know."

"But we go on with the good work, so why worry?"

She nodded slowly.

"Yes, we go on. Maybe it won't be long now."

"And that boy of yours?"

"He thinks I'm travelling around improving my mind." She laughed. "I suppose I am, if you look at it that way. . . ."

And there was a silence.

And in that simple silence began an understanding that needed no explanations. For the Saint always knew exactly what to leave unsaid. . . . And when, presently, he reached out a long arm to crush his last cigarette into an ashtray, glanced at the clock, and stood up, the movement fitted spontaneously into the comfortable quiet which had settled down upon the evening.

"Do you realize," he said easily, "that it's nearly midnight, and we've had a busy day?"

Her smile thanked him, and he remembered it after she had left the room and he sat by the fire smoking a final cigarette and meditating the events of the last twenty-four hours.

Adventures to the adventurous. Simon Templar called himself an adventurer. What other people called him is nobody's business. Certainly he had had what he wanted, in more ways than one, and the standard of enterprise and achievement which he had set himself from the very beginning of his career showed no signs of slacking off. It was only recently that he had started to realize that there was more for him to do in life than he had ever known. . . . And yet, just then, he was quite contented. Simon Templar's philosophical outlook on life was his strong suit. It kept him young.

As long as something interesting was happening he was quite happy. He was quite happy that night.

For complete contentment he required well-balanced alternations of excitement and peaceful self-satisfaction. At the beginning of his cigarette he was enjoying the peaceful self-satisfaction. Halfway through the cigarette, the front door bell rang curtly and crisply, and the Saint came slowly to his feet with a speculative little frown.

He was not expecting to receive callers at that address, apart from tradesmen, because it had never been registered in his own name. And in any case, when he came back to London this time there had been no notices in the newspapers to say that Mr. Simon Templar had returned to town and would be delighted to hear from any friends and/or acquaintances who cared to look him up. For obvious reasons. The Saint had never been notorious for hiding his light under any unnecessary bushels, but he always knew precisely when to remain discreetly in the background. He had learnt the art in his cradle, and this was one of the periods when he applied it energetically. It was therefore a practical certainty that the visitor would be unwelcome; but Simon opened the door with a bland smile, for he was always interested to meet any trouble that happened to be coming his way.

"Why, if it isn't Claud Eustace!" he exclaimed, and stood aside to allow the caller to enter.

"Yes, it's me," said Mr. Teal heavily.

He came in, and oozed through the miniature hall

into the sitting room. Simon Templar followed him in.

"What can I do for you? Do you want a tip for the Two Thousand, or have you come to borrow money?"

Inspector Teal carefully unwrapped a wafer of chewing gum and posted it in his red face.

"Saint," said Teal drowsily, "I hear you've been a naughty boy again."

"Not me," said the Saint. "You must be thinking of someone else. I'll admit I've been to Paris, but——"

Teal's lower jaw ruminated rhythmically.

"Yes," he said, "some of it was in Paris."

Simon leaned against the mantelpiece with a little twinkle of amusement in his eyes.

"Well?"

"In Paris," said Teal, "you doped Lord Essenden and took a couple of hundred thousand francs off him. Before that, while acting as a police officer, you abandoned your duty and connived at the escape of a woman who's wanted for murder. You can't go on doing that sort of thing, Saint. I'm afraid I shall have to bother you again."

"Well?"

The detective's shoulders moved in a ponderous shrug.

"The best thing about you, Templar," he said, "is that you always come quietly."

Simon fingered his chin.

"What d'you mean—'come quietly'?" he asked, with childlike innocence.

"Come for a walk," said Teal. "Or, if you like, we'll take a taxi. I'm sorry to have to pull you in at this hour, but you were out when I called earlier, and if I left it till to-morrow morning you might have gone away again."

"And where are we going to take this walk—or this taxi drive?"

Mr. Teal blinked. He seemed to find it a tremendous effort to keep awake.

"Rochester Row police station."

"In Pimlico?" protested the Saint. "Not that. I'm only taken to West End police stations."

"Not Pimlico," said Teal. "Westminster."

"Worse still," said the Saint. "Members of Parliament get taken there."

Mr. Teal settled his hat, which, like the traditional detective, he had not removed when he entered the flat.

"Coming?" he inquired lethargically.

"Can't," said the Saint. "Sorry, old dear."

"Simon Templar," said Teal, "I arrest you on a charge of——"

"Let's see it on the warrant."

"Which warrant?"

The Saint grinned.

"The warrant for my arrest," he said.

"I haven't got a warrant."

"I guessed that. And how are you going to arrest me without a warrant?"

"I can take you into custody——"

"You can't," said the Saint pleasantly. "I'm behaving myself. I'm in my own flat, just about to go to bed like any respectable citizen. There's nothing you can accuse me of. What you're doing, Teal, is to put up a very thin bluff, and I'm calling the bluff. Laugh that off."

Teal closed his eyes.

"In Paris——"

"In Paris," said Simon calmly, "I stole two hundred thousand francs from Lord Essenden. I admit it. If you like, I'll put it in writing, and you can take it home with you to show the chief commissioner. But you can't do anything about it. The hideous crime was committed on French soil and it's a matter for the French police alone. I'm in England. An Englishman cannot be extradited from England. Sorry to disappoint you, I'm sure, but you shouldn't try to put things like that over on me."

"In Birmingham——"

"In Birmingham," said the Saint, in the same equable manner, "a man known lately as Stephen Weald and formerly as Waldstein was shot by Jill Trelawney. Whether it was in self-defense or not is a matter for the jury which may or may not try her—I suppose you had some sort of a story from Donnell. However, I did my duty and arrested her. I thought I had disarmed her, but in the taxi she produced another gun and stuck me up. I was forced to get into a train with her. Not far north of London, she forced me to jump out. I don't know what happened after that. I lay stunned beside the track for several hours——"

"What kind of a gag," demanded Teal, "are you trying to put over?"

The Saint beamed.

"I'm merely giving you a free sample of my defense, which will also be the means of getting you thoroughly chewed up in the courts if you get nasty, Claud Eustace, old corpuscle. The commissioner should have had my letter of resignation, in which I explained that I was so overcome with shame that I couldn't face him to hand it in personally. It was posted the same evening. I admit I proved to be the duddest of all possible dud policemen, but my well known desire to save my own skin at all costs——"

Teal spread a scrap of paper on the table.

"And this—your receipt to Essenden? I know one of these pictures, Templar, but the other——"

"My wife," said the Saint breezily.

"Oh, yes. And when were you married?"

"Not yet. The tense is future."

The detective closed his eyes again.

"So that's your story, is it?"

"And a darn good story it is, too," said Simon Templar complacently.

"And what about this new home of yours?"

"Since when has it been illegal for a respectable citizen to have a second establishment—or even an alias? . . . But I wouldn't mind knowing how you located it so quickly, all the same."

"I've known about it for months," said the detective sleepily. "When I drew blank at Upper Berkeley Mews, I came straight here."

The Saint laughed.

"And then you go straight home again. Teal, that's too bad! . . . But you ought to have known better, honey, really you ought. Now, are you going to take Uncle's advice and have a glass of barley water before you go, or do you want to argue some more?"

For some moments there was a gigantic silence—on the part of Chief Inspector Teal. The Saint could feel the tremendousness of it; and he was amused, for he knew exactly where he stood. And in his trouser pockets there were two iron fists quietly bunched up ready to prove the courage of his convictions if the challenge were offered. . . .

And then Teal opened his eyes, and his mouth widened half an inch momentarily.

He nodded.

"You always were a bright boy," he said.

"I know," said the Saint.

Teal's smile remained in position. He hitched his overcoat round, and buttoned a button that must have had a tiring day. His heavy-lidded eyes roved boredly over the furnishings of the apartment.

"Sorry you've wasted your time," said the Saint sympathetically. "Don't let me keep you any longer if you're really in a hurry."

"I won't," said Teal. And then his eyes fell on the chair where Jill Trelawney had been sitting.

Simon followed his gaze.

"Been entertaining a friend?" asked Teal, without a change of expression.

"My Auntie Ethel," said the Saint blandly. "She

left just before you came in. Isn't it a pity? Still, maybe you'll be able to meet her another day."

"How old is this Auntie Ethel?"

"About fifty," said the Saint. "A bit young for you, but you might try your luck. I'll send you her address. She might like to see round Rochester Row."

Teal took his hands out of his pockets and loco-moted across the room. Only a man like Teal can possibly be said to locomote.

This locomotion was deceptive. It appeared to be very heavy off the mark, and very slow and clumsy in transit, but actually it was remarkably agile. Teal picked a bag up from the chair and inspected it soberly.

"Your Auntie Ethel has a gaudy taste in bags," he remarked. "How old did you say she was?"

"About a hundred and fifty," said the Saint.

Teal opened the bag and proceeded to examine the contents, extracting them one by one, and laying them on the table after the inspection. Lipstick, powder puff, mirror, comb case, handkerchief, cigarette case, gold pencil, some visiting cards.

"Princess Selina von Rupprecht," Teal read off one of the visiting cards. "Where does she come from?"

"Lithuania," said the Saint fluently. "I have some very distinguished relations in Czecho-Slovakia, too," he added modestly.

Teal put the bag down and turned with unusual briskness.

"I should like to meet this Princess," he said.

"Call her Auntie," said Simon. "She likes it. But

you can't meet her here to-night because she's gone home."

"She'll come back for her bag," said Teal comfortably. "I'll wait. And while I'm waiting I'd like to see round some of the other rooms in this flat."

Simon Templar pulled himself off the mantelpiece, against which he had been leaning, and looked Teal deliberately in the eyes.

"You won't wait," he said, "because I happen to want to go to bed, and I prefer to see you off the premises first. And you won't search this flat, not on any excuse, because you haven't a search warrant."

Teal stood squarely by the table.

"I have reason to believe," he said, "that you're sheltering a woman who's wanted for murder."

"You haven't a search warrant," repeated the Saint. "Don't be foolish, Teal. I may be a suspicious character, but you've got nothing definite against me, apart from the little show in Paris, which isn't your business —nothing in the wide, wide world. If you try to search this flat I shall resist you by force. What's more, I shall throw you down the stairs and out into the street with such violence that you will bounce from here to Harrod's. And if you try to get me for that, the beak will soak you good and proper. Once upon a time you might have got away with it, but not now. The police aren't so popular these days. You'd better watch your step."

"I can get a warrant," said Teal, "within two hours."

"Then get it," said the Saint shortly. "And don't

come in here again bothering me until you've got it in your pocket. Good-night."

He crossed the room and opened the door, and Teal, after a few seconds of frightful hesitation, passed out into the hall.

Simon opened the front door for him also; and there Teal paused on the threshold.

"You *are* a bright boy, Saint," said Teal somnolently. "Don't go to bed. I shall be back with that warrant inside two hours."

"Good-night," said the Saint again, and closed the door in the detective's face.

He came back into the sitting room and found the girl putting her possessions into her bag.

"I heard," she said.

"In five minutes," said the Saint, "Teal will have a man outside this front door to watch the place while he goes off to get a warrant. Meanwhile——"

The shrill, sharp scream of a police whistle sounded in the street outside, and a little smile touched Simon Templar's mouth.

"At this moment," said the Saint, "he's standing on the steps blowing that whistle. He's not taking any chances. He's not going to look for a man—he's going to wait till a man comes to him. He's going to make quite sure that whoever's in here isn't going to slip out behind his back. And the person they want to find here is you."

Jill Trelawney nodded.

"On a charge of murder," she said softly.

CHAPTER VI

HOW SIMON TEMPLAR WENT TO BED, AND MR. TEAL WOKE UP

SIMON had slipped out his cigarette case and absently selected a cigarette. He lighted the cigarette, looking at a picture on the opposite wall without seeing it; and his faintly thoughtful smile lingered on the corners of his mouth, rather recklessly and dangerously. But that was like Simon Templar, who never got worked up about anything.

"Of course," he said quietly, "I've been rather liable to overlook that."

"Why not?" she answered, in a tone that matched his own for evenness. "You can't spend twenty-four hours a day thinking and talking about nothing but that."

He shifted his gaze to her face. Her beauty was utterly calm and tranquil. She showed nothing—not in the tremor of a lip, or the flicker of an eyelid. And unless something were done there and then, she might have less than two months of life ahead of her before a paid menial of the law hanged her by the neck. . . .

Teal's whistle, in the street below, shrieked again like a lost soul.

And Jill Trelawney laughed. Not hysterically, not even in bravado. She just laughed. Softly.

She turned back the coat of her plain tweed costume, and he saw a little holster on the broad belt she wore.

"But I've never overlooked it," she said—"not entirely."

Simon came round the table, and his fingers closed on her wrist in a circle of cool steel.

"Not that way," he said.

She met his eyes.

"It's the only way for me," she said. "I've never had a fancy for the Old Bailey—and the crowds—and the black cap. And the three weeks' waiting, in Holloway, with the chaplain coming in like a funeral every day. And the last breakfast—at such an unearthly hour of the morning!" The glimmer in her eyes was one of pure amusement. "No one could possibly make a good dying speech at 8 a.m.," she said.

"You're talking nonsense," said the Saint roughly.

"I'm not," she said. "And you know it. If the worst comes to the worst——"

"It hasn't come to that yet."

"Not yet."

"And it won't, lass—not while I'm around."

She laughed again.

"Simon—really—you're a darling!"

"But have you only just discovered that?" said the Saint.

He made her smile. Even if her laughter had been of neither hysteria nor bravado, it had not been a thing to reassure him. A smile was different. And he still found it easy to make her smile.

But she was of such a very unusual mettle that he could have no peace of mind with her at such a moment. They were very recent partners, and still she was almost a stranger to him. They were familiar friends of a couple of days' standing; and he hardly knew her. In the days of their old enmity he had recognized in her a fearless independence that no man could have lightly undertaken to control—unless he had been insanely vain. And with that fearless independence went an unconscious aloofness. She would follow her own counsel, and never realize that anyone else might consider he had a right to know what that counsel was. That aloofness was utterly unaware—he divined that it had never been in her at all before the days of the Angels of Doom, and when the work of the Angels of Doom was done it would be gone.

And Teal's whistle was silent. Simon looked down from a window, and saw that Teal had gone. But a uniformed man stood at the foot of the steps on the pavement outside, and looked up from time to time.

"Well?" said the girl.

"He's gone for his warrant," said the Saint. "Cast your bread upon the waters, and you shall find it after many days. We can thank your Angels of Doom for that. If you hadn't made the police so unpopular, Teal would have risked the search without a warrant. As it is, we've got a few minutes' grace, which may run into two hours. Pardon me."

He went through into the bedroom and selected a coat from his wardrobe. He returned with this, and a pillow from the bed.

"Keep over on that side of the room."

She obeyed, perplexedly. He pushed an armchair over against the window, put the pillow inside the coat he had brought, and sat coat and pillow in the chair.

"Now—where's your hat?"

He found the hat, and propped it up over the coat on a walking stick. Then he carried over a small table and set it beside the chair; and on the table he put a small lamp. After a calculating survey, he switched on the small lamp.

"Now turn out that switch beside you."

She did as she was told; and the only light left in the room came from the small lamp on the table by the armchair against the window.

"The Shadow on the Blind," said the Saint. "A Mystery in Three Acts. Act One."

She looked at him.

"And Act Two—the fire escape?"

He shook his head.

"No. We haven't got one of those. Why not the front door? Are you ready?"

He handed her her bag, went out into the hall, and fetched in her valise. This he opened for her.

"Put on another hat," he said. "You must look ordinary."

She nodded. In a couple of minutes she was ready;

and they walked down the stairs together. At the foot of the stairs he stopped.

"Round there," he said, pointing, "you'll find a flight of steps to the basement. Wait just out of sight. When you hear me go up the stairs again, walk straight out of the front door and take a taxi to the Ritz. Stay there as Mrs. Joseph M. Halliday, of Boston. Mr. Joseph M. Halliday—myself—will arrive for breakfast at ten o'clock to-morrow morning."

"And Act Three?" she asked.

"That," said the Saint serenely, "will be nothing but a brief brisk dialogue between Teal and me. Goodnight, Jill."

He held out his hand. She took it.

"Simon, you're not only a darling—you're a bright boy."

"Just what Teal said," murmured the Saint. "Sleep well, Jill—and don't worry."

He left her there, and went and opened the front door.

The constable outside turned round alertly.

"Officer!" said the Saint anxiously.

He looked amazingly respectable; and the policeman relaxed.

"Yes, sir?"

"There seems to be something funny going on in the flat below me——"

The constable came up the steps.

"Which floor are you on, sir?"

"Second."

The eyes of the law studied the Saint's nervous respectability with an intent stare; and then the finger of the law beckoned.

Simon followed the law outside; and the finger of the law pointed upwards. In the first-floor window, a silhouette could be seen on a blind.

"In that flat below you, sir," said the law impressively, "there's a woman ooze wanted for murder."

Simon peered upwards.

"Why don't you arrest her?" he asked.

"Inspector's gone for a warrant," said the constable. "I'm keeping watch till he gets back. Now, what was it you heard in that flat, sir?"

"A sort of moaning noise," said the Saint sepulchrally. "It's been going on for some time. Sounds as if someone was dying. I got anxious after a bit, and went down and rang the bell, but I couldn't get any answer."

"Listen," said the policeman.

They listened.

"Can't hear anything," said the policeman.

"You wouldn't, down here, with the window shut," said the Saint. "It's not very loud. But you can hear it quite clearly on the landing outside the flat."

"She's still sitting there, in that window," said the policeman.

They stared upwards, side by side.

"Sits very still, doesn't she?" said the Saint vaguely.

They stared longer.

"Funny," said the policeman, "now you come to

mention it, she does sit still. Ain't never moved 'arf an inch, all this time we've been watching her."

"I don't like the look of it, officer," said the Saint nervously. "If you'd heard that noise——"

"Can't 'ear no noise now."

"I tell you, it gave me the creeps. . . . Did this woman know you were going to arrest her?"

"Oh, I think she knows all right."

"Supposing she's committing suicide——"

The constable continued to strain his neck.

"Sounds as if I ought to look into it," he said. "But I don't care to leave my post. The inspector said I wasn't to move on any account. But if she's trying to escape justice——"

"She still hasn't moved," Simon said.

"No, she ain't moved."

"I don't see how going inside would be leaving your post," said the Saint thoughtfully. "You'd be just as much use as a guard outside the door of the flat as you are here."

"That's true," said the policeman.

He looked at the Saint.

"Come on up with me," he said.

"L-l-l-like a shot," said the Saint timidly, and followed in the burly wake of the law.

They listened outside the door of the flat for some time, and, not unnaturally, heard nothing.

"Perhaps she's dead by now," Simon ventured morbidly.

The law applied a stubby forefinger to the bell.

A minute passed.

The law repeated the summons—without result.

The Saint cleared his throat.

"Couldn't we break in?" he said.

The law shook its head.

"Better wait till the inspector gets back. He won't be long."

"Come up and wait in my flat."

"Couldn't do that, sir. I've got to keep an eye on this door."

Simon nodded.

"Well, I'll be off," he sighed. "I'll be upstairs if you want me."

"If anything's happened, I expect the inspector will want to see you, sir. May I have your name?"

"Essenden," said Simon Templar glibly. "Marmaduke Essenden. Your inspector will know the name."

He saw the name written down in the official notebook, and went up the stairs. On the landing above, he waited until he heard the constable tramping downwards, and then he descended again and let himself into his own flat.

He was reading, in his pajamas and a dressing gown, when his bell rang again an hour and a half later; and he opened the door at once.

Teal was outside; and behind Teal was the constable. Seeing Simon, the constable goggled.

"That's the man, sir," he blurted.

"I knew that, you fool," snarled Teal, "as soon as you told me the name he gave you."

He pushed through into the sitting room. His round red face was redder than ever; and for once his jaws seemed to be unoccupied with the product of the Wrigley Corporation.

The constable followed; and Simon humbly followed the constable.

"Now look at that!" said Teal sourly.

The Saint stood deferentially aside; and the constable stood in his tracks and gaped along the line indicated by Mr. Teal's forefinger. The Saint had not interfered with the improvised dummy in the chair. He had felt that it would have been unkind to deprive the constable of the food for thought with which that mysteriously motionless silhouette must have been able to divert his vigil.

"And while you were making a fool of yourself up here," said Teal bitterly, "Jill Trelawney was walking out of the front door and getting clean away. And you call yourself a policeman!"

Simon coughed gently.

"I think," he said diffidently, "that the constable meant well."

Teal turned on him. The detective's heavy-lidded eyes glittered on the dangerous verge of fury.

The Saint smiled.

Slowly, deliberately, Teal's mouth closed upon the word it had been about to release. Slowly Teal's heavy eyelids dropped down.

"Saint," said Teal, "I told you you were a bright boy."

"So did Auntie Ethel," said the Saint.

2

Simon Templar, refreshed by a good night's sleep, set out for the Ritz at 9.30 next morning.

He had not been kept up late the night before. Teal, gathering himself back into the old pose of mountainous sleepiness out of which he had so nearly allowed himself to be disturbed, had gone very quietly. In fact, Simon had been sound asleep three quarters of an hour after the detective's return visit.

Teal hadn't a leg to stand on. True, the Saint had behaved very curiously; but there is no law against men behaving curiously. The Saint had lied; but lying is not in itself a criminal offense. It is not even a misdemeanour for a man to arrange a dummy in a chair in such a way that a realistic silhouette is thrown upon a blind. And there is no statute to prevent a man claiming a Lithuanian princess for an aunt, providing he does not do it with intent to defraud. . . . So Teal had gone home.

Suspicion is not evidence—that is a fundamental principle of English law. The law deals in fact; and a thousand suspicious circumstances do not make a fact.

No one had seen the Princess Selina von Rupprecht. No one could even prove that her real name was Jill Trelawney. Therefore no charge could ever be sub-

stantiated against Simon Templar for that night's
work. And Teal was wise enough to know when he was
wasting his time. There was a twinkle in the Saint's
eye that discouraged bluff.

"And yet, boys and girls," murmured Simon to himself, the next morning, as he went down the stairs,
"Claud Eustace Teal is reputed to have a long memory.
And last night's entertainment ought to make that
memory stretch from here to the next blue moon. No,
I don't think we're going to find life quite so easy as it
was once."

The house was watched, of course. As he turned
out into the street, he observed, without appearing to
observe, the two men who stood immersed in conversation on the opposite pavement; and as he walked
on he knew, without looking round, that one of the
men followed him.

There was nothing much in that, except as an omen.

It made no difference to the Saint's intention of
breakfasting at the Ritz as Mr. Joseph M. Halliday,
of Boston, Mass. In fact, it was to allow for exactly
that event that he had left his flat earlier than he need
have done. It was nothing new in Simon Templar's
young life to be shadowed by large men in very plain
clothes, and such minor persecutions had long since
ceased to bother him.

He left the sleuth near Marble Arch, and took a
taxi to the Ritz with the comfortable certainty of being
temporarily lost to the ken of the police; and the pair

of horn-rimmed glasses which he donned in the cab effectively completed his simplest disguise.

He arrived on the stroke of ten, entering behind the breakfast tray. Taking advantage of the presence of the waiter, he kissed Jill like a dutiful husband, and sat down feeling that the day was well begun.

As soon as they were alone—

"The self-control of the police," said the Saint hurriedly, "is really remarkable."

The girl maintained her gravity with an effort.

"Did he go quietly?" she asked.

"To say that he went like a lamb," answered the Saint, "means nothing at all. He would have made a lamb look like a hungry tiger outside a butcher's shop on early-closing day."

He retailed the part of his ruse at which she had not been audience, and had his reward in the way she sat back and looked at him.

"You're a marvel," she said, and meant it.

"All this flattery," said the Saint, "is bad for my heart."

He picked up one of the newspapers that had come in with the tray, and read through the agony column carefully, without finding what he sought. He had no more luck with any of the others.

"He hasn't had time," said Jill.

Simon nodded.

"To-morrow," he said, "for a fiver. Care to bet?"

They spent the day inside the Ritz, very lazily; but neither of them was inclined to take a risk at that moment. Meanwhile, Scotland Yard, lashed by the biting comments of Chief Inspector Teal, tore its hair and ransacked London. The Ritz, naturally, was never thought of; and Mr. and Mrs. Joseph M. Halliday never once set foot outside the hotel.

The advertisement appeared in *The Times* next morning. During the previous day they had amused themselves with speculating about the form it would take; and, as it happened, neither of them had come very near the mark.

INJUSTICE.—*A great wrong may be put right if the Lady of Paris will meet one who is anxious to make restitution in exchange for forgiveness.* —THE LORD OF PARIS.

"It brings tears to my eyes," said the Saint.

"Do you believe it?" asked Jill.

Simon shrugged.

"It isn't impossible," he said. "You say you're certain he had a hand in the framing of your father. Well, we now know a few things about *him*. He's got some reason to respect us. And, as a cautious man, he may think it a wise move to make a treaty."

Jill Trelawney nodded, buttering a slice of toast.

"And yet," she said, "it's a trap."

"Not for the police. Essenden wouldn't dare—not in the face of what we know. For trafficking in illicit drugs, five years' penal servitude."

"No, not the police. Just himself."

Simon lighted a cigarette.

"Do you want to buy?"

"We buy." She looked at him. "Or I buy. I shall see Essenden to-night."

"Where?"

"At his house. I've been there before. Shall I forget it?" She smiled at him, and he laughed. "That's where he'll be expecting me, from to-day onwards. He wouldn't expect me to write—he knows me too well."

"And if he knows you so well," said the Saint, "he'll be expecting trouble."

"Of course."

"And he's going to get it?"

With a cup of coffee in her hand, the girl answered, quite calmly: "A year ago I swore to kill every man who had a hand in ruining my father. Waldstein is dead. I suspect Essenden. If I find proof against him——"

"That was my way, once," said the Saint quietly. "But doesn't it ever occur to you that you might be doing much better work if you looked for the evidence to clear your father's name, instead of merely looking for revenge?"

Jill Trelawney said: "My father died."

Simon had nothing to say.

They spent another inactive day, reading and talking desultorily. To Simon Templar, those long conversations were fascinating and yet maddening. She never spoke of the Angels of Doom, or the charge that lay against her, or the unchanged inflexibility of her pur-

pose. These things remained as a dark background to
her presence: they were never allowed to steal out of
the background, and yet they could not be escaped.
Against that background Simon Templar felt himself
a stranger. Not once yet, in that bizarre alliance of
theirs, had he been allowed to enter into the secret
places of her mind. But he played up to her. Because
she had that air of unawareness, he left her unaware.
He tried no cross-examinations. She was the soloist:
he was the accompaniment, heard, valuable, perfectly
attuned, but subordinate and half ignored. It was one
of the most salutary experiences of the Saint's violent
life. But what else could he do? The mind of a woman
with an Idea is like a one-way street: you have to run
with the traffic, or get into trouble.

She obliterated their forthcoming adventure until
the evening. Until after dinner; when she smiled at
him across the table and his cigarette case, and said:
"Saint, it's very nice of you to be coming with me."

"Very nice of you to be come with," said the Saint
politely.

He offered her a match; but for a moment she
looked past it.

"Does the idea of being an accessory to another
murder attract you?" she asked.

"Tremendously," said the Saint.

"It will probably come to that, you know."

"I've always enjoyed a good murder."

She touched her waist. He knew what she carried
there, under her coat. Since the night before, he had

inspected the weapon again, with a professional eye.

"Have you got a gun?" she asked hm.

"Don't care for 'em," he said. "Nasty, noisy things. Dangerous, too. Might go off."

She laughed suddenly.

"And yet," she said, "you've proved you aren't a fool. If you hadn't, I'd have taken a lot of convincing. . . . Are you ready?"

He glanced at his watch.

"The car should be here now," he said.

They went out to the car five minutes later—a luxurious limousine, with liveried chauffeur, ordered by telephone for the occasion.

Simon handed the girl in, and paused to give directions to the chauffeur.

It was a pure coincidence that Chief Inspector Teal should have been passing down Piccadilly at that moment. The car was not in Piccadilly, but at the side entrance of the hotel, in Arlington Street, which Teal was crossing. He observed the car, as he invariably observed everything else around him, with drowsy eyes that appeared to notice nothing and in fact missed nothing.

He saw a man speaking to a chauffeur. The man wore an overcoat turned up around his chin, a soft hat worn low over his eyes, and a pair of horn-rimmed spectacles. It is surprising how much of a man's face those three things can hide between them—especially at night. Teal thought there was something familiar about the man, but he could not connect up the association immediately.

He stood at the corner of the Ritz and watched the man enter the car. He was not looking for Simon Templar at that moment. He was not, as a matter of fact, even thinking of Simon Templar. He had thought and talked of little else but Simon Templar for the last forty-eight hours, and his brain had wearied of the subject.

Thus it was that he stood where he was, inertly pondering, until the car turned into St. James's Street. As it did so, a woman leaned forward to throw a cigarette end out of the window, and the light of a street lamp fell full across her face.

She was hatless. He saw straight, jet black hair, fine straight black eyebrows, eyes in deep shadow, carmine lips. These things belonged to no woman that he knew.

Thoughtfully he spat out a scrap of spearmint in which the flavour had ceased to last, extracted a fresh wafer from the packet in his pocket, engulfed it, and chewed with renewed enthusiasm. Then, still thoughtfully, he proceeded on his way.

The hiatus in his memory annoyed him, and even when he had filled it up it still annoyed him, for it was his boast that he never forgot a face. This was his first lapse in years, and he was never able to account for it to his satisfaction.

It was nearly an hour later, when he was chatting to the divisional inspector in Walton Street police station, that the blind spot in Teal's brain was suddenly uncovered.

"If you don't mind my saying so, sir," remarked the divisional inspector, "we've probably been combing all the wrong places. A man and a woman like Templar and Trelawney can reckon up some nerve between them. They're probably staying at some place like the Ritz——"

Teal's mouth flopped open, and his small blue eyes seemed to swell up in his face. The divisional inspector stared at him.

"What's the matter, sir?"

"The Ritz!" groaned Teal. "Oh, holy hollerin' Moses! The Ritz!"

He tore out of the station like a stampeding alp, leaving the D.I. gaping blankly at the space he had been occupying. The back exit, a breathless sprint down Yeoman's Row, brought him to the Brompton Road, and he was fortunate enough to catch a taxi without having to wait a moment.

"The Ritz Hotel," panted Teal. "And drive like blazes. I'm a police officer."

He climbed in, with bursting lungs. He had left his sprinting days behind him long ago.

He was wide awake now—when, as he realized with disgust, it was somewhat late in the day to have woken up.

A few minutes later he was interviewing the management of the Ritz. The management was anxious to be helpful, and at the same time anxious to preserve itself from any of the wrong sort of publicity. Teal was not interested in the private susceptibilities of the management. He made his inquisition coldly and efficiently, and it did not take him long to narrow the search down to just two names on the register—the charming Mr. and Mrs. Joseph M. Halliday, of Boston, Mass.

Teal inspected the small suite they had occupied, and heard from the floor waiter the story of how Mrs. Halliday had been in bed with a severe cold ever since her arrival, and how Mr. Halliday, like a truly devoted American husband, had never left her side. This evening was the first evening they had been out. Mrs. Halliday had felt so much better that Mr. Halliday had decided that a short spin in the country, well wrapped up in a closed car, might do her a lot of good.

"On a nice warm winter's night!" commented Teal sarcastically. "And, of course, in the dark she could enjoy the scenery! Yes, that's a very good story."

The source of information was understood to remark that such eccentricities were to be expected of wealthy Americans.

"Yes, very wealthy Americans," agreed Teal.

He picked up a small leather valise. It was empty. Further investigation showed that it was the one and only item of their property that Mr. and Mrs. Halliday had left in the suite.

"Did they take any rugs with them?" asked Teal.

"They borrowed two from the hotel, sir, for the drive."

"It's amazing what a lot of stuff you can carry under

a rug," said Teal, "if you know the trick of packing it."

Returning downstairs to the manager's office, he learnt, as he expected, that the car had been ordered by the hotel on behalf of Mr. Halliday.

"We arrange these things," said the manager.

"And sometimes," said Teal, with a certain morose enthusiasm, "you pay for them, too."

The manager was not entirely green.

"I suppose," he said, "we needn't expect them back?"

"You needn't," said Teal. "That's another eccentricity of these very wealthy Americans."

He hurried back to Scotland Yard, and by the time he arrived there he had decided that there was only one place in England where Jill Trelawney and Simon Templar could plausibly be going that night.

He tried to telephone to Essenden, and was informed that the line was out of order. Then he tried to get in touch with the assistant commissioner, but Cullis had left the Yard at six o'clock, and was not to be found either at his private address or at his club.

Teal was left with only one thing to do; for he had a profound contempt for all police officials outside the Metropolitan area.

At ten minutes to ten he was speeding through the west of London in a police car; and he realized, grimly, that he was unlikely to arrive at Essenden's anything less than two hours too late.

CHAPTER VII

HOW JILL TRELAWNEY KEPT AN APPOINT-MENT, AND SIMON TEMPLAR WENT PADDLING

ESSENDEN poured himself out another drink, and pushed the decanter towards the centre of the table.

It was quiet in Essenden Towers that night. Lord Essenden had seen to that. With some ingenuity, and a solicitude which hitherto he had not been in the habit of manifesting, he had suggested to Lady Essenden that her appreciation of country life would be enhanced by an occasional visit to London. In fact, he said, he had taken a box at the Orpheum Theatre, for that very night.

It was unfortunate that at the last moment, when they had been on the point of setting out for London, Lord Essenden had been overcome by a violent and agonizing attack of toothache. But he refused to allow his misfortune to interfere with his wife's amusement, and insisted that she should go to London alone. He had telephoned to friends and arranged for them to accompany his lady.

That was one thing. The servants had been a second problem. But, in the matter of disposing of the servants, Fate had played kindly into his hand. That night there was a dance in the next village. His staff had previously applied to him for permission to attend, which he had refused. Now he repented, and, in an astonishing burst of generosity, he gave the evening off to every man and woman in Essenden Towers. The butler would have stayed, but Essenden packed him off with the others, saying he would much rather be left alone with his ache.

Thus it had been easy for Lord Essenden to introduce into the house the four men who now bore him company.

They had been carefully chosen. Lord Essenden had very few more criminal acquaintances than any other successful financier, but from the hoodlums of his acquaintance he had selected those four with care and forethought.

They sat round the table, helping themselves from the whisky bottle which he had placed at their disposal—four carefully chosen men. There was "Flash" Arne, a ferrety-faced man with a taste in diamond rings and horsy tweeds, a prominent member of a race gang that many North of England bookmakers had known to their cost. There was "Snake" Ganning, recently released from Pentonville; tall and lean and supple, with the sleek black hair and long neck and beady eyes that had earned him his name. There was "Red" Harver, with the permanent scowl and the huge hasty fists. And there was Matthew Keld, who had once had his face slashed from temple to chin with a razor by a man who was never given the chance to slash another face in his life. Four very carefully chosen men.

Essenden spoke:

"Is everything quite clear?"

He looked round the small circle of faces, and the owners of the faces gazed back at him complacently. Snake Ganning inclined his head on the end of his long neck and answered for them all, in his soft, sibilant voice.

"Everything's quite clear."

"I can't tell you how they'll come in," said Essenden. "I do know that there are only two of them. If I know anything about them, I should say they'd probably walk up to the front door and ring the bell. But they may not. I've worked out the posts I've given you in different parts of the house so that each one of you will easily be able to cover his share of the ground-floor rooms. There are alarms everywhere, and you will all be in touch with one another. The man you will deal with as you like. The girl you will bring to me."

It was the fourth or fifth time that Lord Essenden had repeated similar instructions in his fussy and hesitant way, and the Snake's sunken black eyes regarded their employer with a certain contempt.

"We heard you," he said.

"All right."

Essenden fidgeted with his tie, and looked at his watch for the twentieth time.

"I think you'd better go to your posts," he said.

Ganning rose, uncoiling his long length like a slowed-up jack-in-the-box.

"C'mon," he said.

Arne and Keld rose to follow him, but Red Harver sat where he was. Ganning tapped him on the shoulder.

"C'mon, Beef."

Harver rose slowly, without looking round. His eyes were fixed intently on something behind Essenden. Behind Essenden was a window, with the heavy curtains drawn.

The others, looking curiously at Harver, grasped what he was staring at, and followed his gaze. But they saw nothing. Essenden himself turned, with an abrupt jumpy movement. Then he turned round again.

"What's the matter, Harver?" he croaked.

Harver's huge arm and fist shot out, pointing.

"Did you shut that window?" he demanded.

"Of course I did," said Essenden. "You saw me shut it."

"You shut it properly?"

"Of course I did," repeated Essenden.

Harver pushed the table out of his path with a sweep of one arm.

"Well, if it hasn't blown open," he said, "somebody's opened it. I've just seen those curtains move!"

He stood in the centre of the group, a red-headed giant, and the others instinctively checked their breath.

Essenden shifted away.

Ganning's right hand sidled round to his hip pocket, and Flash Arne buttoned his coat deliberately.

Harver stepped cautiously forward on tiptoe.

The stealthy movement ended in a quick rush. Harver's huge, ape-like arms gathered up all the curtains in one wide sweep, and he held something in the enveloping folds of the curtains like a fish in a net.

He carried his whole capture bodily back into the centre of the room, tearing the curtains down as if they had been held with thin cotton. There he threw the bundle down, and stood back while the intruder struggled into view.

"Well, who are you?" barked Essenden feebly, frm the outskirts of the group.

The man on the floor pulled his cap off his eyes and blinked dazedly about him. He was not a beautiful sight. The suit he wore was stained and dusty. Portions of a pair of vividly striped socks were visible between the frayed ends of his trousers and the tops of a pair of muddy boots. Round his neck, presumably as a substitute for shirt and collar and tie, he wore a red choker. His cap was very purple. It appeared to be several days since he had last shaved, and a black shield obscuring one eye gave his face a sinister and unsavoury appearance. And when he spoke he whined.

"I wasn't doin' no 'arm, guv'nor."

Harver reached out one ham-like hand to the man's collar and yanked him to his feet.

"What's your name?" he demanded.

"George," said the burglar miserably.

"George what?"

"Albert George."

Harver shook his prisoner like a rat.

"And what were you doing there?"

"Oh, lay off him, Red," said Ganning. "He's nothing to do with this."

Essenden came closer.

"We don't know that," he said. "This might be one of her tricks. Anyway, even if he isn't anything to do with it, he may have heard us talking."

Harver shook the captive again.

"How much did you hear?" he snarled.

A look of fear came into the eyes of Albert George.

"I didn't 'ear nuffin', s'welp me, I didn't."

"Liar!" said Flash Arne delicately.

"S'welp me," wailed the prisoner, "I didn't 'ear nuffin'."

Harver chuckled throatily.

"I'll s'welp you," he said, "if you don't remember something. Who told you to come here?"

"S'welp me——"

Harver drove his fist into the man's chest, sending him reeling back against the wall.

"I promised I'd s'welp you," he said, "and I have. Now, are you going to talk?"

He followed up his victim with measured, ponderous strides, and the slighter man cowered back. Arne and Keld and Ganning stood watching dispassionately. The prisoner shrank away, his face contorted with terror. And as Harver came within striking distance again and his fist went back for another blow, Albert George voiced a sharp, shrill yelp of panic.

"S'welp me!"

He ducked frantically, and Harver's fist smashed shatteringly into the wall. George scuttled into a corner and crouched there, but Harver turned like an enraged bull and came after him.

"I'll talk," screamed the prisoner. "Don't hit me again——"

Harver seemed about to refuse the offer, but Essenden put himself between the two men.

"Wait a minute," he said. "There'll be time for that later. We'll hear what he's got to say."

Albert George huddled against the wall.

"It's a cop," he said, between breaths that came in labouring gasps. "But it wasn't my idea. It was a bloke I met this morning in Seven Dials. 'E told me there was a man 'e wanted beaten up, name of Essenden. Is one of you gents Mr. Essenden?"

"Go on," growled Harver.

"There was a lot of money for it, and 'e said there wasn't no risk. I'd just got to open a winder on the ground floor, an' get in. 'E told me where the alarms was, an' 'e drew me a plan of the 'ouse, an' 'e marked the bedroom, an' 'e says, 'You just go in that room and slosh 'im one, an' I'll be waitin' for yer at the Lodge gates wiv a car to tyke yer back to London.' "

"He said he'd be waiting at the Lodge gates with a car?"

Albert George swallowed.

"Yus. What's the time? 'E said 'e'd be there at ten o'clock."

"What was this man's name?"

"I dunno. 'E was a toff. All dressed up, 'e was, like 'im." He pointed to Flash Arne.

"Was there anyone with him?"

"Yus. There was a woman with 'im. She was a toff, too. She'll be in the car, too—she said she would."

Ganning took his hand away from his hip pocket.

"Well, that ought to be easy," he said. He looked at Essenden. "Guess we'd better go down and fetch them in."

Essenden nodded. He could hardly believe his good fortune.

"You'd better all go," he said. "They may be armed. Here, tie this man up first."

He took a length of cord out of a drawer and brought it over. Harver seized the prisoner's arms and twisted them roughly behind him. Keld performed the roping with a practised hand. The prisoner was then dropped into a corner like a sack of coals.

"He won't get out of that in a hurry," said Matt Keld.

Ganning hitched himself round the table.

"C'mon," he said.

The four men trailed out through the French windows.

Lord Essenden, left alone, went and helped himself again from the decanter. This time it seemed that Fate had played right into his hand. Jill Trelawney was clever—he admitted that—but, for once, he had been cleverer. He gazed contemplatively at the unkempt figure which lay huddled in the corner, just where it had been dropped. It struck him that the Saint had showed an astounding lack of discrimination in sending such a man to "slosh him one."

He was at a loss to divine completely what might be the object of these attacks. It was not so long ago that he had been severely beaten up at the instigation of Jill Trelawney by a member of the Donnell gang. Here, apparently, yet another tough had been hired for the same purpose. From her point of view he could see nothing that these attacks might achieve. But, from his point of view, he had to admit that the prospect of being beaten up and sent to hospital at regular intervals was, in a general way, discouraging. He still carried a fresh pink scar on his forehead as a memento of the last occasion, and it burned with reminiscent hatred whenever he thought of Jill Trelawney.

He put down the glass and wiped his lips on a silk handkerchief. Albert George lay huddled in the corner, his chin drooped upon his chest, and his whole pose one of lifeless resignation. Essenden went over and stirred him with the toe of a patent-leather shoe.

"How much were you getting for this?" he barked, and the shaky staccato of his voice was an indication of the strain of anxiety that was racking his mind.

The man looked up at him with one furtive eye.

" 'Undred quid," he said, and lapsed again into his stupor.

Essenden went back and poured another two fingers of whisky into his glass. A hundred pounds was a large sum of money to pay for a bashing. There were many men available, he knew, who would undertake such a task for much less, and if this seedy, down-at-heel specimen was being paid a hundred quid for the job, Harry Donnell must have picked up at least twice that amount. Of course, there were varying rates for these affairs. A man can be put in hospital for a week for a fairly reasonable charge. More is asked for breaking a limb, and correspondingly more for breaking two limbs. These facts are very well known in some circles of which Lord Essenden had more than once touched the fringe. Even so . . .

Even so, that night's incident was but another confirmation of the fact that Jill Trelawney was at no loss for funds to carry on her campaign. So much the police had already observed, when her previous exploits at the head of the Angels of Doom had set them by the ears and roused screams of condemnation for their inefficiency from a hysterical press. And if the Angels of Doom were dispersed, and Jill Trelawney was herself a hunted criminal with a price on her head and the shadow of the gallows on her path, it seemed that she was still able to keep control of the finances which had made her such a formidable outlaw in the past. Of course, the Saint was with her now, and the Saint's resources were popularly believed to be inexhaustible. And there was also the minor detail of the two hundred thousand odd francs that had disappeared in Paris.

The memory of Paris produced an unpleasant feeling of emptiness in the pit of his stomach, and he sent a gulp of whisky down to anæsthetize the void. For the wallet and notebook which had been taken from him at the same time, and the contents of which either Jill Trelawney or the Saint had successfully decoded, contained scraps of information which, adroitly pieced together and studiously followed up, were not incapable of bringing his own name into dangerously close connection with a traffic upon which the law frowns in a most unfriendly way; and which it can, without difficulty, be moved to punish with five years' penal servitude and twenty-five strokes of a nine-thonged whip.

He glanced at his watch again, wondering how much longer it would be before his men returned. And at that moment he heard a bell ring in the depths of the house.

He was so keyed up that the sudden disturbance of the silence, faint as it was, made his hand jerk so that some of the liquor in his glass splashed onto the carpet at his feet. He put the glass down carefully, and touched the heavy metallic shape in his jacket pocket to reassure himself. Then, half hesitantly, and uncertain of the impulse which prompted him to go and investigate, he went out into the dark hall. As he switched on the lights, the summons was repeated.

He opened the door.

Jill Trelawney stood on the threshold, straight and slim in a plain tweed travelling costume, with her own soft hair, freed from the black wig that had so effectively baulked Chief Inspector Teal's celebrated memory, peeping from under the small brown hat that framed her exquisite face. At the sight of Essenden her eyes gave no more than the most cursory flicker of recognition.

"Good-evening," she said quietly.

He stepped back falteringly, perplexed, but without hesitation she swept past him into the hall; and, with the world reeling about his ears, he turned to close the door.

It has been said that she swept past him into the hall. That, in fact, was Lord Essenden's own impression, but actually she was almost on his heels—close enough to press into the small of his back something round and hard which he knew could only be one thing—and when she spoke her voice came from a point close behind his ear.

"Put them up," she commanded, in the same quiet tone in which she had said "Good-evening."

Lord Essenden put them up. His brain seemed to have gone dead—and must, he knew now, have gone dead at least two minutes ago.

She saw the light beyond the door of a room farther down the hall and urged him towards it. He led on, helplessly, his hands held high above his head, back into the room he had just left.

In the centre of the room she stopped him and flung

a glance over her shoulder at the bound figure in the corner.

"Hullo, Saint!" she said.

2

Simon Templar smiled with his lips and his one visible eye.

"Hullo, Jill!" he murmured. "And how have you been keeping all these years?"

The girl backed towards him, still covering Essenden with her little gun; and there was a knife in her left hand. The Saint turned over, and Jill stooped and hacked swiftly and accurately at the cords that held him. In a moment he was free, scrambling to his feet and stretching himself.

"That's better," he remarked. "Brother Matthew has efficient but violent ideas on the subject of roping people. Pull the knots as tight as you can without breaking the rope—that's Matthew. Very sound, but uncomfortable for the victim. However, here we are. . . ."

He was dusting his coat. It was really a very respectable coat, when he brushed off the shabbiness which he had applied with French chalk. The enormous boots, removed, disclosed a neat pair of shoes worn beneath them. The horribly striped socks were dummies, which he unbuttoned and put in his pocket. The red choker, removed also, proved that the impression it conveyed at first sight was false: he actually wore shirt, collar, and tie underneath it, and all three were quietly elegant. Before Essenden's staring eyes, he slipped off the very purple cap and the eyeshade, wiped the blue make-up from his chin with his handkerchief, and so ceased to bear the slightest resemblance to Albert George.

"An ingenious device," he said, "to divide the enemy's camp. But not, to tell you the truth, original. None the less useful for that."

"Did you have any trouble?" asked Jill.

"Not much. Just one rough man. He hit me once, which was tiresome, and he hit the wall once, which must have hurt him quite a lot. Otherwise, no damage was done. And the whole bunch went off to look for the car like four maggots in search of a green cheese."

Essenden, standing back against the wall with Jill Trelawney's automatic centred unwaveringly on his waistcoat, knew fear. There was a gun in his own pocket, but he dared not reach for it. The girl had never taken her eyes off him for more than a fleeting second, and the expression in those eyes told him that her finger was itching on the trigger.

He realized that he had been criminally careless. Even when he saw her outside the front door, he had not been alarmed—so insanely blinded had he been by the story of Albert George. He knew that his four guards would return in a few moments; he was sure also that, whatever she meant to do, she would not do it while he could convince her that so long as she held her hand she had the chance of getting the information his advertisement had offered; he had meant to play up that offer—it was his trump card for an emergency, and he had been convinced that as long as he held that card he could be in no real danger. But the unmasking of Albert George—the revelation that there was not only Jill Trelawney, but also Simon Templar, to cope with—that had upset Essenden's confident equilibrium.

There was something rather horrible about a shifting flicker of snapping nerves in the eyes of such a fussy and foolish-looking little man.

The grimly brilliant scheme that he had elaborated was toppling down like a house of cards. . . .

But Jill Trelawney only laughed.

"Now we have our talk, don't we?" she said; and Lord Essenden seemed to shiver—but that might have been due to nothing but the draught from the French windows which his guards had left ajar when they went out.

By the windows stood the Saint.

"The boys are coming back," he said. "This time, I think, a gun might save trouble."

He stepped over to Essenden, lifted the automatic from Essenden's pocket, and retired to the cover of a bookcase which projected in such a way that it would hide him from the view of anyone entering by the windows.

"And if you'll just take Essenden for a walk," he drawled, "I'll give you a yodel when the collection is complete. It's a bit late in the year, but you might find some mistletoe somewhere——"

"O.K., Big Boy."

Simon watched Essenden removed; and leaned back

against the wall with the peer's gun swinging lightly in his hand.

Voices spoke outside the windows. The voice of Red Harver, booming above the others, said: "A plant, that's what it was——"

And the voice stopped short, on the threshold of the room, it seemed to Simon; and the other voices died down also.

Then Flash Arne spat an unprintable word.

Keld yapped: "He couldn't've got outa those ropes —not by hisself, he couldn't——"

"There's the rope there on the floor where he was," Ganning hissed derisively. "I suppose he just melted and trickled through it and froze again on the other side."

"Don't talk soft," snarled Harver. "We know Albert George was a liar. One of his pals has been in here while we were outside——"

"Quate," said the Saint apologetically. "Oh, quate!"

Harver whipped round, his fists doubling; but the automatic in the Saint's hand discouraged him. It discouraged Ganning, who was renowned for his slickness on the draw, and Flash Arne, who knew some tricks of his own; and it discouraged Matthew Keld, that violent but efficient rope expert.

"Sorry," said the Saint, without regret, "but it's a cop—as George said."

Red Harver, peering savagely at him, recognized him by his voice.

"You——"

"Oh, no," said the Saint in distress. "Never. I hate sitting with my back to the engine."

He herded the four men into a convenient corner, in his briskly persuasive way, and raised his voice to Jill. Lord Essenden came through the door first, and Ganning drew in his breath sharply; but the mystery was solved when Jill Trelawney followed.

"If you'll take over," said the Saint, "I'll go and look for some more rope."

The girl nodded briefly. Her automatic, swinging in a little arc over the latitude of the five prisoners, said all that there was left to say.

Simon went swiftly through the pockets of the group, and brought back four guns, two life preservers, a knife, and a razor, which he deposited in the coal scuttle with a faint gesture of distaste.

Then he sought the kitchen, and presently came back with six fathoms of good cord.

His methods of roping were less primitive than those of Matthew Keld, but they were equally efficient. When he had finished, only four Houdinis could have restored Messrs. Arne, Ganning, Keld, and Harver to the position of mobile actors in the scene. Essenden, however, he left.

"You might," he suggested to Jill, "want to ask his lordship a few questions. And I might want this rope's end to encourage him to answer."

He made a long yard of rope whistle horrifically through the air; but the girl shook her head

"He's already started to answer."

Simon raised his eyebrows.

"Have you rung a bell?"

Essenden spoke in a cracked voice: "Of course I've answered. Why shouldn't I have meant what I said in my advertisement? But I thought you might think my advertisement was a trap, so I had to protect myself. That's the only reason I brought these other men into it."

"A beautiful bunch!" murmured the Saint skeptically. His leisured gaze swept over the quartet like a genial blizzard. "I think I know them all. I know about Red Harver's seven years for manslaughter—which ought to have been a quick hanging for murder. I know all about Brother Matthew and the Waikiki Club. I know how Flash Arne gets the money to buy his diamond rings. And I've met Snake Ganning before. Say 'how d'you do,' Snake."

"I admit all that," said Essenden fretfully, "but——"

"What you mean," said Jill Trelawney calmly, "is that you laid a trap for us, but we've made you the pigeon. You're in the soup you brewed for Simon and me. Your gay little party has kind of bust. And now, to save your skin, you're prepared to reopen your original offer. Having flopped on the double-cross, you're anxious to hurry back to the first bargain. Isn't that it?"

She had no grounds for asking whether that was it. But then, the question was almost purely rhetorical. What she was actually doing was to point out to Essenden the only course of action that was left open

o him. She wasn't asking a question at all—she was
ommanding. Persuasively she spoke, in a quiet and
reasonable voice, with sudden death aimed steadily
from her hand, and murder in the clear tawny eyes like
wo drops of frozen gold.

"Yes," said Essenden hoarsely, "that's it."

"Go on."

Essenden swallowed.

"Your father wasn't framed."

He paused.

"I said—Go on!"

The girl's voice ripped out like a pistol shot; yet she
had not spoken loudly. The likeness came only from
her tone—sharp, swift, distinct, deadly.

"I was in it—I admit that—the thing he was framed
for, but he was unlucky. You don't believe me. But
I can prove it. I've kept the papers—papers that never
came into the inquiry, naturally. If they had, they'd
have made it worse for him. I can show you letters in
his own hand——"

"Where?"

"In my private safe—hidden away——"

"Where?"

Essenden seemed to flinch from the glacial in-
clemency of her voice.

"In the cellar."

"Oh, yeah?" said the Saint unnecessarily.

"There's a door under the main staircase. You go
down——"

"And flop through a patent trapdoor into the castle

drains," said the Saint, unimpressed. "Sorry to dis appoint you, comrade, but we've heard that one before."

The girl answered unemotionally.

"I'll go and see if he's lying," she said. "If he is— well, you can use that rope's end. But we might as well see—in case he's telling the truth by accident."

Simon tossed the length of rope onto the table with a shrug.

"I'll go," he said, "though I don't think it's much use. Let's have some more directions. Down the stairs——"

"You come to the wine cellar," said Essenden. "Go straight through that. There's a door at the far end and the key hangs on a nail beside it. You'll find some more steps down. They lead into what's left of an old secret passage. About twenty yards along, it opens into a sort of cave . . ."

Simon heard out the story.

"Right," he said. "It sounds to me like a feeble attempt to waste time, but I'll go. I'm just warning you that if it *is* a waste of time—oh, Marmaduke, my pet, you're going to wish you'd never had that bright idea."

"I'm not wasting time," said Essenden.

The Saint looked at him. He had a dim suspicion that there was something in Essenden's eyes that should not have been there; but he could not be sure. And yet—what could the trick possibly be? Not more than a device to get rid of the man, in the hope that the woman would be easier to deal with.

Regarded in that way, the idea became ludicrous—
to anyone with a scrap of imagination and the slightest
knowledge of Jill Trelawney. Yet Simon turned in the
doorway and spoke a ridiculous warning.

"Jill," he said, "it's just possible that he's expecting
to do something clever when he's got you alone. But
the dangerous four are safely trussed up, and Marmaduke's a very silly little man and not at all necessary
to the cause of Empire Free Trade—so if he does raise
up on his hind legs——"

"You should worry," said the girl. "That's just what
I'm waiting for. I've got both eyes on his lordship, and
they're not blinking till you come back."

"Good enough, baby," said the Saint, and drifted
out.

He went down the hall and found the door under
the main staircase without any difficulty. Opening it,
he found a switch, and went down a long flight of stone
stairs, finding the wine cellar at the bottom, as he had
been told he would. By his side, at the foot of the
stairs, he found another switch, and with this he was
able to light up the cellar. The door at the far end was
of massive and ancient wood, heavily barred, and
studded with iron. He would have expected such a
door to be heavily dusted and cobwebbed; but a faint
trace of oil about the hinges was enough to tell his
keen eyes that he would not be the first person to
penetrate into the passage.

He took down the key. It was bright and newly
burnished, and the lock turned easily. Beyond the
door, when he had opened it, he found another switch,

and this lighted up a row of frosted bulbs along the tunnel that faced him.

A breath of damp, musty air struck his face. He went on cautiously, and with a faint feeling of illogical alertness tingling up his spine—a feeling almost amounting to apprehension. He scowled at the feeling. There was no reason for it—no basis beyond the fact that he had imagined he had caught in Essenden's eye a flicker of an expression whose interpretation had baffled him. But he went on, calling himself every manner of fool, and kept his hand on his gun.

The passage sloped steeply downwards, and the last ten yards were almost precipitous. He descended them gingerly by the aid of well-worn crevices in the stone paving that must once have been another flight of steps, before they had been worn away into mere ridges in a steep slope.

The roof of the passage, which had been low at the beginning, did not descend with the slope. It remained at its old level, so that the space above his head became loftier as he went down. At the foot of the slope the passage took a sharp turn. He rounded the corner and found himself suddenly in the place that Essenden had described as "a sort of cave." It was certainly a sort of cave, but of a sort that the Saint had never expected to find in such a place. Where he entered it the roof was not very high, and the light from the last of the row of bulbs which had led him there illuminated it. But of the extent of the cavern he could not judge. It stretched away beyond the rough semicircle of illumination, its ultimate depths of darkness dwarfing the light at that one end. He spoke a few pointless words with some idea of testing the dimensions of the cave, and the echoes of his voice reverberated backwards and forwards with a wild and swelling intensity until they almost deafened him, and then gradually rolled and rattled away into the bowels of the earth. And when the echoes had stopped, in the utter silence and loneliness of the place, he had no inclination to burst into tears because his instructions did not compel him to penetrate any farther into that gigantic crypt.

He turned. The aperture through which he had come seemed now, in perspective with the rest of the place, to have a puny and insignificant appearance, like a mouse hole in a cathedral wall; but on the right of the entrance he found what he had been told to look for. In the centre of the wall of the cave, about a dozen feet apart, were two sets of chains hanging from iron staples cemented into the rock. He was to look between these.

He went forward. At the foot of the cavern wall, between the wall and himself, ran a kind of dark stream, about four feet wide. Standing on the edge of this, he was able to see, in the wall opposite him, a flat square slab like a flagstone let into the natural rock—exactly as he had been told he would find it.

With a sigh he retired a few paces, removed his shoes and socks, and turned up his trousers. Then he stepped delicately into the dark, ice-cold water.

It could not have been more than six inches deep.

CHAPTER VIII

HOW JILL TRELAWNEY MADE A SLIP, AND THERE WAS A LOT MORE PADDLING AND GENERAL MERRIMENT

LORD ESSENDEN shifted his feet.

More than ten minutes had passed since the Saint had left the room. Essenden's arms, wearied almost to paralysis by the strain of the position of surrender which he had been compelled to adopt, had sagged lower and lower until now they hung straight down and aching at his sides.

Jill Trelawney had permitted the movement—it was the only thing to do. Sheer fatigue enforced it. But she never let her eyes stray an inch from their relentless concentration, and the gun she held was as unwavering as if it had been gripped in the hand of an automaton. And Essenden was too wise to attempt to put into practice any of the bold bids for freedom that flashed in theory through his brain. He knew that, so far as Jill Trelawney was concerned, there could be little to choose between any of the possible excuses for rendering vacant the barony of Essenden in the county of Oxford.

But the time passed; and Jill Trelawney, tirelessly

watching her prisoner, was troubled by the first stir-
rings of anxiety.

She owed much to Simon Templar. Whatever questions might be asked about her association with him,
and the various conflicting debits and credits therein
involved, there was one fact that stood away above all
discussions or dispute. Forty-eight hours before, he
had thrown up a new and promising career to rescue
her from under the very nose of the law. That was an
item on one side of the ledger which could hardly be
cancelled by any number of contra accounts.

And still Simon Templar had not come back.

She had no idea what could have happened to him—
if anything had happened. But it was not in her nature
to dawdle along and hope for the best. He should
have returned by then, and he had not returned. The
reason for the delay might be made apparent in due
course; but she was not inclined to leave it to chance.

"Essenden!"

Her voice crisped into the silence that had fallen
upon the room with Simon Templar's exit; and Essenden started.

"The Saint has been gone a long time," said the
girl—quietly and sufficiently.

"He may have met with some difficulty——"

"Or he may have met with some—accident."

The sentence was an accusation, and she was watching Essenden closely, but his face betrayed nothing.

"The slab in front of the safe may have stuck——"

"Then we'll go and help him to open it."

Essenden's eyes evaded her searching scrutiny.

"I don't see——"

"But I do!" She was sure now. "Essenden, you'll come down to that cellar—with me!"

A muscle twitched in the shadow of Essenden's drooping moustache; and again the girl spoke.

"You don't want to go down there. Exactly. There's something down there which might be dangerous. . . . Oh, yes, I saw it in your face! And that's why we're going."

She opened the door.

"March!"

"I don't——"

Jill Trelawney's eyebrows lowered over her frosty stare.

"I said—*March!*"

Essenden opened his mouth, and closed it again. He went to the door.

"Get a move on."

"It's your own funeral, if you insist on going down there."

"I do insist. *Get on!*"

He obeyed. The door under the main staircase was open, and the light was on. Essenden led straight to it; and Jill followed, tensely alert for the faintest hint of treachery. They went down the flight of steps. The iron-barred door at the far end of the wine cellar had also been left open by the Saint in his passage.

They followed the tunnel, with Essenden moving slowly and hesitantly in the lead, hardly spurred on by the girl's tongue, and Jill Trelawney keyed up to a tingling wariness. But he went on without an attempt at active resistance, and scrambled in front of her down the last ten yards of steep furrowed slope. She descended after him, slowly, with infinite precautions against a false step that might have given him a chance to turn the tables.

"Where now?"

"This is the cave."

He turned the angle of the passage, and she followed quickly.

But not quite quickly enough.

He had played his card superbly—with such an innocent naturalness had he vanished for one instant from her sight. But when she herself rounded the corner, she could not see him.

Then he stepped out of a dark crevice in the rock beside her, and grappled desperately.

He had a hold on her gun wrist before she could move. He was not really such a silly little man as the Saint had called him, and he was much too strong for her. His sudden vicious wrench at her wrist took her unawares, and her automatic clattered down to the stone.

He pushed her roughly away and picked up the gun.

"Now look at my cave!"

She retreated before him. He had changed completely. He was confident, cruel, bestial, transformed. He pointed.

"And Mr. Templar!"

She saw. Simon Templar lay stretched out on the floor of the cavern. He was alive. She heard his breath come in a long tortured gasp. About his bare left ankle was locked a contrivance of shining steel, like a pair of skeleton jaws at the end of a length of chain which vanished into the dark stream beside him.

"An invention of my own," said Essenden, in a queerly high-pitched voice, "for the discouragement of poachers. But it has caught something better than a poacher to-night!"

He laughed, squeakily; and suddenly she realized that he was mad.

"Caught!" he babbled. "I hid it in the stream. Whatever happened, I meant to send him down here. Then he would have to step into the stream to get at the safe. Safe! I put that slab in yesterday, myself, just to catch him. I knew that when he didn't come back, you'd bring me down to look for him, and then I'd catch you as well. Those four men upstairs were only part of the surprise I had waiting for you. If I'd seemed too easy, you'd have suspected something. And didn't you see that that was why I pretended I didn't want to come down here? That was to make you all the more determined to bring me down. And it worked!"

He laughed again, a shrill giggle that pricked the hairs on the nape of the girl's neck.

"But he isn't moving!"

"Of course he isn't," leered Essenden. "It has a very strong spring, my little contrivance—and yet the turn of a small key will release it. I have the key in my pocket. But until the key is used, it will go on hurting."

"You—devil!"

The Saint turned his head with a set twisted smile on his lips.

"No vulgar abuse, Jill," he said huskily. "I haven't used any—and I've been lying here ten minutes, and I dropped my gun in the stream and couldn't find it again."

"My dear!"

"God bless you," said the Saint through his teeth, "for those kind words."

She ran to him, falling on her knees beside him, careless of what Essenden might do. The Saint's face was white with pain, but he kept smiling.

And he said, in the ghost of a whisper: "Liar—gun —left-hand coat pocket—you have it. Your need may yet be greater than mine, sister. . . . Watch your chance——"

Essenden came closer. He flung out his left hand in a grandiose gesture.

"My little cave!" he cackled. "Look at it well, because it's the last thing you'll ever see. The tunnel was bricked up once, but I opened it up again—and this is what I found. But I've never explored it properly. You might get lost, and then if you were caught by the tide——"

He shook to another burst of maniacal merriment.

"You see, this is one shore of a huge underground lake, and it has its own tides, twice a day. When the tide comes up, it reaches nearly to the low part of the roof over your head. That's why the last few steps are so worn away. The water does that. . . . It's long past low tide now. In less than two hours the tide will be up. Oh, yes, and you'll be here to see it . . . creeping up . . . while you're chained here. Till it comes right over your heads . . . up and up . . . and up——"

"And up," murmured the Saint.

"And you will be here—both of you." Essenden turned his pale eyes upon the girl. "Both of you. I'd have saved you, Jill, but you're too dangerous. You'll have to stay here, too. And I shall wall up the tunnel again, with my own hands, and no one will ever know."

The girl knelt beside the Saint. With one hand she stroked the damp hair back from his forehead; the other hand crept slowly, infinitely slowly, towards his pocket. But the gun that Essenden held still covered them both, and there was the cunning of madness in his eyes.

"I shall chain you up here, and leave you," he rambled on. "Then I shall go upstairs and send the others home. I shall pay them well, and they will ask no questions. . . . Aaaaah!"

He pounced, suddenly, like a tiger; and the girl let out an involuntary cry. Her hand was in the Saint's pocket, but it had encountered the muzzle instead of the butt of his automatic. Foolishly, she tried to work round to the butt. The gun came out of the Saint's

pocket as Essenden tore at her wrist; then it fell onto
the rock.

Simon rolled over and snatched at it. Essenden
kicked. The gun shot away from under the Saint's
fingers, spun clattering over the uneven floor, and
plopped into the stream a dozen feet away.

"You must have played football for Borstal," said
the Saint appreciatively.

He grabbed swiftly at Essenden's ankle, and Essenden kicked backwards. His heel struck the Saint between the eyes, half stunning him. . . .

Jill felt herself hurled backwards. She caught
Essenden's right wrist, and he stumbled and tripped.
They fell together into the shallow stream. Then, with
the strength of madness, he pinioned her arms and
heaved her up against the rock face. He groped around
with one hand, holding her there with his other hand
and the weight of his body. A chain was brought
across her body; then she heard it grate metallically
through a socket. There was a click, and he stepped
back, panting.

"That's got you!"

She kicked savagely at him; but he dropped on one
knee and gathered in her legs. A second chain snapped
about her knees, holding her helpless. And Simon
Templar, with the whole world still reeling about him
from that savage kick between the eyes, was straining
at the relentless grip on his ankle with the strength of a
prisoned giant.

"Got you!" babbled Essenden. "Got you both! But I dropped my gun——"

He splashed about in the stream on all fours, muttering to himself, searching. Then presently he stood up, empty-handed.

"It doesn't matter. I don't need a gun now."

"You do!" rapped the Saint. "I've got another—somewhere——"

He was straining at something that seemed to have caught in his hip pocket.

Essenden screamed, and leapt on him.

And the Saint laughed.

This time he did not miss his hold.

As Essenden fell on him, Simon fastened two sinewy hands upon the peer's throat.

On the floor, the two men rolled and fought together like wild beasts. Simon Templar had the strength and speed of a tiger, but insanity had suddenly made Essenden superhuman. Pinned to the floor by the steel trap as effectively as if he had been anchored to a mountain, the only chance that the Saint had lay in keeping his hold on Essenden's windpipe, and on that effort alone he concentrated, while Essenden kicked and writhed and tore at face and fingers with claw-like hands. They rolled over and over, gasping. Simon knew it could not last.

He was weak with pain. He thought his left ankle might be broken, and certainly his left leg seemed to have severed connection with his body from the knee downwards. Unless Essenden weakened soon . . .

Well, there would be plenty of opening for other candidates for the distinction of being the two most unpopular plagues inflicted upon Scotland Yard. The Saint held on desperately, feeling his strength ebbing with every second of that nightmare struggle; but Essenden, a man possessed, seemed to be breaking every known law of human endurance. He fought on, when anyone else should have been unconscious.

And then one of his flailing fists caught Simon in the face.

It was not for the first time in that fight. But this time it so happened that Simon was on his back, his head lifted a bare inch from the floor. And the blow dashed the Saint's head with sickening force against the stone.

A wave of spangled blackness swept over his vision, and all the remaining strength went out of him. He felt his fingers torn easily away from Essenden's throat, and heard Essenden draw breath in one long, quavering sob. The Saint was rolled away like a child.

As his sight cleared, he saw Essenden crawling away out of his reach.

He lay still, his chest heaving, utterly done in, and watched Essenden scramble to his feet at a safe distance.

"Beaten you—again. . . . And you won't—get—another chance!"

Essenden gasped out the words in a rasping clamour of triumph. He reeled towards Jill Trelawney, one hand caressing his larynx jerkily, and stood swaying before her with his face contorted.

"You too, my beauty! You don't know what a lot of trouble you've given me. You ought to pay for my trouble. I meant to leave you here and go back at once. But there's plenty of time before the tide comes up——"

"You fool! D'you think you can get away with this?"

Jill Trelawney stood with her head held high, the contempt undimmed in her imperious eyes, and her beauty made more vivid by its unwonted pallor. Her voice never faltered.

"Why not?" demanded Essenden hazily.

"Because the police are coming here. Because I told the police to come here in time to arrest you——"

"Arrest me?" Essenden chuckled. "There's nothing to arrest me for. There aren't any papers. You didn't believe that story, did you? The only evidence there is is *here!*" He tapped his forehead. "But I'll never give it. I could clear your father's name, but I never will. He was a meddler, and he had to go. Now you've started meddling as well, and you've got to go, too."

"The police will search the house," said Jill steadily. "They can't help finding this place. And then they will take you and hang you."

And even as she spoke, she knew that her bluff fell on deaf ears. Essenden paused to let her speak, but her words made no impression on his brain. Probably he never even heard them.

"Now you've got to go," he mouthed. "But not—before—I've made you—pay for my—trouble!"

He lurched forward, reaching out pawing hands.

And Simon Templar, lashing himself to the last bitter effort, tore futilely at the chain that held him.

In so doing, he rolled over on his face. And right under his nose was a little cluster of gleaming metal shapes.

A bunch of keys!

2

He stared at them like a man in a trance. And then, like a man in a trance, he gathered them into his hand and felt them, felt the smooth hard cold contact of them, wondering if that ghastly adventure had unhinged his brain.

But the keys might have fallen out of Essenden's pocket in the fight.

He shot a sidelong glance at Essenden; but for the moment Essenden had forgotten his existence.

Even so, he could not take a chance.

He rolled away, still seeming to wrestle with his chain, and splashed into the little stream.

Under cover of the water, he could try every key on the bunch without being observed.

"Hold on, Jill!"

His voice rang in the cave with the old unconquerable Saintly lilt as clear in it as sunlight, and Essenden turned to bare his teeth again and laugh.

"You'll never get away, Templar! I made sure of

that when I anchored the trap. But you can try. . . ."

His hands pawed again at the girl's dress.

"But you, Jill," he crooned—"Jill! Such a pretty name, Jill! Pretty Jill—do you still hate me? You shouldn't hate me. . . ."

The Saint worked frantically.

The icy water in which he was half immersed did more than cover his movements. The chill of it stung his aching wearied body into new life.

He found a key that fitted, and felt a fresh surge of hope.

Jill Trelawney had not once cried out. She had not spoken. She had not even answered his encouragement. But as the key he tried turned in the lock, and the steel jaws snapped away from his ankle, he heard her choke back a little moan.

The sound made him forget that for half an hour his left ankle had been locked in the crushing grip of Essenden's man trap. He tried to leap at Essenden, and felt stupidly surprised when his leg gave under him and sent him sprawling.

Essenden whipped round in a flash.

"So you've got loose!"

"I have so," said the Saint.

He had scrambled up onto one knee when Essenden's rush bowled him over again; and once more they were entangled in a mad battle.

If the Saint had ever fought with the frenzy of despair, this was that time. It was his second chance. One chance he had been given, and he had lost out on it. Now he was given the second chance which he had no right to ask; and if he threw that away, he could not expect another. This time he had to win.

And he heard Jill Trelawney speak.

"Oh, Simon! Good man!"

He could not spare the breath to answer. The bunch of keys was in his pocket now; and with Essenden out of the way, he could release the girl in a moment. But to dispose of Essenden . . .

The man had the strength of ten, while the Saint's strength had already been cut down by half by the various punishings he had received. The strongest part of the Saint was his fingers, and with these he strove to take up again his first grip. He reached up for Essenden's throat, found it, circled the windpipe, tightened his hold crushingly. Essenden's face went red. His eyes dilated enormously, and the air wheezed painfully into his starved lungs; but he fought on like an animal at bay.

Simon dropped his chin on his chest and tried with his arms to ward off or at least break the force of the blows that Essenden rained upon him. But when he was guarding his face, Essenden drove his fist into his stomach. In the ordinary way, he would have made nothing of the blow, but at that moment he was weakened and unprepared for it. He gasped and rolled over, fighting down a flood of nausea that threatened to choke him, keeping his stranglehold grimly.

It so happened that the stone floor jutted up immediately under his arm.

It caught him in the elbow, in such a way that a twinge of numbing agony shot up his arm like an electric shock. The fingers of his right hand relaxed, and with a snarl of exultation, Essenden tore both his hands away and breathed again.

Hardly knowing what he did, the Saint wrenched one arm free and lashed out blindly.

He felt the punch jar a thinly covered bone, and Essenden sagged sideways, suddenly limp.

Simon dragged himself to his feet and limped over towards Jill, fumbling in his pocket.

The stream beside the wall had been four feet wide when he had first seen it. Now it was twice that width, and there was a turbulent flurry in its dark waters.

Essenden must have mistaken the time of the tide. And it rose with an appalling speed. While the Saint fought with the lock that held Jill's chains, he felt the cold water creeping up his legs; and when the chains fell away it was up to his knees. The stream was now a racing river as many yards wide as it had once been feet, and one edge of it was still spreading over the floor of the cave.

And Essenden was getting up again.

"Look out!" cried the girl.

Simon turned; and as he did so his bare foot fell on a familiar hardness.

Even so, it was a miscalculation on his part to try to pick up the gun.

He got it into his hand; but Essenden kicked his wrist, and the automatic fell into the stream again.

Essenden plunged frantically; and the Saint, with only one sound leg to stand on, was sent staggering back against the wall. And by some miracle Essenden's hand found the gun without a second's groping.

With the face of a fiend, Essenden took deliberate aim. And the Saint, flattened against the wall, looked death in the eyes.

The second chance—thrown away.

Of course, he ought to have settled Essenden thoroughly, when he had the advantage, instead of relying on a lasting effect from the lucky blow he had landed on the man's jaw.

The strengthening current, an inch above the Saint's knees now, seemed to be trying to pluck his feet from under him and whirl him away. That underground tide must grow in a few more minutes into something with the power and ferocity of a maelstrom. And the Saint would be shot, and the tide would carry him away with it into the unfathomed depths from which it rose. Without a trace. . . . And that would be the end. . . .

With a queer feeling of carelessness, Simon Templar gathered his muscles for the shock of the bullet.

Then he saw Jill Trelawney moving.

She was struggling towards Essenden; and in another step her movement would bring her into the line of fire.

With a cry, the Saint hurled himself forward.

He fell. It was impossible to hurl oneself effectively through that swelling torrent. As he went down, he heard the report of Essenden's shot go booming and reëchoing through the cave.

Then his hand closed upon an ankle.

He jerked, with all his force; and as he fought up through the flood he saw Essenden spinning into the water.

One hand especially he saw—a hand holding a gun, waving wildly as Essenden fell.

In shallower water, Simon caught the hand and the gun, and twisted the gun right round so that it aimed into Essenden's own body.

"Now shoot!" gasped the Saint.

Essenden squinted at him.

"You're another meddler," said Essenden, and tightened his finger on the trigger.

CHAPTER IX

HOW SIMON TEMPLAR KISSED JILL TRE-
LAWNEY, AND MR. TEAL WAS RUDE TO MR.
CULLIS

ESSENDEN was gone. As his body went limp, the rising mill-race fury of the stream whipped him up and swept him away into the dark depths of the cave, further than the ineffectual light at the entrance could penetrate.

The water was coming up higher. It was thigh-deep now, and against its tearing speed it was difficult to stand upright. In fact, the Saint, with one useless leg, would probably never have escaped if it had not been for Jill Trelawney. When one would have thought that she needed all her own reserve of strength to escape herself, she yet managed to find enough strength to spare to help the Saint along beside her. Stumbling and splashing desperately, often on the verge of falling where one false step would have meant certain death, they reached the end of the passage by which they had come.

There they found some sort of haven, with calmer waters lapping up to their waists. If they had been in the full force of the stream at that point they could scarcely have got out alive. As it was, it was hard enough to scale the precipitous slope at the end of the passage. Somehow they dragged themselves up, and lay gasping on the dry stone above the level of the water.

Minutes later, Jill pulled herself to her feet.

"Feeling better?" she asked.

"Miles," said the Saint.

He pulled himself up after her; and they covered the rest of the passage together, Simon leaning some of his weight on an arm placed round her shoulders.

When they had reached the wine cellar, the girl locked the door through which they had come and carefully replaced the key on its nail.

The Saint's shoes and socks had been swept away by the tide in the cave. He limped into the library, and there, after comparing the size of his feet with those of the four tough guys, proceeded, without apology, to remove the footwear of Flash Arne and put it upon himself. The pattern of the socks offended his æsthetic principles, and he would have preferred to ask for shoes of a less violently lemon colour, but a beggar could not be a chooser.

More or less comfortably shod, he stood up again.

"You boys," he said, "may stay here as long as you like. Make yourselves at home, and spend your spare time thinking out the story you're going to tell when the servants come back and find you here."

The replies he received have no place in a highly moral and uplifting story like this.

He went out with Jill, and limped down the drive beside her.

"The water's got into my watch and stopped it," he said, "but we ought to be just about on time."

They were on time. As they reached the lodge gates the lights of a car came up the road.

Jill Trelawney had sent the chauffeur off to buy a bottle of brandy in a neighbouring village; and the probable time he would take on the errand—with necessary refreshment for himself *en route*—had been carefully calculated.

"And that bottle," said the Saint, "may easily turn out to be one of the greatest inspirations either of us has ever had—if you feel anything like as cold as I do."

In the darkness, their drenched and draggled condition could escape notice. They climbed into the car, and Simon took delivery of the Courvoisier and directed the chauffeur.

"And so—the tumult and the shouting dies, the sinners and the Saints depart."

The cork of the bottle popped under his expert manipulation, and the luxurious fittings of the car provided glasses. The liquor gurgled out in the dimness.

"An inferior poison, as compared to beer, but perhaps more warming," he said.

They drank gratefully, and felt the cold recede from the radiant trickle of Three Star. And then the Saint gave her a cigarette and lighted one for himself.

"Where did you tell the chauffeur to drive?" she asked.

"Reading. We can go on to London from there in the morning: I don't want too many people to know all our movements. Teal found my Sloane Street address quickly enough, but it was never my best hidey-hole. I've got another little place in Chelsea that I'll swear he's never even dreamed about. You can make that your home, and I'll go back to Upper Berkeley Mews quite openly, just to annoy Claud Eustace. I might even ring him up and ask him to toddle over and chew some gum with me."

He could see her face in the faint glow as she drew at her cigarette.

"I suppose the Saints have to depart?" she said.

He struck a match to see her better, and his eyebrows went up with the trickle of smoke he exhaled.

"Why?"

She hesitated. Then—

"I thought you meant you were cutting out."

"Jill, you should know me better than that!"

"But I never knew that this kind of thing was in your line."

"The righting of injustice, the strafing of the ungodly, and the succouring of a damsel in distress? Oh, Jill! . . . Did you never hear of Galahad?"

"Ye-es."

"My stage name," said the Saint.

The match went out, and he leaned back on the cushions. His strength was sweeping back into him like a steady stream. He had already made certain that his ankle was not broken, and that was all that had really worried him. In a couple of days he would be prancing around like a puppy off the leash. He was almost satisfied.

"Of course," he murmured, "we have been criminally careless. We have been persistently bumping off the very birds who might have saved us a lot of trouble. I admit Essenden bumped himself off, but that was due to a misunderstanding. It's the principle of the thing. Jill, if we're going to vindicate Papa, we're going to have to be awful careful we don't bounce Number Three on the programme before he's sung his song."

"We shall."

"And then," said the Saint dreamily, "you'll have your hands full looking after that boy friend back in Gee, Wis., won't you?"

There was a silence.

Then she said: "And you?"

"Oh," said the Saint, "you won't want me there, will you?"

She laughed.

"Won't you be going back to someone?"

"Who knows!"

The Saint's cigarette end reddened to a long inhalation, and faded.

"You butted in where you shouldn't have butted in," he said. "This story started mostly as a joke, as I told you one time. I always have been crazy. But I certainly didn't mean to get landed into all this. Since I'm here, I'm enjoying myself; but the entertainment was not among those listed for this season. However, here we are, and here is nobody else, and I always believe in making the best of a good job. Possibly you noticed the tendency at breakfast yesterday."

"Oh!" said the girl.

"There is," said the Saint firmly, "a piffling idea abroad among the sub-hominoids of Suburbia that a man may not kiss a girl for no other reason than that he simply wants to kiss her. Now that is obviously absurd, because although you've just saved my life I'm going to kiss you very passionately for no other reason than that I want to—and you are going to like it."

2

Inspector Teal arrived at Essenden Towers later, before the servants returned from their ball, and found four blasphemous men in the library. His great regret ever afterwards was that, in spite of the extraordinary circumstance of their discovery and their known reputations, he could never find a substantial charge to bring against them in connection with that night's mystery. It was even more suspicious because the stories they told were perfectly true, and they could not be made to contradict either themselves or one another under the most searching examination. Besides which, there were many scraps of circumstantial evidence to bear them out. And it is not a crime for four gangsters, however notorious, to be the guests of a peer.

This annoyed Teal, because he was unable to find any trace of the principal actors in the mystery. And even a minor scapegoat would have been better than none.

He went down through the wine cellar and found the flooded cave. When the waters had subsided, an extensive search was made with electric torches, but still the extent of the cavern and the source of its strange subterranean tides could not be discovered. And no human eyes ever saw Lord Essenden again.

It was late the following afternoon when a sleepless, but not more than ordinarily sleepy, Chief Inspector Teal returned to Scotland Yard to prepare his report.

"I don't suppose Essenden will ever be seen again," he told the assistant commissioner gloomily.

"He was murdered, of course?"

"Probably he was. But how are we ever going to prove that if we can't produce a body? You know the law as well as I do."

Cullis rasped his chin.

"Waldstein first, then Essenden. There must be a connecting link somewhere."

"Of course there is. Trelawney believes that her father was framed, and she's out to get the men who did it. Her idea is that there was a ring of first-class crooks working in with an accomplice right inside this building. Sir Francis Trelawney was the man they wanted here, though—and they couldn't get him. What was more, he was getting hotter on their trail

every day. So he had to go. He was framed, with the
help of their police accomplice; and we know the rest.
That's her story, and somehow or other she's made the
Saint believe it."

"But that's ridiculous! There were only two people
concerned in the show that really put the finger on
Sir Francis Trelawney. The chief commissioner was
one, and I was the other. I told Templar the story
myself. If you're suggesting that one of us was taking
graft from Waldstein——"

"I'm suggesting nothing," said Teal. "I'm just telling you the tale we're up against."

Cullis frowned.

"It's a tale that's making more trouble for us than
we've had for years—there was another leading article
in the *Record* this evening," he said sourly. "Something has got to be done about it, or the chief will be
wanting resignations all round. If there's anything at
all on Trelawney's side, there'll be a clue to it in the
Records Office somewhere—if we can only find it."

Teal nodded.

"It would help us if we could," he said. "She'll be
going after this accomplice in the Yard itself next, and
if we knew whom she was going to pick on, we'd be
ready for her. I wouldn't be worrying so much if the
Saint wasn't in it, but when I see his trade-mark anywhere I know there's going to be no bluff about the
trouble. I wouldn't put it above him to kidnap the
chief commissioner single-handed and flood out Records
with back numbers of the *Vie Parisienne.*"

"He'd have to be a clever man to do it," said Cullis, who had no sense of humour.

"The Saint is a clever man."

Cullis grunted.

"I'll go through that Trelawney dossier again myself," he said.

That dossier was put before Mr. Assistant Commissioner Cullis the very next day; and he spent a whole twelve hours with it, neglecting all other business.

This record of Jill Trelawney was of great interest to Mr. Cullis, for it dealt with the career of that dangerous lady for some time before she had burst upon London as the leader of the Angels of Doom. It went back, in fact, to the event which had led to the creation of the Angels—the time when Sir Francis Trelawney, her father, himself at one time assistant commissioner, had been detected almost in the act of betraying his position and submitting to bribery and corruption. And after his death, which some said was directly due to his discovery and disgrace, had come the Angels of Doom, with his daughter at their head. . . .

As he went through that dossier, Cullis remembered the day, nearly three years ago, when he himself, then only a superintendent, had helped to bring home the charge—the day in Paris when he had gone there with the chief commissioner to watch Sir Francis in the very act of betraying a police secret.

And Cullis remembered the day after that. An afternoon in Scotland Yard when, in the presence of Trelawney and the chief commissioner, he had opened a box taken from the Chancery Lane Safe Deposit, and had found in it a bundle of new five-pound notes which it had been possible to trace back directly to Waldstein. He remembered Trelawney's protestations— that he had never put the notes in his strong box, that he had never seen them before, that he could not explain how they came to be there at all. And the chief commissioner's cold, accusing eyes. . . .

All these memories came back to Cullis as he went through page after page of the dossier, and they were still with him when he went home late that night. For although Teal was humanly inclined to spread himself on the subject of his pet aversion, there was no doubt even in Cullis's mind that the Saint was a factor to be reckoned with, and anyone might have been pardoned for wondering what was going to happen next.

But the next morning there seemed to be no more reason to wonder, for when Cullis arrived at the Yard and went up to his office he found Chief Inspector Teal waiting for him there, and there was something in Teal's lugubrious countenance which foreboded bad news; and, since Cullis's mind was full of Jill Trelawney, he was not so surprised as he might have been when he discovered what that bad news was.

"Weren't you the last man to handle that Trelawney dossier?" asked Teal, coming straight to the point.

Cullis nodded.

"I should think so. I had it out all yesterday afternoon."

"I believe you returned it to Records yourself?"

"That's right," said Cullis. "It was late when I left,
and I turned it in on my way out."

Teal jerked his thumb at the commissioner's desk.

"Take a look," he said.

The folder was there, with its neat label. Cullis
opened it and was moved to a profane exclamation.

The first thing that met his eye was a sheet of paper
bearing a sketch like many others that he had seen
before, and one line of writing:

With compliments and thanks.

Under the note was a blank sheet of paper. Under
the blank sheet the third was also blank. There were
twenty-seven blank sheets altogether—he counted
them.

"When was this discovered?"

"About an hour ago," said Teal. "I sent down for
the file myself to look something up. You'll find that
every sheet relating to the original Trelawney affair
has been taken. The rest has been left, and the bulk
made up with those blank sheets."

"But it's impossible!" snapped Cullis.

"Absolutely," agreed Teal acidly. "And yet it's
been done."

The trials that it had been enduring of late had not
improved the detective's temper.

"No one could raid Scotland Yard," Cullis persisted. "Was there any sign of the files having been tampered with?"

"None at all."

"Then it must have been someone in the building—somebody actually in the Records Office."

Teal extracted a battered piece of gum from his mouth as if he disliked the taste of it. Or it may have been something else that he disliked.

"If we go on making progress at this rate," he said morbidly, "one of the stunt newspapers will be running us as modern reincarnations of Sherlock Holmes."

Cullis scowled.

"That doesn't get us much further. Even if someone in the Records Office was responsible, it might have been any one of a dozen men you could name."

Teal shrugged.

"And which?" he asked tersely.

"There'll be an inquiry, of course."

"And what will that find out? We know the Angels had a lot of money, and I know the Saint still has. Suppose they've bought someone actually in the Yard, why should it be one man more than another?" Teal reached out a slothful arm and picked up one of the blank sheets. It was creased down the centre, as were the other sheets. Teal shuffled the pile together and folded them over the crease. "They'd go into a man's breast pocket," he said. "It's cheap and ordinary paper —the kind they use in a few hundred offices. We shan't find any clue there."

He picked up the note.

"What do you make of that?" asked Cullis.

"It's almost the same handwriting as the note they left on Essenden in Paris, isn't it?"

"Not exactly the same, though. But the writing was disguised, anyway. A man can't write a disguised hand as consistently as he writes his own natural fist."

"Man?" queried Cullis sharply.

"Simon Templar," said Teal sleepily. "I'll swear he wrote that note to Essenden in Paris, anyway."

"And this one?"

"Simon Templar," said Teal, somewhat inconsequently, "is a very clever young man."

Cullis looked at him. He remembered that the feud between Chief Inspector Teal and the Saint was one of the epic legends of the force. There had been truces from time to time—truces and breezy interludes—but the fundamental feud had never finished. And if anything had been wanting to reawaken in Teal's expansive breast the ambition to be the first man to lag Simon Templar, it should have been supplied to him on the night in London, such a very short time ago, when the Saint had balked him of a coveted prey by a trick which a babe in arms should have spotted and which a middle-aged police constable had somehow failed to spot.

"A very clever young man," said Teal.

"Have you any idea where he is now?"

"He's in London, living in his own home. I saw him last night."

"You saw him?" exclaimed Cullis incredulously. "But——"

"Need we have any more of that?" asked Teal wearily. "I'm tired of being told I ought to arrest him. I'm tired of explaining that we can't do anything against him in England for robbing Essenden in Paris. And I'm tired of explaining that you can suspect what you like about him and Jill having been at Essenden's the night Essenden disappeared. But you can't prove anything, and Simon Templar knows it. He can admit anything he likes in private conversations with me, but that evidence disappears the moment I walk out into the street again. He's made a fool of me once, and I'm not going to give him the chance of making a fool of me again by charging me with unlawful arrest. Don't you know that the Saint has never yet been inside?" he added.

"With his record?"

"He hasn't got a record," said Teal. "He's a suspicious character, and an absconding policeman, but that's the worst you can say about him without paying damages for slander—except for that affair in Paris, which we can't do anything about. Once upon a time there were other things we could have held him for, but he got a pardon and wiped all those out. Heavens above, sir," Teal broke out, in a kind of helpless exasperation, "haven't I spent years of my life trying to find something I could put on the Saint? I've had men he's beaten up, in the old days, and he's told me himself he did it, and I couldn't make one of them say a word against him—not a word we could have acted on, I mean. I've had the Saint on the run, once, with a bundle of evidence against him all tied up in my office and a real warrant in my pocket, and then he went and saved a royal train and had all his sins forgiven. I've stood and *watched* him blow a man to blazes, and I haven't been able to prove it to this day. I'm not a miracle man, and I'm not even a convincing liar. I'll tell the world the Saint has beaten me in every game I know and some I'd never heard of before I met him, and I'll try to smile while I'm saying it. But I won't even try to tell a deaf-and-dumb half-wit that I could pull the Saint in to-morrow and have him sent down for so much as seven days in the second division, because I know all I should get would be the horse laugh."

"But he's known to be an associate of Trelawney's."

"And what then?"

"He was Trelawney's accomplice at Essenden's."

"Accomplice?" queried Teal patiently.

"He was with her. He must know where she's hiding now."

"Of course he must. But who's going to prove that in a court of law? We shouldn't do anything by pulling him in, even if we could. No, our best hope is to go on watching him and hoping that sooner or later he'll lead us to Jill Trelawney. And I can't help thinking that that's not much of a hope—with a man like Simon Templar."

Cullis's eyes returned to the ransacked dossier.

"The chief will have to be told about this," he said.

"I've already told him," said Teal. "He was all set to turn Scotland Yard inside out, only I was able to persuade him not to. I'd like a chance to do something on my own before the whole world hears what fools we are."

He stood up. He had been seated in the assistant commissioner's chair throughout the interview, leaning back and chewing gum as if the office belonged to him; for Mr. Teal was a very privileged person. His extraordinarily apathetic acceptance of that morning's startling discovery puzzled his chief. It is not every day that important papers are abstracted without trace from the Records Office, yet Teal seemed as wearily resigned to the fact as if he had only had to inform the commissioner that a plumber had been arrested the previous night for being drunk and disorderly in the Old Kent Road. Cullis was puzzled, for he seemed to detect a thread of melancholy fatalism behind the few remarks that Teal had made on the subject.

"I'll be getting along," Teal said glumly.

Cullis stood by the window with three deep furrows of thought in his forehead. As Teal reached the door he roused out of his abstracted concentration.

"That man Gugliemi?" he said.

"He's being shipped off to-morrow. The deportation order came through this morning. What about him?"

"Where is he now?"

Teal raised his mournful eyebrows.

"Brixton, I think. I'll find out for you. Why?"

"I've got an idea."

"I had one of those myself, once," said Teal reminiscently. "What is this idea?"

"I'm thinking of taking a leaf out of the Saint's book. Dyson was useful to him, if you remember, and I have an idea that Gugliemi may be useful to me. Every one of the men we've put on to watch Trelawney and Weald has been worse than useless. Gugliemi might get by where an ordinary plain-clothes man would be spotted a mile off. Also——"

He paused abruptly.

"Also?" prompted Teal.

Cullis closed his mouth.

"That will keep," he said.

And he kept his idea to himself, and Teal had to go out with his curiosity unsatisfied.

Gugliemi was duly located in Brixton Prison half an hour later, and Cullis, receiving the information, spoke personally to the governor of the prison over the telephone.

Within the hour Gugliemi arrived at Scotland Yard in a taxicab between two warders, and was taken straight to the assistant commissioner's room. And a little while later the two warders returned alone.

Teal, an inquisitive man, returned to the assistant commissioner's room later in the afternoon, and found that Gugliemi had mysteriously disappeared, although no escort had been detailed to conduct him back to the prison.

"The deportation order will be stayed for seven days," said Cullis in answer to Teal's inquiry.

"What's the big idea?" asked Teal.

"Gugliemi," said Cullis heavily, "is an enthusiastic collector of butterflies. I've told him that a very rare specimen of butterfly, called Trelawney, has been seen in England, and I have agreed to let him go out with his butterfly net and try to find it before he's sent back to Italy."

Mr. Teal was not amused.

CHAPTER X

HOW SIMON TEMPLAR SPOKE OF BIRDS-NEST-ING, AND DUODECIMO GUGLIEMI ALSO BE-CAME AMOROUS

IT MUST be admitted at once that Duodecimo Gugliemi had never been cited as an advertisement for his native land. A sublime disregard for the laws of property would alone have been enough to disqualify him in that respect; as it was, he was affected also with an amorous temperament which, combined with a sudden and jealous temper, had not taken long to make Italy too hot to hold him. Leaving Italy for the sake of his health, he had crossed the Alps into Austria; but the Austrian prisons did not agree with him, and, again for the sake his health, he had taken another north-ward move into German territory. He had seen the insides of jails in Munich and Bonn, and had narrowly escaped even more unpleasant retribution in Leipzig. In Berlin he had led an unimpeachably respectable life for six weeks, during which time he was in hospital with double pneumonia. Recovering, he left Berlin with an unspotted escutcheon, and migrated into France; and from France, after some ups and downs, he came to England, from which country, but for the intervention of Mr. Assistant Commissioner Cullis, he would speedily have departed back to the land of his birth. Actually the thirteenth child of a family that had been christened in numerical order, he had been permitted to slip into the appellation of a brother who had died of a surfeit of pickled onions at the tender age of two; but that, according to his own story, was the only good fortune that had come to him in a world that had mercilessly persecuted his most innocent enterprises.

He was a small and dapper little man, very amusing company in his perky way, with a fascination for barmaids and an innate skill with the stiletto; and certainly he looked less like an English plain-clothes man than anything in trousers. Which may account for the fact that Simon Templar, sallying forth one morning from Upper Berkeley Mews, and alert for waiting sleuths, observed two large men in very plain clothes on the other side of the road, and entirely overlooked Duodecimo Gugliemi.

These large men in very plain clothes were among the trials of this life which Simon Templar endured with the exemplary patience with which he faced all his tribulations. Ever since his first brush with the law, on and off, he had been favoured with these attentions; and the entertainment which he had at first derived from this silent persecution was beginning to lose its zest. It was not that the continual watching annoyed him, or even cramped his style to any noticeable extent; but he was starting to find it somewhat tiresome to have to shake off a couple of inquisitive shadowers every time he wanted to go about any really private business. If he made a private appointment for midday, for instance, at a point ten minutes away from home, he had to set out to keep it half an hour earlier than he need have done, simply to give himself time to ditch a couple of doggedly unsuccessful bloodhounds; and this waste of time pained his efficient soul. More than once he had contemplated addressing a complaint to the Chief Commissioner of Police for the Metropolis on the subject.

That day, he had a private appointment at noon; and, as has been explained, he allowed himself half an hour to dispose of the watchers. He disposed of them, as a matter of fact, in twenty minutes, which was good going. He did not dispose of Duodecimo Gugliemi—partly because Gugliemi was rather more supple of intuition than the two detectives, and partly because he was unaware of Gugliemi's existence. So soon as he found that the two large men had fallen out of the procession, he went on to his appointment by a direct and normal route, in ignorance of the fact that Duodecimo was still on his heels.

The return from Reading had presented no serious difficulty to a man of the Saint's ingenuity and brass neck, although he had known quite well that by the following morning there would be patrols of hawk-eyed men watching for him at every entrance to London. In a suit which had not been improved by the previous night's soaking, and which he had deliberately made no effort to smarten up, he had interviewed the proprietor of a garage and spun his yarn. He was an ex-service man down on his luck; he had been a haulage contractor, and a run of unsuccessful speculations had forced him to sell up his business; now a windfall had come his way in the shape of a transport job that was worth twenty-five pounds to him if he could only find the means to carry it out. And he secured the truck that he wanted, and the loan of a suit of overalls as well, and so drove boldly into London under the very noses of the men who were waiting for him at the Chiswick end of the Great West Road, with Jill Trelawney under a tarpaulin in the back. And after that, it had been a childishly simple matter to smuggle her stealthily into the studio at dead of night; where he had indicated a cupboard plentifully stocked with unperishable foods, and marooned her. There he visited her frequently, to report news and replenish the larder—that morning, as a matter of fact, he carried a dozen kippers, a loaf of bread, half a pound of butter, and two dozen eggs with him in an attaché case.

She met him at the door.

"Bless you," she said. "If you hadn't come to-day, I think I should have blown up in hysterics. You've no idea what it is to be stuck indoors with nothing to do but read and eat for twenty-four hours a day."

Simon set up the attaché case on an easel which had never carried a canvas.

"And I've only been away since the night before

last," he said. "The girl's starting to love me, that's what it is."

She offered him a cigarette, and took one herself.

"What's been happening?"

"Nothing much. Teal's been in again. Started by threatening, got the bird, tried to be cunning, got the bird, tried to be friendly, got the bird, tried to bribe me, got the bird, and went home. Now he's going to retire and start a poultry farm on that capital. Policemen disguised as gentlemen still follow me everywhere——"

"How can you be certain you've shaken them off?"

"When I can't hear their boots squeaking, I know I'm at least three blocks in the lead. Oh, and Records Office has been burgled."

She looked down at him in his chair.

"What's that?"

"Burgled. Feloniously entered, and important secret papers unlawfully abstracted from. Jill Trelawney, dossier of, subsection M 3879 xxi (*b*). . . . Incidentally, that's an exaggeration. Give the police some credit. The burglary theory was discarded after the first five minutes, as a matter of fact, and the crime is now held to have been an inside job, carried out by some corrupt official in the pay of the Saint."

"When was this?"

"Night before last."

"When you were here?"

"Exactly. My alibi is perfect."

"You left at midnight?"

"Not of my own free will."

She smiled.

"But you said you had an appointment?"

"I did."

"Did you have an appointment?"

"Did I say I had? Jill, I won't be cross-examined. You must keep that for your American boy friend, when you've hooked him. I had to see a man in Camden Town about a second-hand Pomeranian, and he sold me a pup. How's that?"

Jill smiled again. Then she pointed to a litter of newspapers on a side table.

"This is the first I've heard about that Records Office affair," she said, "and I'll swear the rest of the world is as much in the dark as I am."

"It is—mostly."

"Then how do you know anything about it?"

"I have secret sources of information," said the Saint.

He yawned monstrously. His head settled lazily back against a cushion, and his eyes closed.

Jill looked at him for a few seconds. Then—

"Simon!"

"Hullo," sighed the Saint, starting up.

"What's the matter with you?" she demanded.

"Sorry," said the Saint. "I've had hardly any sleep for the last couple of nights, and I'm dead tired."

"What have you been doing?"

Simon stretched himself.

"Jill," he said, "you ought to have more faith in me. I haven't been on the tiles. I've been darn near them, though——there was a nasty bit of drain-pipe work on the way, and one hideous moment when I thought the gutter was going to come to pieces in me 'and. But it turned out all right, though I did some damage to the ivy——"

"You didn't break into Scotland Yard?"

"Who said I did?" asked the Saint, opening wide, childlike eyes of innocent astonishment.

The girl came over and sat on the arm of his chair. In her plain blue frock, with her lovely face innocent of the make-up which it never needed, she might have posed for a picture that would have made that studio famous, if Simon Templar had been an artist; and the Saint admired her frankly.

"That American boy is going to have a busy life bumping off aspiring co-respondents some day," he murmured idly.

"What were you doing—on drain pipes?"

"Birds-nestin'."

"Simon!"

"All right, teacher. If you want to know, I'm going into the plumbing trade, and I wanted to do my studies on the cheap."

She stood up impatiently; and Simon laughed, and pulled her down again by a hand which he had not released.

Absent-mindedly, he kissed the hand.

"Thank you."

"Not at all," said the Saint politely. "Look here, will you believe me if I swear that Scotland Yard was robbed the night before last, and I didn't do my drain-piping till last night—or rather the small hours of this morning?"

She looked him puzzledly in the eyes.

"Yes," she said, "I will. But what are you getting at?"

The Saint grinned.

"Then hold on," he said, "because your faith in my word is going to get a shock."

He slipped a hand into his breast pocket and brought it out with a heavy envelope.

"Take a look. No charge for inspection."

She turned the envelope over. It was not sealed. Turning back the flap, she drew out a thick bundle of papers and unfolded them.

At the sight of the first one, her face changed. Then she glanced rapidly through the rest. She turned to the Saint with a frown on her eyebrows and a half-smile on her lips.

"You—blighter!"

"I told you your faith would take a toss."

"But why not tell me right away?"

"Tell you what?"

The innocence of the Saint's wide blue eyes was blinding.

"Why not tell me at once that you'd bust the Records Office?" she said.

"Because," said the Saint blandly, "it wouldn't have

been precisely true. I'm always very particular about telling the precise truth," he said virtuously.

"It's either true, or it isn't——"

"Talking of macaroons," said the Saint hurriedly, "have you noticed the last sheet?"

She looked.

"It's blank."

"A valuable curiosity. Once upon a time some person or persons whom we will call unknown unlawfully obtained private papers from the files of Scotland Yard. In place of said papers, the said person or persons left an equivalent number of blank sheets. The blank sheet you hold in your hand is a specimen of the same. Very interesting."

She stared.

"One of the sheets that were left in the file?"

"No. An identical sheet, out of the block from which the sheets left at the Yard were taken. Now here"—the Saint dived into another pocket—"is one of the sheets that were left at the Yard. If you compare the two——"

Jill Trelawney took the second sheet in her hand.

She said breathlessly: "But how the——"

Simon Templar smiled seraphically.

"My spies are everywhere," he said. "I have resources at which you cannot even guess. Excuse me."

He took all the papers out of her hand, restored them to the envelope, and replaced the envelope in his pocket.

The girl put a hand on his shoulder.

"You're playing some clever game," she said. "I want to know what it is."

The Saint tapped his pocket.

"There are papers here," he said, "which cannot be duplicated. They are the only genuine dromedary's drawers. There is, for instance, the original letter giving warning of an impending raid, written on Scotland Yard notepaper on the typewriter which was in your father's office, which went part of the way towards substantiating the charges against your father. There is evidence which cannot be taken again. And there are details of the case which, without these papers, nobody might remember, after all this time. Small details, but important to some people. If, for instance, the chief commissioner should for any reason decide to set up a fresh inquiry into the circumstances of your father's dismissal——"

"Why should he do that?"

"Isn't that what you want?"

She did not answer.

"Isn't that what the Angels of Doom were for?"

"Yes," said Jill, almost in a whisper, "that's what they were for—originally."

"To wipe the noses of the guys who framed Papa because they couldn't buy him. Exactly."

"And that's all," said Jill huskily. "That's all they ever did. There was Waldstein and Essenden. Essenden made some sort of confession—but Essenden's dead, and no one would credit my evidence and yours. And it was the same with Waldstein. I'm beginning to think that there's no chance of doing anything but take revenge."

"Waldstein and Essenden," said the Saint—"Numbers One and Two. There's still Number Three; it's always third time lucky, lass."

"Are we going to do any better there?"

"We ought to, after all the practice we've had. If you keep your heart up, old girl——"

She raised her head.

"I still don't know," she said, "why you should be in this with me."

"Child," said the Saint, "is that still biting?"

"The others were in it for money."

"I took a hundred thousand francs off Essenden in Paris. It would have been two hundred thousand if we hadn't gone into partnership. Yes, I know—you're a dead loss to me. But there was that little joke I've mentioned more than once, if you remember."

"Is that your secret?"

"One of them. Didn't I tell you I always have been crazy? That's very important. If I hadn't been crazy, there'd have been no joke, and the Lord alone knows what would have happened to the Angels of Doom; but certainly there'd have been a lot less mirth and horseplay in history than there is now. . . . One day, when this story's over, I'll tell you all about it. All I can say now is that there was one thing I vowed to do before I went respectable; and I can tell you it was well worth doing. Will that do for to-day, Jill?"

He saw the smiling perplexity in her face and the

whimsical shake of her head, and laughed. And then he looked at his watch and stood up.

"Do you mind if I go?" he asked. "It's my bed-time."

"At one o'clock in the afternoon?"

He nodded.

"I told you I hadn't had any sleep to speak of for two nights. And to-night I'm going to call on a most respectable relative, and I don't want to look too dissipated. He mightn't be so ready to believe in my virtues as you are."

She was surprised into an obvious remark.

"I didn't know you had any relatives."

"Didn't you? I had a father and a mother, among others. It was most extraordinary. The papers at the time were full of it."

"You mean the *Police News?*"

"I don't remember that the *Police News* was interested in me just then," said the Saint gravely. "I rather think their interest developed later."

She had dropped into banter to cover up her breach of good criminal manners; but she was still inquisitive enough to try to press a serious question.

"Have you honestly got any relatives who still know you?"

It was beautifully put—that touch of sympathetic curiosity, the quiet assumption that they were now intimate enough to exchange notes. But Simon only laughed.

"To tell you the truth," he said, "this isn't a really

truly relative, although I call him Auntie Ethel. But
he views my indiscretions with a tolerant eye, and still
believes that I shall reform one day. Now let's talk
about supralapsarianism. I can't promise when I'll be
in again, Jill, but it'll be as soon as I can make it. . . ."

She went with him to the door and watched him
down the stairs, and felt unaccountably lonely when
he had gone.

Simon went straight back to Upper Berkeley Mews.
He had not been joking when he spoke of going to
bed. He would have to be up again that night, and
Heaven alone knew when he would get his next full
night's rest.

But since he had not noticed Duodecimo Gugliemi
before, the Saint did not miss him on the way home.

2

The Saint had been gone eight hours when a peal
on the bell rang sharply through the studio and set
the girl's heart pounding against her ribs.

No one should have rung that bell. The Saint himself had a key, and no tradesmen ever called, for
obvious reasons. Who it could be outside, therefore,
except a detective whom the Saint had not been so
clever in shaking off as he had believed . . .

As she stood by the table with her brain in a whirl
the ring was repeated.

She went to the window and looked out and down
into the street, but there was nothing out of the

ordinary to be seen there—no signs of a cordon or even of one or two men told off to wait for an escape by another exit. As for the man at the door, it was impossible to inspect him; for the entrance of the studio was on the third and top floor of the building, and the architect, not knowing that his building was ever to be used for sheltering a wanted criminal, had omitted to provide a window looking out onto the landing, or any other similar means of inspecting callers before opening the front door.

Jill Trelawney thought all this out in a flash, and made her decision.

Whoever it was, she would gain nothing by refusing to open the door. If it were the police, the block would be well surrounded, and the door would eventually be forced if she refused to answer the bell. If it were anyone else . . . She had no idea who it could be, but she must still answer.

The little automatic that she was never without in those days was in her hand when she went to the door and opened it.

The first sight of the man outside was reassuring. Certainly he was not a detective, whatever else he might be—he was far too small and slim ever to have succeeded in entering the ranks of the metropolitan police, even if he had wanted to. A second glance told her that he was not likely even to have wanted to; for there was something unmistakably un-English about the exaggerated nattiness of his attire which would have marked him for a foreigner anywhere, even without the evidence of his thin dark features and his restless dark eyes.

"Mees Trelawney?"

After only a fractional hesitation she admitted the charge. His manner was so confident that she realized immediately that a bluff would carry no weight. At the same time, although he seemed so certain of her identity, there was nothing menacing or even alarming about his manner.

But in a moment he explained himself.

"I come from the part of Meester Templar. He has been arresting."

A sudden fear took her by the throat.

"Arrested? When?"

"Very near here. He meet me last night and say he has work for me. This morning I meet him again, he bring me along here, and he tell me to wait outside while he go in, and then we go off together and he tell me what it is to do. Then we get a little way from here, and a man recognize him in the street and say 'I want you.'"

The visitor waved his arms expressively.

"And Mr. Templar told you to come here?"

"Oh, no. But he look at me, and I know what to do."

She understood. The Saint could not have said anything before the police without giving her away.

"Who are you?" she asked.

"I am Duodecimo Gugliemi," said the little man dramatically. "Now I tell you. Meester Templar, he get in a taxicab with the detective, and I get in another taxicab and I follow. Then a piece of paper come out of the taxicab window, and I stop my taxicab and pick it up. Here it is."

He flourished a muddy scrap of paper, and she took it from him and deciphered the smudged scrawl:

Wait in car outside Scotland Yard ten o'clock.

S.

"Why didn't you come before?" she snapped. "If this was only just after he left here——"

"I had to get a car. It is outside now. A friend of mine is driver. Meester Templar, he know my friend also."

"Wait a minute."

She left him at the door and was back in a moment, slipping into her coat and cramming her hat onto her head. Her little gun was in its holster at her side, under her coat.

"Now we'll go."

The Italian was scuttling down the stairs in front of her, and she followed quickly. There was a closed car standing by the curb, and Gugliemi opened the door for her. She stepped in, and he followed, and the car began to move off almost at once.

It was only then that she saw that thin gauze blinds were drawn across all the windows. She sat quite still.

"What are those curtains doing?"

"You must not see where we go. It would be dangerous for you to see."

She sat in silence, with a delirious kaleidoscope of

conflicting speculations whirling over in her brain. She was sure only of one thing, and that was that she had been incredibly stupid. She peered at the man beside her, but he was gazing steadily ahead, and seemed to have temporarily forgotten her existence.

Presently, when her watch told her they had been driving for nearly half an hour, Gugliemi spoke:

"We arrive. You must let me put this over your eyes."

There was a flash of a white handkerchief in his hand.

"Is—that—so?"

"I am afraid you cannot refuse. I must tie this over your eyes, and you must not make me be violent about it, because I do not like being violent."

She waited. The blur of white moved towards her, and she felt the soft caress of silk on her face. And then she twitched her automatic from its holster and rammed it into the man's ribs.

"You're moving too fast, Duodecimo," she said softly. "Think again—and think quickly!"

The Italian continued imperturbably with his task.

"I'll count three," she rapped. "You can start say·ing your prayers now. *One*——"

"And then the car stop, the police come, and you are arresting," he replied calmly. "But do not trouble, Mees Trelawney, I have already unloaded your gun."

She realized that the car had stopped, and could have wept with rage against herself.

"Will you get out?"

She could feel rather than see the stronger light that

entered as the door was opened; but she had been well blindfolded. She could not even get a glimpse of the ground under her feet. Even a chance to lift the bandage for a moment was not given her, for both her wrists were firmly grasped.

"There are some steps down———"

He guided her along what seemed to be a passage, up a few more steps that grated like bare stone under her shoes, round a corner.

"Now there are some stairs."

She climbed them with his hand on her arm guiding her—four flights—and then he opened a door and led her through. In a few more paces he checked her, and she felt something hard pressed against the back of her knees.

"Sit down."

She obeyed. She felt his hands at her wrists, the rough contact of tightening leather straps, and the cold touch of a metal buckle. . . . Then the same thing at her ankles. . . . Four straps held her as firmly as steel chains; and then the handkerchief was untied.

The room in which she found herself was small and dingily furnished. The paper was peeling off the walls, and the carpet was patched and frayed at the edges. There was a truckle bed in one corner, and on a rickety table stood a bottle, a few glasses, and the remains of a sandwich reposing on a piece of newspaper.

She was sitting in a solid oaken chair which seemed to have no place in that room and might even have been acquired for the occasion. The straps which he had just fastened pinned her wrists to the arms of it, and her ankles to the legs, and she knew at once that she would never be able to free herself unaided if she sat there for the rest of her life. So much she knew even before she pitched all her strength against the seasoned leather, and found the little Italian watching her with a kind of detached amusement.

"I do not think you will escape, Mees Trelawney," he said, "so I will excuse myself. I will send my friend away, and then I will come back and talk to you." The bright little eyes gleamed under the brim of his hat. "I have very interesting things to say to you—very interesting."

And as the door closed behind him something like a cold ghostly hand seemed to touch the back of her neck, sending a clammy tingle over her scalp and an icy numbness sinking down into the pit of her stomach.

Now that she knew he had nothing to do with the Saint, she wondered if the Saint knew anything about him—if it were possible that the Saint might have noticed him at some time. It meant, at least, that the story of the Saint's arrest was probably untrue, mere bait for the trap into which she had walked so blindly. But how soon would the Saint find out, and, even then, what could he do? Such a little time could make so much difference. . . . And on the upturned dial of her wrist watch, almost under her eyes, three impersonal hands traced the crawling of time into eternity.

She watched their remorseless movements with a dull apathy of fascination, and saw the plodding minutes lengthen into an hour. She had no idea what Gugliemi could be doing; it did not seem to be useful to wonder. Probably he was drinking. . . . One hour became two. Something seemed to snap in her brain and make her insensible to the passage of time. What would the Saint be doing? . . . She was getting cramp and her nose was tickling. . . .

And then footsteps sounded outside, and the handle of the door turned with a rattle that made her heart leap into her mouth and flop back into a furious hammering. A crazy hope that it might even be the Saint himself swept through her head—she had unconsciously attained to such a faith in the Saint, had fallen so deeply under his spell, without knowing it at the time, that she could have believed him capable of any miracle. . . . But the sound heralded only the return of the dapper Gugliemi, now lightened of his hat and coat.

He came into the room and locked the door behind him, and the girl raised her head.

"You've been a long time with your friend," she remarked.

"Yes." He smiled. "He was a little difficult. But I have sent him away now, and he will not come back for two hours. That will give me plenty of time. I hope you are becoming interested."

"Not enough to raise my temperature. And I didn't invite you to sit down. Even if you are disguised as a gentleman——"

"Mees Trelawney——"

"Or perhaps you aren't disguised as a gentleman. I admit the disguise wasn't very successful, but I thought that was what it was meant to be."

Gugliemi adjusted his tie with delicately manicured hands.

"Do you know what is going to happen to you?" he inquired.

His English had become more fluent, perhaps because his first agitation, which had not been entirely simulated, was wearing off.

"I told you I wasn't interested," she said.

Watching him, she appreciated the circumstances cold-bloodedly. Even her useless automatic had been taken from her; and she knew, from the grip that he had once taken on her wrists, that even if she had not been strapped to the chair he could have handled her as he pleased, slight as he was. And then . . . Of course, the story of the Saint's arrest might possibly be true; but it was unlikely. Her thoughts were muddled by the feeling of exasperation which ran through them. For her, after turning the laws of England inside out, and making enough trouble to whiten the hair of every man in Scotland Yard, to have fallen for a bushel of birdseed like that! But how long would it be before the Saint missed her?

Since she had been installed in the studio he had called at least every other day. Sometimes on consecutive days. At the best, reckoning upon his previous habits, he could not be expected to call again before to-morrow; and two hours, according to Gugliemi, were all the time that there was to spare.

And yet things were moving faster than they had been before, and it was more than possible that the Saint might have reason to see her again that night.

And when once he missed her, he wouldn't be likely
to accumulate so much moss under his feet that it
would seriously interfere with his travelling. But could
she hold out so long—long enough to give him the
time he would require to make up the lost ground?

"It is necessary," said Gugliemi, "that you should
be killed. I have been told so, and I myself have been
paid to do it. I did not know before that these things
were done in England, but now I am told that they
are. In Italy, of course, if anyone is a trouble he disappears—poof!—like that. But I did not know it was
done in England until I was told that you must disappear. And they told me that if you disappeared
completely they would not send me back to Italy. That
is very important, because if I went back to Italy I
should be sent to prison at once."

She stared at him, hardly believing her ears.

"Who told you this?" she asked in a strained voice.

"I was told," said Gugliemi. "But I was not told to
do it like this. This was an idea of my own. I was told
to take my little gun and find out where you lived, and
go in and shoot you and walk out again, and no questions would be asked. But I saw you once, when you
looked out of the window I was watching in the street
outside, and I decided that it could not be done like
that. Not with anyone so young and beautiful."

He kissed his fingers to her, elegantly.

"So I have brought you to my little home. You
have disappeared, and so the police will be satisfied.
As for me, I also will be satisfied, and everything will
be quite all right."

The ridiculous preciousness of his speech and gesture made the situation grotesque, and yet . . .

She looked round the bare, mean room, made dingier, if possible, by the fact that it was lighted only by a feeble gas jet in one corner. And while Gugliemi deliberated his next sentence, rocking gently in his chair, she listened in the silence, and heard no other sound in the house. Probably it was empty—Gugliemi would not have risked leaving her ungagged in a place where she might cry out and attract attention.

He seemed to read her thoughts with the restless dark eyes that searched her face with blatant appreciation of her beauty.

"No," he said, "there is no one here. We are in Lambeth, and this is the caretaker's room over an empty warehouse. You can cry out if you like, but no one will hear you. And as soon as you promise me that you will behave yourself, I will take those straps away and you will be free."

"So," she said calmly, "Mr. Templar hasn't been arrested?"

He spread out his hands.

"How should I know? That was a story I made up. When he left your house, I did not follow him any more. I was not interested in him. Perhaps he has been arrested, perhaps he has not. Who can say?"

She grasped that one fact as a drowning man might clutch at a straw.

And then, as if in answer to her thoughts, somewhere down in the depths below there was a thunder of knocking on the door.

CHAPTER XI

HOW SIMON TEMPLAR INTERRUPTED A PARTY, AND MR. CULLIS WAS AT HOME

GUGLIEMI must have thought that it was his friend returning, for his dark eyes opened wide when he saw Simon Templar.

"What do you want?" he demanded.

"Who are you?" inquired the Saint, inspecting him from crown to toe with a disparaging eye.

"I am the caretaker."

"Then I hope you will take great care," said the Saint.

The Italian was starting to push the door in his face, but Simon pushed harder, and walked in.

"What do you want?" asked Gugliemi again, and this time he asked it more dangerously.

Simon carefully detached a fragment of cobweb from his sleeve. He was in his dinner jacket, without hat or overcoat, and his shirt gleamed snowy white in the dim light.

"I really don't want you to think me interfering, Signor Oleaqua," said the Saint diffidently. "But don't you think it's time you let Miss Trelawney go home?"

"I know nothing about Mees Trelawney."

"But, my dear Signor Gazebo," protested the Saint, in accents of shocked innocence, "think of the proprieties! Think of what the bishop would say if he knew that you were alone with a fair lady at this hour!"

"I do not understand," said Gugliemi stubbornly. "I know no Mees Trelawney, I tell you."

The Saint's eyebrows lifted half an inch.

"Really?" he said. "But a friend of yours has just told me that he brought her here with you."

Gugliemi shrugged eloquent shoulders.

"Perhaps you make the fairy tale?" he said.

"Perhaps," agreed the Saint. "But of course you'll let me have a look round, just to make sure, won't you?"

"I shall not." Gugliemi straightened up. "You have forced your way in here, and if you do not go quickly I will call for the police."

Simon straightened up also.

"Your ideas of hospitality are deplorable," he remarked genially. "But I'm sure you don't mean it. You're just one of these strong men with no trimmings, and you wouldn't be really troublesome for the world, would you?"

A shining automatic had appeared from nowhere in his hand. He flourished it airily, and Gugliemi became aware of an unpleasant sinking feeling.

"I'm not very used to these little toys," said the Saint mildly, as the gun flourished round and settled down directly opposite the sinking feeling. "I am a

man of peace, though nobody ever seems to believe it.
But I understand that if you squeeze these gadgets
in the wrong place they go bang and make holes in
things. I should be frightfully interested to see if that's
true. Do you happen to know, by any chance?" His
fingers flickered carelessly over the trigger, and Gugliemi went pale. "But what's the idea, my little *andante
capriccioso?* A spot of kidnapping? Some of this heavy
desert love stuff you've seen on the cinematografo?"

He waggled his automatic perilously with every
question.

Gugliemi reached behind him, but the Saint was a
little quicker. He reached out and caught the Italian's
wrist in time, and Gugliemi dropped his gun with a
yelp of pain. Simon pushed him away and picked
it up.

"And what are your views," asked the Saint con-
versationally, "on the subject of supralapsarianism?
They should be valuable. Only a few hours ago——"

"All right," snarled Gugliemi. "I find you Mees
Trelawney. Only put that gun away."

"Not till I know you aren't going to pull any more
slapstick comedy, sweetheart," said the Saint. "Where
is she?"

"Upstairs."

"Dear—me!" The automatic nuzzled again into
Gugliemi's fancy waistcoat. "I hope you haven't been
forgetting your manners?"

"I will show you."

"You certainly will," said the Saint pleasantly. "But

I'm afraid that if you *have* been forgetting your manners, I shall be forced to do things to you which will be not only painful, but permanently discouraging. . . . Lead on, Rudolph."

Gugliemi led on, and the Saint followed him into the upper room. He saw the light that came to the girl's eyes as he entered, and bowed to her with a laugh—the entrance happened too obviously upon its cue, and anything like that was bliss and beauty for the Saint, who was nothing if not melodramatic. And he turned again to the Italian.

"Remove the whatnots," he ordered operatically.

Gugliemi bent shakily to obey. The straps fell from the girl's wrists, then from her ankles.

"And now, Jill, has the specimen behind this tie pin been getting what you might call uppish?"

"He was——"

"Ah-ha!" The Saint revolved his automatic. "I don't want to be premature, Antonio, but this looks bad for your matrimonial prospects. If you remember what I was saying just now——"

"But you got here in time," Jill protested. "What are you going to do?"

"Oh!" said the Saint, almost reluctantly. "Hasn't he been really nasty?"

"Not really."

The Saint sighed.

"The old story book again," he murmured unhappily. "You know, I've always wondered what would happen if the hero missed his train and blew in half an hour too late. And I suppose we shall never know. . . . But what was the idea?"

She told him, exactly as Gugliemi had told her, while the Italian stood pallidly silent under the continued menace of the Saint's automatic. And when, at the end of the story, Simon turned suddenly on him, Gugliemi almost jumped out of his skin.

"You really mean to tell me the police passed you that yarn?" demanded the Saint. "And you expect me to believe it?"

"But it is true, sair."

"Which policeman?" inquired the Saint skeptically.

"A big man—with a moustache—like this——"

Gugliemi frowned down his eyebrows, twisted his mouth, and thrust out his jaw in a caricature which the Saint recognized at once. So did Jill.

"Cullis!"

Simon sat down on the bed, regarding the Italian with a thoughtful air.

"But how did you get here?" Jill was asking.

"Oh, I breezed along," said the Saint. "As a matter of fact, I was coming round to see you. My respectable friend thought he'd like to meet you, so I was sent off to bring you along. Just as I turned the corner by the studio I saw you get into a car and drive away. There wasn't a taxi in sight to give chase in, and in the circumstances I couldn't raise happy hell in the street. But I nailed down the number of the decamping dimbox, and then it was easy enough to find out who the owner was."

"But how did you do that?"

"I consulted a clairvoyant," said the Saint, "and he told me at once. It took a bit of time, though. However, I got the man just as he was putting the car away in the garage. He was persuaded to talk——"

"You made him talk?"

"I hypnotized him," said the Saint blandly, "and he talked. Then I came right along here."

The girl shook her head ruefully.

"I'm luckier than I deserve to be. If I'd thought I should ever live to fall for a gag like that——"

"It's an old gag because it's a good one, darling. Given the right staging, it never fails. So I shouldn't take it too much to heart. And now let's go home, shall we?"

He stood up, and Jill Trelawney was at a loss for anything more to say at that moment. She could only think of one feeble remark.

"But what are we going to do with—this?"

She indicated Gugliemi, and Simon looked at the man as if he had never seen him before.

"I'll take him back to Upper Berkeley Mews," he said. "I think I'd like to have a little private talk with him; that break of yours might turn out to be the most useful thing you ever did."

And take Gugliemi he did, with one hand holding the man's arm and another jamming the muzzle of the automatic into his ribs, all the way from Lambeth to the studio in Chelsea, in a taxicab which they were lucky enough to find as soon as they emerged onto the main road. He left Jill at the studio, saying that he would return in an huor; and he himself went on in the taxi with Gugliemi to Upper Berkeley Mews.

He was as good as his word. It was almost exactly an hour later when she heard his key in the lock, and the next moment he walked in, as calm and unperturbed as if nothing of any interest whatever had happened that evening.

By that time she had collected her wits, and she was ready for him.

"Did you have a good talk?" she inquired.

"Charming," said the Saint, stretching himself out on the sofa and lighting a cigarette. "What about a brace of those kippers I brought in this morning? My respectable friend gave me a slap-up dinner, but I've still got room for some good plain food."

"What did you talk to Gugliemi about?" she persisted.

"About Judas Iscariot."

"Don't be funny."

"But I'm dead serious, Jill. In that famous name you have the whole conversation in a nutshell. He didn't take much persuading, either, and we parted bosom friends."

"Do you mind giving me some straight talk? What's this game you're playing now?"

Simon grinned.

"That," he said, "must still be one of my own particular secrets. But I can satisfy you about Gugliemi, who has a very kind heart when you dig down to it, although his methods are rather low. In fact, I gather that he was really getting quite fond of you before I arrived and spoilt his evening."

"I quite believe that," said the girl grimly.

"Joking apart," said the Saint, "he's an interesting psychological specimen: I'd figured that in the first few minutes. He was quite ready to put you out of the way in his own fashion—for a fee—since he had been told that you were a political nuisance. But I had a much better story to tell him. I didn't even have to beat him up, which I was quite prepared to do. I took him into my confidence. I dosed him with a bottle of Chianti I found lying around. I told him he'd been humbugged all the way down the line, and I was able to produce a bit of evidence to convince him."

"What evidence was that?"

"Never mind. But he was really quite ready to be convinced, because, as I said, you'd made a great impression on him. And when he saw what the game was, what with his native chivalry and another litre of Chianti and my persuasive tongue, he switched right round the other way. And now I believe he'd go out after Cullis with a gun in each hand and a stiletto behind his ear if you asked him to. Did you know his first name was Duodecimo? That's a jolly sort of name, that is. We were getting as matey as that before the end. . . . The really interesting point is our assistant commissioner's psychology."

The girl was lighting a cigarette.

"Go on," she said.

"You see his point," said the Saint. "You're getting troublesome, so Cullis employs Gugliemi to bump you off. If Gugliemi doesn't get caught, so much the better. If he does get caught, and tries to tell anyone that the assistant commissioner employed him to take you for a ride, they'd just think he was raving. It was really beautifully simple. My respectable friend will just love that story."

The girl looked at him curiously.

"Who is this respectable friend you keep talking about?"

"Auntie Ethel," said the Saint lucidly. "She has a very fine sense of humour. For instance, she simply roared over the story of those papers that were taken from the Records Office."

Jill Trelawney watched him with narrowed eyes. She had not seen him in this mood before, and it annoyed her. When they had joined forces in Birmingham, and throughout the adventures which followed—even in the earlier days of bitter warfare—everything had been perfectly straight and aboveboard. But now the Saint was starting to collect an aura of mystery about him, and she realized, almost with a shock, that in spite of the fantastic manner in which he played his part there was something very solid behind his fooling.

She had always been used to being in the lead. The Angels of Doom had followed her blindly. But Simon Templar had challenged her from the very beginning, and from the very moment when he had elected to catapult them into a preposterous partnership he had been quietly but steadily usurping her place. And now, when he calmly produced a dark secret which he would not allow her to share, while he knew everything that he needed to know about her, she felt that she had fallen into a definitely subordinate position. And the bullet was a tough one for her to chew.

But the Saint's manner indicated no feelings of triumph, or even of self-satisfaction, which was really so surprising that it made the situation still more irritating to her. If he had been ordinarily smug about it she could have dealt with him. But he had a copyright kind of smugness that was unanswerable. . . .

"The papers," said Jill deliberately, taking up his remark after it had hung in the air for some seconds, "which *you* took from the Records Office."

"Oh, no," said the Saint. "The papers which Cullis took from the Records Office!"

She was startled into an incredulous exclamation.

"Cullis?" she repeated.

Simon nodded.

"Yes. The night before last I was up all night watching his house. He lives in Hampstead, which is a dangerous thing for a man like that to do, in a house which stands all by itself with a garden all round. French windows to his study, too. I sat shivering in the dew behind a bush, and watched him when he came in. I didn't know then what the papers were, of course, but I gathered from his expression that they were something pretty big. Next morning I heard about Records Office being robbed, and I guessed what it was."

"You never told me how you learnt that."

"Through the clairvoyant I mentioned before," said the Saint fluently. "A very useful man. You ought to meet him. . . . Last night I went down and did my burglary. I had to do the drain-pipe work I mentioned and get in on the first floor, because there were some very useful burglar alarms all over the downstairs window—a new kind that you can't disconnect; and I duly collected the papers, as you saw. You see, Cullis is getting the wind up."

Jill Trelawney gazed at him without speaking.

"Cullis is getting the wind up," repeated the Saint comfortably. "Our blithe and burbling Mr. Cullis is feeling the draught in the most southerly quarter of his B.V.D.'s. He's already afraid of the inquiry on your father being reopened, so he abstracted certain important papers from your dossier. And he knows you're dangerous, so he employed Duodecimo to move you off the map. Yes, I think we could say poetically that our Mr. Cullis is soaring rapidly aloft on the wings of an upward gale."

"I see," said Jill softly.

"But you didn't see before?" asked the Saint. "Didn't you realize that there were really only two men concerned in catching your father—the chief commissioner himself, and Superintendent Cullis as was. Putting the chief commissioner above suspicion, we're left with Cullis. He could have written the raid letter on your father's typewriter. He could have telephoned the fake message which sent your father to Paris, and then taken the chief commissioner along to see the fun. And he was the man who took your father's strong box out of the safe deposit and opened it in the Yard. If Cullis was in league with Waldstein, what could have been easier than for him to pretend to discover notes which could be traced back to Waldstein in your father's box?"

The girl had been gazing intently at nothing in particular while the Saint released that brief theory. But now she turned suddenly with an extraordinarily keen query in her eyes.

"When did you figure all this out?" she asked.

"In my spare time," said the Saint airily. "But that doesn't matter. The thing that matters is that Assistant Commissioner Cullis has put himself in the cart. He has pulled his flivver, and you and I are the souls who are going to take the buggy ride. Partly by luck, and partly by our own good judgment, we've got the bulge on him—for the moment. And the letter I'm going to write to him to-night will let him know it. I'll put it in his letter box myself, and sit in the garden and watch him read it—it'll be worth the rheumatism. And when he's thoroughly digested that letter, I'm going to have an encore entertainment figured out for him that will make him feel like a small balloon that's floated in between an infuriated porcupine and a bent pin by the time the curtain comes down!"

2

He left soon afterwards, without elucidating his riddle, and she was alone with her perplexity.

She tried to compose herself for a night's rest, but sleep would not come. She was too preoccupied with other things, and she was not a girl who could be satisfied to remain in a state of mystified expectancy. She had to take every bull by the horns. And while inactivity would have irked her no less at any other time, that vexation was now made a thousand times worse by the feeling that it implied her own retirement from a sphere of active usefulness.

For an hour she tossed about in her bed. Sleep lay heavy on her eyes, but her brain was too restless to let her relapse into that void of contented lassitude which merges into dreams. And when, presently, she heard the chimes of a neighbouring clock striking the half-hour after midnight, she rose with a sigh, lighted a cigarette, pulled on her kimono, and went back into the studio.

The embers of the fire still glowed in the grate; she raked them over, put on some more coal, and watched the flames lick up again into a blaze. And then she began to pace the room restlessly.

There was a big cupboard in one corner. She saw it every time she passed in her restless pacing. It fascinated her, caught her eye from every angle, until she was forced to stop and stare at it. Perhaps even then the germ of what she wanted to do was budding in her brain. The cupboard was locked—she had tried the door before, when she had been looking for a place to hang her clothes. What could there be inside it? She found her mind reaching out covetously towards the obvious answer. That studio was admittedly the Saint's most secret bolt hole. And how could a man of such flamboyantly distinctive personality and appearance be sure of keeping even the most cautious bolt hole indefinitely secret? Only by one means. . . .

And almost without her conscious volition, she found herself digging a plain household screwdriver out of a drawer in the kitchen.

The cupboard was locked, certainly, but it was the kind of lock that exists for the purpose of discouragement rather than actual hindrance. She slid the blade of the screwdriver into the gap between the two doors, and levered with a gently increasing pressure. . . . The lock burst away from the flimsy screws that held it with less noise than the sound of a book dropped on a bare floor.

Jill Trelawney lighted another cigarette and inspected her find.

She knew she could only make one find that would be of any use to her. Reckless as she might be, and thoughtlessly as she might have dashed off to the rescue of an arrested Saint without a moment's heed for the risk to herself, in any enterprise such as she was meditating then there were sober and practical considerations to be reckoned with. She would gain nothing by throwing a single point in the game anyway.

But if that locked cupboard provided the means of
saving that single point, just in case of accidents . . .

And it did.

As the doors flew open, she looked at three complete outfits hung in a little row—a set of workman's
overalls, a suit of violently purple check and a Shaftes-
bury Avenue nattiness, and a filthy and ragged costume such as a down-at-heels sandwichman might wear.
And neatly arranged on adjacent shelves were the
shirts, socks, ties, mufflers, overcoats, hats, and shoes
to complete the disguises down to the last minute
detail.

For a few seconds she surveyed the treasure trove;
and then, with slow deliberation, she crushed out her
cigarette. . . .

The outfit she contrived for herself from the mate-
rials at her disposal was a heterogeneous affair, but it
was the best she could do. A shabby pair of trousers,
with the ends tucked up inside the legs and secured
with safety pins, fitted her passably well; but tall as
she was, there was no coat in the collection that she
could wear. A stained and tattered mackintosh, however, could be made to pass, with the sleeves treated in
a similar manner to the legs of the trousers; and a
gaudy scarf knotted about her neck would conceal the
deficiencies of her costume in other respects. She pulled
a tweed cap well down onto her head, tucking her
hair away out of sight beneath it. From the kitchen
she was able to grub out enough grime to disguise her
face and hands against any casual scrutiny; her own

low-heeled walking shoes were heavy enough to pass
muster. And then she inspected the completed work
of art in a full-length mirror, and found that it was
good. . . .

And thus, after one searching glance round, she
went out in quest of her share of the adventure.

The only thrill she felt was not due to anything like
nerves. It was simply a vast relief to be clear of the
studio, in which she had been practically a prisoner for
the last ten days, and to be out again on an active
enterprise instead of merely sitting at home and having enigmatic information, which was really worse
than no information at all, brought to her by the
Saint.

The Saint, at any rate, had told her enough about
Mr. Assistant Commissioner Cullis to decide her that
Simon Templar's simple plan, whatever it was, could
not be good enough.

It wasn't for Jill Trelawney to sit tight and wait for
Cullis to come out of his hole and fight. Far from that
—she was going out to meet Mr. Cullis.

A faint tingle of unleashed delight vibrated through
her as she walked. She hummed a little tune; and the
melancholy droop of the unlighted cigarette attached
to the corner of her mouth had no counterpart in her
spirits. The cool freshness of the night air went to her
head; after the wearisome atmosphere of the studio, it
came like a draught of wine to a parched man. Respectable restraint and Jill Trelawney definitely failed
to blend. For days past she had been feeling that the

enforced idleness had been crushing her into an intoler
able groove, even sapping from her the very person
ality without which she would become nothing but a
ordinary unadventurous woman—a ridiculous idea to
anyone who had ever known her, and most intolerabl
of all to herself.

In her elation she hardly noticed the passage of tim
or distance, and picked her route almost by instinct
Almost before she realized how far she had travelled
she had passed Belsize Park Underground Station; sh
paused there a moment to pick up her bearings, and
then, a hundred yards farther on, she struck away
down a dark side street within measurable distance o
her goal.

She rounded first one corner and then another, and
paused under a lamppost to light her cigarette. The
action was more instinctive than necessary: in the
whole of her body there was not a nerve quivering for
need of the sedative, but the draught of velvety smoke
helped to collect her thoughts and lent balance to her
impetuosity; and she felt, in a moment's touch of self
mockery, that it was a debonair thing to do. It wa
the sort of thing the Saint would have done. . . .

From where she stood she surveyed the lie of the
land.

It was simple enough. The house stood away from
the road, exactly as the Saint had described it, in it
own rather spacious grounds, and there was not a
light showing anywhere. To find it almost withou
hesitation had been easy enough. The studio in Chel

sea had been amply equipped for the simple prepa-
ration of any such excursion. There had been a
telephone directory from which to discover Cullis's
address, a street directory in which to find the exact
location of his house, and a large-scale map from
which to read the most straightforward approach.
These three references alone would have been material
enough even for anyone less accustomed to rapid and
concise thinking than Jill Trelawney, and the investigation had not taken her more than three minutes.
After which she had a faultlessly photographic memory in which to hold the results of that investigation in
their place. She remembered that at the back of the
house there was a piece of land on which no buildings
were marked on the map; but under the faint light of a
half-fledged moon she could see the dark masses of
scaffolding and unfinished walls in the background,
and marked down that terrain as a convenient avenue
of escape in case of need.

In her own way she had had her fair share of luck.
The last patrolling policeman she had seen had been
near Baker Street, and the road in which she now stood
was deserted. Knowing the habits of policemen on
night patrol, her keen eyes probed deep into every
patch of shadow around her, but there was no one
there.

She turned off the road and slipped noiselessly over
the low gate into the front garden.

The Saint had kindly warned her about the alarms
on the ground-floor windows. He had also been good

enough to explain his method of approach by way of
the drain pipe. But she did not feel confident to cope
with drain pipes. Ivy was easier, if more risky and
more noisy, and at the back of the house there was a
patch of ivy running to a very convenient window on
the first floor.

She went up as if she had been born in a circus.

The ledge of the window came easily under her
feet, and she found that the latch was not even fastened. She slid up the lower sash with the merest rustle
of sound, and lowered herself warily over the sill.

The darkness inside was impenetrable, but that
meant nothing to her. She moved through the room
inch by inch, with her fingers weaving sensitively in
front of her, and reached the door in utter silence after
several seconds. Not until she was out on the landing,
with the door closed again behind her, did she dare to
switch on her tiny electric torch.

By its light she found the stairs and went down
them into the hall. Crossing the hall, she opened a
door on the far side and cautiously closed it again
behind her. Then she went over to a window, located
the alarms with her torch, disconnected them, and
opened the window wide, drawing the heavy curtains
again when she had finished.

The beam of her torch filtered through the darkness, flickering over every part of the room. A massive safe that stood in one corner she ignored without
a moment's hesitation—Cullis would never have taken
the risk of keeping anything incriminating in a place

which would be the obvious objective of any chance intruder. She went over the bookcase shelf by shelf, shifting the books one by one and searching expertly for a dummy row or a panel concealed in the back of the case, but she found nothing. The pictures on the walls detained her for very little longer: there was nothing concealed behind any of them. And then she lighted another cigarette and looked around her with a rather rueful frown.

In any modern house, she knew, the range of possible secret hiding places was limited. Secret panels and ingenious flooring arrangements cannot be installed without structural alterations that involve too much curiosity to be effective. And yet, somehow, that was the room in which she had expected to find something—if there was anything to find. In Cullis's own bedroom, on the other hand . . . possibly. But not probably. Thus her intuition answered her, and she returned to a second search of the study with a little tightening of determination on her lips.

Eventually the search narrowed itself down to an ornate Chippendale bureau which stood between the windows. She went over it patiently. None of the drawers was locked, and for that very reason she spared herself the trouble of investigating their contents. But she pulled each one out and measured it against its fellows and against the desk itself in the hope of finding some telltale discrepancy; and she found none. But she did decide that there was a rather curious thickness of wood in the construction of the writing surface. She went over it inquisitively, tapping it with her fingernails: it seemed to give back a hollow sound, and her heart beat a little faster. Then she observed a slight gap between two of the pieces of wood of which it was composed.

She slid the blade of a penknife into the gap; but it must have been one of her elbows which touched the necessary control, for part of the back of the desk seemed to give way under her unconscious pressure, and the two pieces of wood between which her knife was moving suddenly flew back with a click, and she found herself looking down at a thin, flat, japanned deed box.

And at that moment she heard the creak of a hinge behind her, and spun round with her gun in her hand as the lights went on.

There was a silence.

Then—

"Good-morning, Mr. Cullis," said Jill.

Their guns covered each other steadily—the deadlock was complete.

"What do you want?"

Cullis spoke harshly. His eyes, straining behind her, rested on the open top of the desk, and she saw a slight quiver of movement under his moustache.

"It should be obvious," said the girl.

His eyes held hers. He could not have recognized her, but an intuitive idea seemed to flash into his brain. She could almost read its arrival in his face, and stood without flinching as he took a pace forward and scanned her more closely.

"Jill Trelawney!"

She saw the gleam of understanding that flashed under his lowered brows, and answered with a sudden tense urgency in her voice as she saw the stirring of his index finger behind the trigger guard of his revolver.

"Quite right. But don't you think you'd better hear one thing before you shoot?"

In some subtle way, her tone commanded audience. Cullis relaxed a fraction.

"Why?"

"Because it might save you from doing something very foolish."

"You're very thoughtful."

"I'm careful," said the girl quietly. "Cullis, have you heard so little about me that you really believe I'd be so easy to catch as this? Did you even think I came here alone? . . . Your wisdom teeth are not cut yet. Perhaps you'd forgotten—the Saint!"

He shifted his feet without answering, and there was a grim purposefulness in her voice which dominated him in spite of himself. And she followed up her advantage without an instant's pause.

"I didn't come here alone. I have some nerve, Cullis, but burgling an assistant commissioner's house single-handed wants a bit more nerve even than I've got. I took this room while the Saint went over the rest

of the house—looking for you! . . . I don't know
how you missed each other, but you wouldn't have
heard him, or even seen him. He's like a cat in the
dark. He might have found you in a passage, or on
the stairs—anywhere. But maybe he didn't want to.
Maybe he just followed you like a ghost, waiting for
his best chance. Maybe he's coming up behind you
now"—her voice rose a little—"and when he's right
behind you—— GET HIM, SAINT!"

She spoke with a sudden fierce sharpness, like the
crack of a gun, and Cullis took the bait . . . for a
sufficient fraction of a second.

He jerked his head half round involuntarily, and
that was enough. Enough for Jill Trelawney to shift
her automatic unerringly and touch the trigger. . . .
The roar of the explosion battered against the walls,
drowning the metallic smack of her bullet finding its
mark. But she never missed. Cullis's right hand went
strangely limp; his revolver flopped dully into the carpet, and he stood staring stupidly at the pulped wreck-
age of his thumb.

"Don't move." She stepped back towards the curtains, and the weapon in her hand never wavered from
its mark by one millimetre. Gently she edged herself
between the hangings, and stopped there a moment
to speak her farewell.

"I might have finished the job with that shot," she
said, "but I still want you alive. . . . I expect you'll
be hearing from me again."

At that very moment she heard a heavy footfall

behind her, but she could not wait. Whoever it might
be, she must take her chance—that single shot she had
fired, ringing through the open window, must have
thundered over the half of Hampstead, and her luck
could not be expected to hold out till the end of the
world.

Her deduction was right: she heard a shrill scream
of a police whistle as she leapt swiftly backwards and
spun round. Of the man whose footsteps she thought
she had heard she could see nothing, and she was not
interested to pursue him. But she could see an unmis-
takable shape at the gate by which she had entered,
and without hesitation she turned towards the back
of the house and went racing over the lawn.

Running footsteps sounded distinctly on the gravel
behind her, and then there was a shot, and a bullet
sang past her head; but it was too dark for Cullis to
take a good aim, and with his right hand incapacitated
he would be lucky to touch her. And at that moment
she felt, for some reason, supremely confident in the
efficacy of her own luck against his.

At the end of the lawn her feet sank into the soft
earth of flower beds; beyond, she saw a low wall. She
tumbled over it anyhow, picked herself up, and
stumbled over the deserted ground ahead.

She could hear voices behind her, and once when
she glanced back she saw the light of a bull's-eye lan-
tern bobbing about in the dark behind.

The going was treacherous and uneven, but she
hurried along as swiftly as she could. Her luck held.

Once a loose scaffold pole caught her foot and almost brought her down, and once she ran straight into a low pile of bricks that barked her shins and grazed her knuckles; but she made her way across the rest of the ground without further damage, and presently turned out of a deeply rutted track into the road behind.

There she slowed up her steps, and went on with a leisurely slouching stride. At any moment someone might come running past to investigate the uproar, and she had no desire to attract attention. But the road was apparently deserted, except for a small two-seater drawn up by the curb a little way ahead.

At least, she thought, the road was deserted, but as she drew nearly level with the two-seater she heard a quick step behind her. A hand gripped her arm.

She whirled round, her hand reaching again for the butt of her automatic, and looked into the smiling face of the Saint.

"It's a cop," he said. "And now, will you walk home, or shall we ride?"

And he was calmly climbing into the car and feeling around for the starter while she still stared at him.

CHAPTER XII

HOW SIMON TEMPLAR WENT HOME, AND CHIEF INSPECTOR TEAL DID NOT

THERE was silence for some distance before Simon Templar condescended to make a remark or Jill Trelawney could think of one. Then—

"Lucky I rolled up," said the Saint calmly. "Saved you a taxi fare home."

She did not venture to inquire what he had been doing there himself, but a few minutes later he volunteered an explanation.

"But you oughtn't to be poaching on my preserves," he said aggrievedly. "I told you I was watching this place. After I'd left you, I went right back home and changed into more ordinary clothes and came along here in my own time. I just arrived in time to hear your bit of fancy shooting. Did you kill him?"

He put the question with such a cheerful carelessness that she had to laugh.

"I wasn't even trying to," she said mildly. "I probably shall one day, but that'll keep. Did you see much?"

"Only the exteriors."

"Then you must have seen the police," she said. "But you didn't offer to lend a hand."

He smiled.

"I was minding my own business," he said. "Your way out was easy enough, and I'd never heard you wanted chaperoning on these parties. If I'd thought you were likely to get in a jam, I'd have horned in; but since I saw the policeman waddling along a hundred yards astern with his suspenders bursting under the strain, and you skipping away like a young gazelle, I didn't see anything to get excited about. I've run too many races against the police myself, in my younger days, to get seriously worried about any policeman who's less than three miles in the lead when he starts chasing me. But it does them good to run, Jill—it shakes up their livers and stops their kidneys congealing."

"Did you mean to do the same thing as I did?"

"Something like. I've been over that room with a small-toothed comb myself more than once, and plenty more of the house likewise; but it was only to-night I got your inspiration about the desk, and I was meaning to try your very own experiment on it."

"But I thought you said you didn't see anything inside the room?"

"Did I really?"

She looked at him with something like a grimace.

"Are you still being difficult?"

"Oh, no. . . . But let's revert for a moment to the absorbing subject of supralapsarianists. Do you really believe they wear barbed-wire underwear and take off their socks when they pass an infralapsarianist in the street?"

She pouted.

"If you don't mean to talk turkey," she said, "you don't have to give me applesauce. I'm not a fish."

"O.K., baby. But how much of that cache did you get through before Cullis butted in?"

She was lighting a cigarette from the case he handed her, and she shook her head ruefully over the match.

"I didn't get through any of it," she said. "It was just a waste of time finding it. The door behind me and the false top in the desk must have opened just about simultaneously. There was a despatch box, and I think there were one or two odd papers underneath; that's all I saw before the fun started. It was hearing you outside that beat me. If that hadn't made me decide that the tall timber was the best next stop for Little Girl, I'd probably have lifted anything I could see and hoped I'd get something good."

"It wouldn't have helped you much," said the Saint. "There can't be many documents in existence that would incriminate Cullis, and it would have been a thousand to one against your collecting the right ones in your handful."

"And now," said the girl bitterly, "if there ever were any incriminating papers in that cache, he'll have them out and burn them before he goes to bed to-night. He won't take a second chance with me."

Simon shrugged.

"Why should he ever have taken a chance at all?"

"It's the way of a man like that," said Jill. "He may have wanted to gloat over them in private. Or he may have just kept them for curiosities."

Simon was steering the two-seater round the big one-way triangle at Hyde Park Corners, and he did not answer at once.

Then he said: "I wonder what incriminating papers there might have been."

"So do I. . . . But to-night's work may put the wind up him a bit more, which is something."

The Saint drove on in silence for a while, and his next remark came as a bolt from the blue.

"Would you object to being arrested?" he asked.

She looked at him.

"I think I should be inclined to object," she said. "Why?"

"Just part of that idea I mentioned recently," said the Saint. "I'll think it out more elaborately over-night, and tell you the whole scheme to-morrow if I think there's anything in it."

She had to be content with that. The air of mystery which had been exasperating her so much of late had somehow grown deeper than ever that night, and he was very taciturn all the rest of the way to Chelsea.

He left her at the studio, and would not even come in for a last drink and cigarette before he went home.

"I want to sleep on it," he said. "It is now after half-past three. I shall be asleep at half-past four, and I shall sleep until half-past four this afternoon. When

I wake up I shall have something to come round and tell you."

For his own convenience he had decided to spend the night at the apartment in Sloane Street instead of going back to Upper Berkeley Mews. He parked the car in a garage close by and walked round to his flat, and, as he crossed the road, he happened to glance up at the windows. Something that he saw there made him halt in his stride, slip his hands in his pockets, and stand there gazing up thoughtfully at the windows for quite a long time. Then he went back to the garage and returned with a couple of spanners from his tool-box.

Standing on the pavement below, he sent one span-ner hurtling upwards with an accurate aim. It smashed through one window with a clatter and tinkle of broken glass, and in a moment the second spanner had followed it through another window.

Then Simon stood back and watched two thick greenish clouds rolling down towards the street like a couple of ghostly slow-motion waterfalls.

As he stood there, a heavy hand tapped him on the shoulder.

" 'Ere," said a voice behind him, "what's this?"

"Chlorine," said the Saint coolly. "A poisonous gas. I shouldn't go any nearer: it would be unhealthy for you to get under that stream."

"I saw you smash those windows."

"That must have been amusing for you," mur-mured the Saint, still gazing thoughtfully upwards.

"But since they're my own windows, I suppose I'm allowed to smash them."

The policeman stood beside him and followed his gaze upwards.

" 'Ow did that gas get there?"

"It was left there," said the Saint gently, "by an assistant commissioner of Scotland Yard who has a grudge against me. I might have walked right into it, only I happened to look up at the windows, and I remembered leaving them open last time I went out. They were closed before I opened them again with those spanners, and that made me look hard at them. You could see a sort of mistiness on the panes, even in this light."

The constable turned, and suddenly a gleam of recognition came into his eyes. He peered at the Saint more closely, and then he released a blasphemous ejaculation.

"I know you!"

"You're honoured," said the Saint affably.

"You're the gentleman who told me that funny story about that very flat the week before last, and got me the worst dressing down I ever 'ad from the divisional inspector!"

He did not call Simon a gentleman.

"Am I?" said the Saint.

"You'll come along with me to the station right now."

Simon turned to him with a bland smile.

"Why?"

"I shall take you into custody——"

"On what charge?"

"Suspicious loitering, an' committing a breach of the peace."

"Oh, for the love of Pete!" said the Saint. "Why not throw in arson and bigamy as well?"

But he had to submit to the arrest, because a humble constable—especially one with good reason to remember him—could not be expected to appreciate the same arguments as Chief Inspector Teal had followed only too clearly.

It took Simon another hour to obtain his liberty, and more than another hour after that to get the last traces of the gas out of his apartment.

It did not take him anything like so long to discover the means by which it had been introduced. There were pieces of glass on the floor which had not come from either of the broken windows. He was able to piece a few of them together into the curved shape which they had originally had. And in the frame of his front door, level with the keyhole of the Yale lock, had been bored a neat hole no thicker than a knitting needle—almost invisible to the casual glance, but as obvious as the neck on a giraffe to the Saint's practised eye.

"Another of the old gags that never fail—sometimes," he murmured. "And glass bulbs of the stuff in an attaché case ready to heave in. He'd probably just got back from this job when Jill met him. . . . Our Mr. Cullis is waking up. If he hadn't had to shut the windows, or I hadn't remembered how I'd left them, I might have been cold mutton draped on the umbrella stand by this time. Oh, it's a great life!"

The first pallor of dawn was lightening the sky when he eventually pulled the sheets up to his chin and closed his eyes; but even then it seemed that he was not to have the undisturbed rest he so badly needed. He seemed to have slept hardly ten minutes before he was roused by the ring of his front-door bell; but when he opened protesting eyes, his watch told him that it was eleven o'clock.

He tumbled sulphurously out of bed, pulled on a dressing gown, and went to the door.

The cherubic visage of Chief Inspector Teal confronted him on the threshold.

"You again?" sighed the Saint, and turned on his heel without another word, leaving the door open behind him.

Teal followed him into the sitting room.

"Had a thick night?" inquired Teal sympathetically. "Sorry I had to disturb you."

"You didn't have to," said the Saint. "If you'd looked twice, you'd have seen that you only had to push your tie pin into that hole beside the lock, and the door would have opened as wide as a whale's yawn. Or are you going to tell me you hadn't heard that one before?"

Teal began to unwrap a piece of chewing gum.

"I hear you've had some trouble."

"Nice of you to come round and see if I was all

right," said the Saint pleasantly. "As it happens, I'm still in the best of health. Now do you mind if I go back to bed?"

"You're not the only man who had trouble last night," said Teal sleepily.

"Been eating too much again?" said the Saint solicitously.

"Some men," said Teal, "bite off more than they can chew."

The Saint sank into a chair with a sigh.

"Have you been sitting up reading a detective story, and then come round to work off some of the jokes on me?" he demanded.

"Up late last night, weren't you?"

"No," said the Saint. "Up early this morning."

"Enjoy yourself in Hampstead?"

Simon wrinkled his brow.

"I believe I've heard of that place before," he said. "Doesn't one of the buses go there, or something?"

Teal chewed stolidly.

"I know roughly what time you got back here," he said, "because I was able to find that out at Rochester Row. I also know what time somebody not quite unknown was busting Mr. Cullis's desk. There were fresh footprints in one flower bed and the same footprints over that patch of building land at the back. It's rather a distinctive kind of mud on that bit of building land. Funny I should have seen the same kind of mud on the floor boards of your car. I went to the garage this morning before I called in here, just to have a look."

The Saint smiled.

"Did Cullis see the man who bust his desk?"

"He did."

"Is he certain he could identify him?"

"Fairly certain."

"Then," said the Saint, "you might fetch him along and ask him to identify me."

Teal shook his head.

"Oh, no," he said. "Yours weren't the only footprints. And the other set of footprints are the ones which Mr. Cullis can identify."

Simon raised Saintly eyebrows.

"Then why bother me?"

"I just had an idea."

"Headlines in the *Daily Scream*," murmured the Saint irreverently, " 'Scotland Yard a Hive of First-class Brains!' But you must take care you don't get too many of these ideas, Claud. I don't know how far your skull will stretch, but I shouldn't think it would hold more than two at a time. . . . Now is that all you've got to say, or do you want to charge me with anything?"

"Not yet," said Teal. "I just wanted to see whether I was right or not."

"And now you either know or you don't," said the Saint.

He picked up a small black notebook from the table and stuffed it into the detective's breast pocket.

"You can have that," he said. "It's an exact transcription of a book that the late lamented Essenden lost in Paris. You may have heard the story. Personally decoded and annotated by Simon Templar. There are about twenty-five names and addresses there, with full records and enough evidence to hang twenty-five archangels—all the main squeezes in the organization that Waldstein and Essenden were running. You may have it with my blessing, Claud. I'd have dealt with it myself once, but life is getting too short for these diversions now. Take it home with you, old dear, and don't tell anyone how you got it; and if you play your cards astutely you may make some mug believe you always were a real detective, after all. And I'm going back to bed."

Teal followed him into the bedroom.

"Templar," said Teal drowsily, "are you still sure it wouldn't be worth your while to come across?"

"Quite sure," said the Saint, closing his eyes.

Teal masticated thoughtfully.

"You're taking on a lot," he said. "You've been lucky so far, but that doesn't say it's going on for ever. And sooner or later, if you keep on this way, you're going to find a big hunk of trouble waiting for you round the corner. I'm not looking forward to anything like that happening. I'll admit you've scored off me more than once, but I'm ready to call that quits if you are."

"Thanks," yawned the Saint. "And now do you mind shutting your face?"

"You're clever," said Teal, "but there are other bright people in the world besides you, and——"

"I know," drawled the Saint. "You're a bright boy yourself. That bit of sleuthing over the mud in the car was real hot dog. I'll send the chief commissioner an unsolicited testimonial to your efficiency one day. Good-night."

2

Teal departed gloomily.

He was very busy for the rest of the day with other business, but that did not prevent him taking frequent peeps at the notebook which the Saint had pressed upon him. The entries were almost shockingly transparent; and Teal did not take twenty minutes to realize that that little book placed in his pudgy hands all the loose threads of an organization that had been baffling him on and off for years. But the realization did not uplift his soul as much as it might have done. He knew quite well that once upon a time the contents of that book would, as Simon Templar had frankly admitted, have remained the private property of the same gentleman under his better-known title of the Saint, and there would have been twenty-five more mysterious deaths or disappearances, heralded by the familiar trade-mark, to weed some more of the thinning hairs from Chief Inspector Teal's round pate. The Saint's own statement, that the old game had lost its charm, and that he was on the eve of another of his perennial lapses into virtue, Teal was inclined to regard skeptically. It seemed almost too good to be true; and Teal had never been called an incorrigible optimist.

He waded through his divers affairs with a queer certainty that something was shortly going to shatter the comparative peace of the past few days; and in this surmise he was perfectly right.

It was not until after dinner that he returned to Scotland Yard; but by that time he had formed a distinct resolve, and he had not been in the building five minutes before he was asking to see the chief commissioner.

The answer which he received, however, was not what he expected.

"The chief commissioner has not been in all day."

Teal raised his eyebrows. He happened to know that the chief commissioner had had a particular piece of work to do that day and also a number of appointments; and he knew that his chief's habits were as regular as clockwork.

"Has he sent any message?"

"No, sir. We've heard nothing of him since he left yesterday evening."

That was less like the chief commissioner than anything, to disappear without a word to anyone; and Teal was a rather puzzled man as he made his way to his little office overlooking the Embankment.

He worked there until ten o'clock; for in spite of the air of massive boredom which he was never without, he was, as a matter of fact, absorbed in his profession, and regular office hours meant nothing to him when he was on a case. In this he was totally different from his immediate superior, Mr. Cullis, who always grudged giving one minute more of his time than the state purchased with his salary.

He prepared to leave at last, however, and as he emerged into the corridor a hurrying constable collided with him violently.

A buff envelope was knocked out of the man's hand by the impact, and Teal good-humouredly stooped to pick it up. As he did so he noticed the address.

"Hasn't Mr. Cullis gone home?" he inquired.

"No, sir. He's still in his room."

"Can you wait half a minute?"

Without waiting for a reply Teal went back into his office, taking the telegram with him. Under the constable's goggling eyes Teal carefully sponged the back of the envelope and eased up the flap with his paper knife. Then he extracted the form and read the message.

He actually stopped maltreating a well-worn pellet of spearmint as he read.

Then, with ponderous deliberation, he refolded the form and replaced it in the envelope, freshened up the gum on the flap from a pot of paste on his desk, and dried his handiwork carefully before the gas fire.

He returned the telegram to the messenger.

"Now you can take that on to Mr. Cullis," he said. "But you needn't mention my name."

"No, sir."

The vestige of a smile twitched at Teal's mouth as the constable departed. It was perhaps fortunate for him that the messenger owed a recent promotion entirely to Teal's good offices, and might therefore be safely counted upon to obey his somewhat eccentric injunction.

The messenger had closed the door behind him; but as his footsteps died away along the corridor, Teal rose silently and opened the door again. Turning out the light he waited close by the switch, listening patiently.

He heard the constable return and go down the stairs, and five minutes later he heard a different footfall coming towards him.

Cullis's office was at the far end of the same corridor, and Teal stepped silently out of his darkened doorway as the assistant commissioner reached it.

"Heavens, you gave me a start!" said Cullis peevishly. "I wish you wouldn't creep about in those rubber soles."

"Regulation boots, sir," said Teal phlegmatically, falling into step beside the assistant commissioner. "Get the order changed, and I'll get the rubbers taken off. Nice day it's been to-day, hasn't it?"

Cullis was not disposed to discuss the weather. He left Teal abruptly at the foot of the stairs, and Teal gazed at his departing back with an expressionless face. Then he turned and went through the passage into Cannon Row police station and found the man he was wanting to see.

"What's the news about Templar?" he asked. "Has he slipped you again?"

The plain-clothes man nodded ruefully.

"Same as he always does, Mr. Teal."

"When was this?"

"About four o'clock, sir."

"And hasn't been back since?"

"He hadn't up till half-past nine, when I was relieved."

Teal glared at him.

"Then why the blue monkeys didn't you let me know before?"

"Chiefly because you weren't in, Mr. Teal," said the man truthfully.

Teal turned on his heel and went back into Scotland Yard, and was lucky enough to catch the day telephone operator, who was just going home.

"They tell me there's been no message from the chief to-day," said Teal. "But are you certain he didn't speak to anyone on the phone?"

"Yes, Mr. Teal, he did. He spoke to Mr. Cullis about six o'clock. The lines got crossed while I was putting somebody else through, as a matter of fact, and I heard him tell Mr. Cullis to stay on to-night until the chief sent him word again."

Teal nodded.

"Thanks. That's all I wanted to know. Goodnight."

"Good-night, sir."

Teal changed his mind about going home himself.

Instead, he returned to his office, took off his overcoat again, and sat down in the dark with a fresh piece of gum.

The departure of Mr. Assistant Commissioner Cullis from his usual routine was explained, even if nothing else was. But there were still far too many things about which Mr. Teal was in the dark; and he meditated those things for an hour and a half before light dawned on him in a blinding flash that made him shoot out of his chair as if he had been stung.

A moment afterwards he was tearing through a time-table. And he swore fluently when he found that he had missed the last train to the place where he wanted to go.

He descended the stairs at a surprising speed for a man of his languid appearance, and a few seconds later he was barking at the first man he met.

"Get me a fast Flying Squad car," he said, "and a couple of men with it. And they'd better be armed!"

The car and the men were outside the Yard within five minutes, and Teal climbed in.

He gave the name of an obscure village in Surrey, and fumed at the delay while the driver consulted a map.

"It's near Guildford, anyway," snapped Teal. "Make for Guildford, and I'll look out the rest while we're going along."

He knew the place was near Guildford, because that was where the telegram which he had intercepted had been handed in; and the prosaic words on the tape pasted across the Inland Telegraph form seemed to stand out in the blackness in letters of fire when he closed his eyes, although they merely conveyed information which should not have been in the least disturbing to a man of Teal's experience.

Have taken Trelawney and Templar. Come down at once.

The message had been signed with the name of the chief commissioner, and it had been sent from Guildford at nine o'clock. An address was given at the end of the message.

It had taken Teal a whole ninety minutes to read between the lines of that simple statement, and, even so, when he thought it over afterwards at his leisure, he was not disposed to consider himself slow on the uptake.

CHAPTER XIII

HOW SIMON TEMPLAR SURRENDERED, AND CHIEF INSPECTOR TEAL WAS NOT HELPFUL

EVERY light in the house seemed to be on when Cullis arrived at the gate of the little garden. It stood in a dark side road; and, so far as he could make out, it was one of those picturesque places often to be found in country byways which modern enterprise has taken and improved without damaging the picture—a small, two-storied house with outside beams and a gabled roof, and an atmosphere of comfortable serenity about it which seemed about to be belied that night.

He went up the short path and mounted a couple of steps to the front door. His hand was actually on the bell when he noticed that the door was not completely closed, and with a slight frown he pushed it open and stepped into the hall.

"Is that you, Cullis?"

The voice came down from the top of the stairs and startled him, though he recognized it at once as that of the chief commissioner.

"Yes, sir."

"Come along up, will you?"

Cullis mounted the stairs. At the top he found a

small landing, and on the landing was the chief commissioner with an automatic pistol in his hand.

"You got my message? Good. I'm glad to see you."

"Where are they?" was Cullis's first question.

"In there." The chief commissioner jerked his thumb at a closed door. "I ran them to earth here, and here I was stuck. They've locked the door on the inside, but they can't get out through the window, because it's barred. They've been working away on the bars, but they haven't been able to get out yet. They can't get out through the door, because I'm waiting for them here. But they're armed themselves, and I didn't feel like committing suicide by trying to force my way in alone."

"But are you alone, sir?"

The commissioner nodded.

"Of course I am," he said testily. "That's how I got stuck. If you can tell me a way for one man to guard an inside door and an outside window at the same time I'll be glad to hear it."

Cullis made a movement towards the door, and the chief reached out and jerked him back.

"I should stay where you are," he said. "They've had one or two pot shots at me through the door as it is, and you mightn't be so lucky."

He pointed to three bullet holes neatly drilled through the woodwork.

"Couldn't you get to the telephone?" asked Cullis.

"There is no telephone."

"Then how did you send that telegram?"

"That was a bit of luck. I picked them up in Guildford and heard them give the address to a taxi driver
at the station. So I waited to send off that wire before
I followed along here. . . . Listen!"

Cullis listened and heard, inside the locked room,
the rasp and tinkle of metal.

"They're still trying to break through those bars,"
said the chief commissioner, "but I don't think they'll
get out that way in a hurry."

Cullis pulled out his cigarette case.

"How did it all happen?" he asked.

"I got a squeal. It came from a man named Pinky
Budd, who was one of the old Angels. He came up to
my house last night and said he'd run into Trelawney
at Guildford. He was hard up, and tried to get some
money out of her, but she gave him the air. Budd
felt nastier and nastier about that all the way home,
and when he got to London he'd made up his mind
to squeal. But when he found me all he could say was
that he'd gathered that Trelawney and the Saint were
living near Guildford, and also that they were coming
up to town on a rush visit to-day. So I went down to
Guildford and spent half the day in the station watching all the trains until they arrived."

"Without a word to anyone?"

"There's been too much inefficiency on this case
already. I forget how many times that man Templar
has slipped the men who are always supposed to be
watching him. I was getting a bit tired of it, and when

this squeal came through I made up my mind to settle the thing myself."

"And then you followed them down here——"

The chief accepted a cigarette.

"And even then it wasn't all plain sailing," he said. "I saw the lights go on upstairs, and thought it was going to be easy, went in through a French window on the ground floor—and found a man waiting for me. Duodecimo Gugliemi! You remember, the man who should have been deported the other day."

Cullis nodded.

"I got the order postponed. I was thinking the same thing as you about the men that Templar was always shaking off, and I wondered if someone who looked less like a detective might be able to do more."

"Instead of which," said the commissioner grimly, "he appears to have joined up with them. Anyway, there he was, loading a gun when I walked in. Fortunately I'd been very quiet about it, and he didn't hear me at first. His back was towards me, and I got quite close before something must have made him look round. The gun was in his hand, but he'd still got the magazine out and it wasn't much use to him. He let out a yell and heaved it at my head, but I ducked and caught him one behind the ear with the butt of mine. That settled him, but the alarm was raised. I sprinted out into the hall and saw a skirt whisking round the top of the stairs. Trelawney can't have had her gun on her at the moment, otherwise it might have been quite a different story. As it was, this door

slammed just as I reached the landing, and I heard the
lock turn as I went at it with my shoulder. Next
minute a bullet came through a panel an inch from
my ear, and I took cover. But I'd got them both in
there together, which was a bit of luck, and the best
thing I could do was to stand guard here and hope
you'd get a train as soon as my telegram arrived."

"And what about Gugliemi?"

"He's still downstairs, unless he's woken up and
sloped off. I've had to keep one eye on the stairs all
the time in case he tried to shove in his oar again, but
there hasn't been a sound. As a matter of fact, he's
probably still dreaming. When I hit him, I hit him
hard. Since you're here, I think you'd better go down
and see if there's any sign of him before we do anything else. You brought a gun, of course?"

Cullis tapped his pocket.

"I shouldn't have come without one," he said, and
went down the stairs at once.

In the room below, which the chief commissioner
had indicated, Cullis found the Italian sitting on the
floor with his head in his hands. Certainly the man
was awake—Cullis heard him groan.

"Here, you!"

Cullis took him by the collar and yanked him to
his feet, and Gugliemi turned a white scared face to
his.

"Signor," he wailed, "it was an accident——"

"What was?" snarled Cullis. "Your double-crossing
me?"

"I do not understand——"

Cullis thrust the trembling man roughly into chair.

"You know quite well what I mean," he said, an the first brutal savagery of his voice had calmed dow to something worse—quiet, frozen ferocity. "Do yo remember the last time you saw me?"

"Yes, sair."

"You were to find this girl Trelawney and get ri of her. That's what I promised you a hundred pound and a clear way out of England for. I didn't tell yo to turn round and join her gang—you rat!"

"I can explain, sair."

"Can you?" said Cullis, and his pale eyes never lef the Italian's face. "I don't think you can explain i any way that will satisfy me. You're a traitor, and have a way with traitors."

"But, if you will listen, sair——"

"Be quiet!"

Cullis dropped the words like two flakes of red-ho metal. He had been jumpy enough earlier in the eve ning, but now he was master of himself, and ther was no humanity in his face.

He pointed to the floor where Gugliemi's gun, witl the magazine beside it, still lay.

"You see that?" said Cullis.

Gugliemi nodded dumbly.

"You were loading it when the commissioner cam in. When I came in just now you had woken up an finished loading it, and you were waiting for me.

had to shoot you in self-defense. Do you understand? It will be quite simple for me to put the magazine in the gun and put the gun in your hand when you have finished with your treacherous life."

His finger was tightening on the trigger even as he spoke. Gugliemi could see the whitening of the knuckle, and his eyes bulged wide with horror. Cullis saw the man's mouth open for a scream and grinned savagely.

But the shot he heard did not come from his own gun. It came muffled through the ceiling above him, and a second report followed a moment later. Then the chief called, rather huskily:

"Cullis!"

Cullis cursed under his breath. His plan could not be put into execution then: it was too late for his explanation to hold water now. Another pretext must be thought of. But meanwhile——

He caught Gugliemi by the lapels of his coat and pulled him towards him. Reversing his gun with a swift movement, he struck callously. . . .

As the man crumpled to the floor at his feet, Cullis heard the commissioner call his name again.

He raced up the stairs. At the top he found the chief leaning against the wall with one hand clutched to his shoulder.

"They got me," said the chief gruffly. "I heard them talking and I went closer to listen. Then a shot through the door. But I fired back, and I think I hit something."

Cullis listened, and inside the room he heard a stifled groan. Then, through the door, Simon Templar spoke:

"We're surrendering," he said.

The key grated in the lock, and the door opened. The Saint stepped out, holding his gun, butt foremost, at arm's length in front of him. His blue eyes swept the assistant commissioner with cool contempt as Cullis took the weapon and dropped it into his pocket.

"Jill's hit," said the Saint. "That was a lucky shot for you."

Cullis went in. He found himself in a small bedroom, and a glance at the barred window showed him that the prisoners had been well on the way to making the gap big enough to squeeze through. Then his eyes fell on the bed, and he saw Jill Trelawney lying there with a red stain spreading on her white blouse.

"It's only a flesh wound," said the Saint, "but it's good enough. You'd better send for a doctor."

He turned to see the chief commissioner stuffing a folded handkerchief inside his shirt.

"I'm sorry I didn't get a better bead on you," said the Saint pleasantly.

The chief commissioner grunted.

"You'd better get her downstairs, Cullis," he said. "I'll go out and find a telephone. You're in a better condition to look after this bunch than I am."

But Simon Templar pushed Cullis unceremoniously aside and picked Jill Trelawney up in his arms as

lightly and tenderly as if she had been a baby. They
went downstairs in procession to the room where
Gugliemi was, Cullis covering Simon from behind, and
the chief commissioner bringing up the rear. Downstairs, Simon laid the girl gently on the sofa, but when
he would have moved away she caught his hand and
held him.

The chief commissioner was looking at the prostrate
Italian.

"He's moved," he said, "so I didn't kill him."

"He was waking up when I came down," said Cullis.
"When I heard the shot and you called me I hadn't
time to do anything but knock him on the head again
and leave him."

"Well, we've got them all together now. If you'll
watch them I'll be getting along down the road. I
think I noticed some telephone wires leading to a
house about a hundred yards farther on."

"Are you sure you'll be all right, sir?"

"I'm all right, Cullis. It's messed up my shoulder a
bit, but I can make that hundred yards without any
trouble. You stay here and keep your eyes skinned.
I'll be back as soon as I can."

He went out, and they heard the front door slam.
Presently the gate clicked. . . .

And then Cullis turned to the Saint.

"So this is the end of your cleverness?"

Simon Templar eyed him coldly.

"I'm not so sure," he said. "I never stop being

clever. And I shouldn't bet on this being the last word, if I were you. It may be my last adventure, but there are so many possible endings."

Cullis showed his teeth.

"You'll get seven years for this night's work alone," he said.

"And how long do you think you'll get, old dear?" asked the Saint very gently.

Cullis returned his gaze stonily.

"I think," he said, "that it won't help you much to try that sort of bluff."

"But suppose," said the Saint—"just suppose, sweet Cullis, that it wasn't entirely a bluff. I admit that for the moment you have us under the lid of the tureen, so to speak. But that's only a bit of luck: a chance shot through a door that ought to have missed both of us by miles. But it was good enough that Jill couldn't get away through that window—couldn't have run for it, even if we'd come out and put up a fight. And yet, Cullis, it mightn't turn out to be all jam."

"How, for instance?" asked Cullis, as if the idea amused him.

"When your desk was opened last night——"

"Yes?"

"Did you go through your papers after the police had come?"

"I did."

"Carefully?"

"Yes."

"You can't have done," said the Saint. "If you had, you'd have realized what we got away with."

Cullis laughed.

"You didn't have a chance to get away with anything. I came into the room just as she got the secret panel open, and she didn't go back again."

"I know she didn't go back," said the Saint, swaying gently on his toes. "But I did."

"You?"

"Me. Of course, you didn't realize I was there. But I was—impersonating a rhododendron in the middle distance. When you followed Jill outside and shot after her as she went across the lawn, I slipped in through the window, took what I wanted, and slipped out again."

Cullis's eyes gleamed.

"And what did you take?"

"Only this."

Simon slipped a hand in his pocket and brought out his wallet. From the wallet he took a piece of paper and unfolded it, holding it up before the assistant commissioner's eyes. It was a new five-pound note.

"Recognize it?" asked the Saint, in that very gentle tone. "Don't you hear its little voice chirruping to you and calling you Daddy?"

"It means nothing to me."

"But it was one of many which you had tied up in that deed box in your very ingenious desk, my pet. There must have been a couple of thousand pounds'

worth all together. . . . Oh, Cullis, did you forget
what your old grandmother told you, and did you let
your avarice get the better of your caution? You
couldn't bring yourself to destroy them, and yet you
didn't dare pay them into your bank or try to dispose
of them in any other way."

Cullis stiffened.

"And why do you think that was?" he asked quietly.

"Because," said the Saint deliberately, "the number
of this note—which was the top one of the bunch I
found in your desk—is the very next number after the
last number of the wad which was taken out of Sir
Francis Trelawney's safe deposit, and which was
traced back to Waldstein. And when the matter comes
to be investigated, I wouldn't mind betting that this
note will be found to have been drawn out of Waldstein's bank at the very same time!"

2

There was a long silence, tensed up almost to breaking point by the measured tick of a cabinet clock somewhere outside in the hall. And through that silence
the Saint lounged at his ease against the revolving
bookcase which he had selected for his support, and
his bleak eyes rested unwaveringly on the assistant
commissioner's face. Jill Trelawney lay still on the
settee, and on the floor Duodecimo Gugliemi groaned
and rolled over, with his fingers twitching; there was
no other movement.

For a space of five or six taut and significant seconds
. . . and then a glimmer of the old Saintly mockery
twinkled back into Simon Templar's gaze, and he
laughed.

"Which is all very unfortunate for you—isn't it,
Algernon?" he drawled; and Cullis's mouth tightened
up like a steel trap under his moustache.

"I see," he said softly.

"Cheers!" said the Saint. "Do you mind if I
smoke?"

He helped himself to a cigarette from the box on
the table and struck a match.

"So that's the yarn you propose to tell, is it?" said
Cullis.

"It is," said the Saint tranquilly. "And I think it's
a damned good yarn, if you ask me. At any rate, it'll
keep your brain ticking over, working out what sort
of an answer you're going to make."

Suddenly Cullis laughed.

"And you really think anyone will believe you?"

"I don't know," said the Saint. "I shall do my best
to spread the glad news around, and when I get going
I have no mean spread. With all the accumulated
evidence——"

"What other evidence?"

"Duodecimo's, for instance. He has a little story to
tell of his very own which ought to cause quite a
sensation."

Cullis sneered.

"A crook lying to save his skin! Do you think that

his word will have any weight? With a reputation like
his——"

"Oh, but he hasn't got to rely on his reputation
alone, comrade. There is a very important bit of cor-
roborative what's-it, or circumstantial how's-your-
father."

"And what might that be?"

"I'll tell you that later," said the Saint, "if you
remind me. But for the present I'm just fascinated to
hear what fairy tale you think you're going to tell
about that fiver."

"Do you really think you'll be able to use that
against me?"

"I do."

"Let me tell you," said Cullis, "that you're going
to be disappointed. There's one thing you seem to
have forgotten, but I remember it quite well. Waldstein himself, under the name of Stephen Weald, was
at one time a member of Trelawney's precious gang.
Did you know that?"

"I did."

"Then," said Cullis deliberately, "what is more
natural than that *you* should have in your possession
a five-pound note which can be traced back to Waldstein's account?"

The Saint looked at him. And the Saint smiled, and
shook his head.

"Not good enough," he said. "That might possibly
be made to account for this note which I've got here;

but will it account for the others which can probably still be found somewhere among your belongings?"

"Which you could have planted there."

"That excuse didn't save Sir Francis Trelawney," said the Saint, cold as a judge. "Why should you think it will save you?"

Their eyes met for a long while, and then Cullis took a slow step forward. His face had become a mask of granite.

"I see," he said again, very slowly.

"So glad you appreciate the point," said the Saint. "It *is* going to be a bit awkward for you, isn't it? But it ought to go a long way towards clearing Sir Francis Trelawney's name."

"And who," said Cullis, in the same soft voice, "is going to make a search of my possessions before I have time to get those notes out of the way?"

And the Saint smiled again, rocking gently on his heels.

"Thank you," he said, "for admitting that you have got the other notes."

"And suppose I admit it," said Cullis calmly. "You've still got to answer my question. Who's going to make that search—and prove anything?"

"I might arrange it," said the Saint. And he said it so quietly and naturally that it was hard to read any blind bluff into the words.

Cullis looked closely at him, and a little pulse began to beat in Cullis's forehead.

"There's something funny about you, Simon Templar——"

"We are amused," said the Saint politely.

"But perhaps," said Cullis, "even you couldn't have prophesied what was going to happen to you when you'd told me that story."

"Tell me."

"You're a dangerous criminal, and your accomplice is wanted for murder. Seeing that the game's up, you're going to make one last desperate effort to beat me and get away. And in self-defense I shall have to shoot you——"

"Just like you had to shoot Gugliemi," said the Saint, almost in a whisper; and Cullis went white to the lips.

Then the mask-like features contorted suddenly.

"How did you know that?"

"I am a clairvoyant," said the Saint easily.

"And yet," said Cullis, "the trick is still good enough——"

"Not quite good enough," said the Saint. And there was a sudden swift urgency in his voice, for at that moment he saw death staring him in the face— death in Cullis's pale blue eyes, and death in the twist of Cullis's lips, and death quivering in Cullis's right hand. "Not quite good enough. Because there's one more instalment to my story—and you'd better hear it before you shoot!"

For a moment he thought that Cullis would shoot and chance the consequences, and he loosened his muscles for a desperate leap. And the assistant commissioner's pose slackened by a fraction.

"I'll hear what you have to say. But you needn't expect to get away with another bluff like the one Trelawney put over last night."

"And it was such a good bluff, too," said the Saint sadly, with one eyebrow cocked at the assistant commissioner's bandaged thumb.

And then he smiled into Cullis's eyes.

"But we don't need to use bluff any more," he said. "I'm strong for having everything in its right place, and the place for bluff has gone by, Cullis."

"Get on!"

"I am a brilliantly clever man," said the Saint, in his airy way, "and picnics like this are sitting rabbits to me. I worked this one out for your special benefit, and you've enjoyed it so much, too. . . . You see, it would have been perfectly easy to bump you off, but that wasn't all we wanted. Waldstein and Essenden had been bounced too rapidly, and we weren't making the same error over you. We wanted to hear you sing to us here before you passed on to join the herald angels; but we quite appreciated that we weren't a sufficient audience. Jill and I are simple souls whom the world has used hardly, and Duodecimo is another piece of shop-soiled driftwood on the sea of life——"

"Cut the cackle," rasped Cullis, with a new venom in his voice. "If you're just trying to gain time——"

"I'm unbosoming in my own style, brother," said the Saint plaintively. "Give me a break. And now where was I? . . . Oh, yes. Duodecimo is another piece of shop-soiled driftwood on the———"

"I'll give you three minutes more. If you've got anything to say———"

"O. K., Algernon. Then let's put it that your word would probably outweigh anything that Jill or I or Duodecimo could say. So there had to be a witness who couldn't be challenged. And who could be a more ideal witness than the chief commissioner himself?"

The Saint saw Cullis's eyes narrow down to mere pin points, and laughed again.

"I went to the chief commissioner. I borrowed his own house. We came down here this evening and set the stage very carefully. Those bullet holes which you saw in the door upstairs were placed there three hours ago by special permission of the proprietor. The bars on the window were installed this afternoon and chopped about while you were travelling down. I personally staged the scene, wrote the dialogue, and produced the soul-stirring drama now drawing to its close—and all in one rehearsal. A microphone behind that picture of an indecently exposed lady throwing geraniums at a nightingale has been picking up all your winged words and relaying them, if not to all stations, at least to one—with a sergeant sitting on his Pitman diploma at the other end and taking them all down. Another connection upstairs gave up the personal lowdown on every word of your recent backchat with Duodecimo—which would have been enough to hang you by itself. But we are thorough. We didn't even

stop there. Half a minute after you heard the front
door slam behind the chief commissioner just now,
he was creeping in through the back door and sprinting up the back stairs to hear some more of the story
from his private broadcasting station. No, I shouldn't
even shoot now, Cullis, because I think I heard Auntie
Ethel coming back——"

Cullis heard the rattle of the door behind him, and
spun round.

The chief commissioner stood on the threshold. And
now he showed no signs of the injury which had at first
impressed his assistant. His bearing was erect, he no
longer clutched his shoulder, and there was a glitter
in his eyes which had nothing to do with anything he
had said to Cullis before he left.

Also, there was an automatic in his hand.

"I heard you," he said; and Cullis stepped back a
pace.

Cullis still held a gun in his hand, but it hung loose
at his side, and he knew that the least movement would
be fatal. He stood quite still, and the chief commissioner went on speaking.

"You ought to know," he said, "that I've been
watching you for some time. I think I first had my
suspicions when those papers were taken from the
Records Office; and then the Saint came to me with a
story which I couldn't ignore, fantastic though it was."

"You believed a crook?" said Cullis scornfully.

"For my own reasons," said the commissioner. "He
was, perhaps, something more than an ordinary crook

when he came to me, and I was able to believe him when I shouldn't have believed anyone else in his place. Even you should admit that the Saint has a certain reputation. There was a warrant out for his arrest at the time." The commissioner's lips twitched. "It was one of many that have been wasted on him. But he placed himself unreservedly in my hands, and it seems as if the result has justified us."

Cullis looked around him, and saw that Simon Templar also held a gun; and Jill Trelawney was sitting up on the sofa, mopping at her blouse with a handkerchief.

"Only red ink," explained the Saint sweetly.

Cullis stood like a man carved in stone.

And then he nodded slowly, and the ghost of a smile twitched at his mouth.

"I needn't bother to deny anything," he said quietly. "It's all quite clear. But it was a clever piece of work on your part to get the story from my own mouth as you have done."

He looked the chief commissioner in the eyes.

"You may as well hear it in full," he said. "I framed Sir Francis Trelawney under your very nose. Waldstein and Essenden were the leaders of the combine that Trelawney was out to smash, and I was strapped at the time. They offered big money, and I came in with them. Trelawney was dangerous. In another month or so he'd probably have had them, if he'd been able to keep on. The only thing to do was to get

him out of the way, and we fixed that up between us.
It wasn't so difficult as it might have been, because he
was always a man who worked on his own. We knew
that if once he was discredited, no one else would be
able to take up his work at the point where he left off.
I paved the way by writing that warning about the
raid on his typewriter. Then I telephoned the message
which was supposed to have come from you, which
sent him over to Paris and helped us to catch him out
at Waldstein's hotel. After that, the rest was easy. I
had Waldstein's money in my pocket when I opened
his strong box in front of you, and I'd practised that
little conjuring trick for weeks. It wasn't very difficult.
The notes came out of his box in front of your very
eyes, and there was nothing he could say about that.
Later on, Waldstein, under one of his aliases, joined
up with the girl to keep her out of mischief. He
called himself lucky when he met her on the boat coming over from New York to start the work of the
Angels. . . . The trouble started when the Saint
came after me—when my house was burgled and my
desk broken open last night."

"I heard about that," said the chief commissioner.

Cullis nodded.

"From the Saint, I suppose? Well, it was a neat
piece of work, although it was the girl who did it.
Even before that I'd decided that Jill Trelawney was
getting too dangerous, and I sent Gugliemi out after
her; but he turned against me, as you know. Even

when my desk was opened, I didn't think anything had been taken, and when you told me to come down here I thought I'd got a chance."

"Until Templar showed you that five-pound note?" murmured the chief.

"Quite right. . . . Is there anything else you want to know?"

"I don't think so."

Cullis's eyes shifted round the room.

"But there's one thing I should like to know," he said.

"What's that?"

"When the Saint came to you with that story, why should you have taken any more notice of it than if anyone else had brought it to you?"

A dry smile touched the commissioner's lips.

"Because I happen to know him well," he said. "When he got his pardon, I coaxed him into the Secret Service to keep him from getting into more trouble. His methods have always been rather eccentric, but they're effective. Some time ago he got an idea that there was something more in the Trelawney business than ever came out, and I let him take up the case in his own way. He's been working at it in his own way ever since: his police appointment was only part of the job, and his very irregular resignation was only another part."

There was one person who was more surprised than Cullis, and that was Jill Trelawney.

"*You*, Saint?"

"When we first met," said the Saint sadly, "I told you I'd reformed, but you wouldn't believe me. And in the last few days I seem to have done nothing but talk to you about my respectable friend. Let me introduce you—Sir Hamilton Dorn, Chief Commissioner of Police for the Metropolis, commonly known as Auntie Ethel. Pleased to have you meet each other."

Sir Hamilton bowed slightly.

"I never was the hell of a policeman," said the Saint apologetically. "Scotland Yard will probably survive without me—though I can't help thinking I might have pepped them up a heap if I'd stayed on."

For that one moment Simon Templar was the central figure, and there was not an eye on Cullis. And then the Saint, out of the tail of his eye, saw Cullis's right hand leap up, and shouted a warning even as he turned. But his voice was drowned by the roar of Cullis's automatic, and he saw the chief commissioner's gun drop to the floor, and saw a red stain suddenly splashed on the chief commissioner's wrist.

He raised his own gun, but the hammer clicked on a dud cartridge, and he threw himself down on the floor as Cullis's automatic barked again.

He heard the bullet sing over his head and smack into the wall behind him with a tinkle of glass from a smashed picture, and spun his legs round in a flailing semicircle that aimed at Cullis's ankles. Even so, he did not see how Cullis could possibly miss with his next shot. . . .

He missed his kick . . . but he had forgotten Jill

Trelawney. As he scrambled up, he saw both her hand
locked upon Cullis's wrist, and Cullis's third shot wen
up into the ceiling. Then he himself also had hold o
the wrist, and he twisted at it savagely. The gun wen
to the floor, and the Saint kicked it away.

He did not see Cullis snatch up the bronze statuett
from the table behind him, but if he had not turned hi
head—more by intuition than by calculation—it woul
certainly have cracked his skull. As it was, the glancin
blow half stunned him and sent him reeling, with hi
hold on Cullis's wrist broken. Jill had let the man g
as soon as the Saint grappled with him.

As he climbed dizzily to his feet, with his head sing
ing, and wiped the blood out of his eyes, he saw th
chief commissioner groping blasphemously for one o
the fallen guns with his sound left hand—saw the ope
French windows, and Jill Trelawney vanishin
through them.

"Come back, you fool!" yelled the Saint huskily.

But she could not have heard him. She was gone
and he followed, staggering.

There was a patter of footsteps down the grave
path along the side of the house, and he saw her whit
blouse as a pale blur in the darkness.

He caught her up at the corner of the house, an
standing beside her, saw Cullis turning through th
garden gate.

Then he started to run again, for he knew that i
Cullis turned again at the next corner, as he would b
likely to do, he would stumble straight upon the chie

commissioner's car, which had been left standing there with the lights out.

And Cullis turned that way. Whether it was simply that he wanted to get clear of the principal road and attempt to shake off pursuit in the darkness and more open country, or whether it was that the luck which had been with him so long was disposed to help him yet a little while longer, could never be known. But he did come upon the car, and he was flinging himself into the driving seat as Simon turned the corner after him. An instant later the self-starter brought the engine to life, and the car was starting to move as the Saint flung himself at the luggage grid.

He hung there for a few seconds, getting his last resources of nerve and muscle together. He was still dazed, practically knocked out on his feet, after the murderous blow that he had taken on his head. And the blood that persisted in trickling into his eyes from a shallow scalp wound half blinded him. But he held on.

And then he pulled himself together and moved again. It had to be done, for his hold was precarious, and he could not have kept it for much longer in the state he was in. And by that time the car was travelling at forty miles an hour, and a slip, a fall in the road, would very easily have put an end to the adventure in quite a different way from that which he had intended.

He got his hands over the furled top, hauled himself up, and tumbled over onto the cushions of the back seat.

With a sigh of relief, he eased his aching muscles and for a while he lay there, dead beat, hardly able to move. His head felt as if it were splitting, and crimson specks danced in a grey haze before his eyes.

But the car drove on. The driver, intent only on the road that showed up ahead in the blaze of the headlights, never noticed his arrival.

Gradually the sick feeling in the pit of his stomach passed off. He was still weary from his reckless effort, but his brain was clearing. He mopped at his forehead with his handkerchief and opened his eyes.

Then he pulled himself up onto his knees.

As his eyes came over the level of the front seat, the blaze of another pair of headlights that were racing over the road towards them flooded into his eyes.

"There's no more speed limit," said the Saint unhappily, in Cullis's ear, "but you're still breaking it and I shall have to arrest you, Cullis, really I shall. Driving to the danger of the public, that's what you're doing——"

As Cullis heard his voice the car swerved perilously, and then straightened up again.

"At least," said Cullis over his shoulder, "I'll take you with me."

Simon took him by the throat, but Cullis's hands still clutched the steering wheel rigidly.

The oncoming car was less than twenty yards away. In any other circumstances, with the road to themselves, Simon might have been able to shoot Cullis, or

even simply hit him over the back of the head with the
butt of his gun, and trust to being able to keep the car
straight while he clambered over and pushed the man
out of the way and took the wheel. But there and then
there was no chance to do that. In another second or
two they would smash head on into the other car. . . .

Cullis's intention was obvious.

With a desperate wrench the Saint rammed Cullis's
face down between the spokes of the steering wheel;
and for a moment the car was out of control. Then,
pushing Cullis sideways, Simon grabbed the wheel and
wrenched the car round.

The oncoming headlights blazed straight into his
eyes, hurtling towards them. The driver of the other
car swerved, but he could hardly manœuvre on that
narrow road, and there was no time for him to pull
up.

Simon heard the futile scream of brakes violently
applied, and thought he would die smiling.

"Here we go," he thought, and held the wheel
round on a reckless lock.

He only just failed. For one horrible instant he saw
the off-side wing light of the approaching car leaping
directly into the off-side wing light of the car in which
he rode. Even so, he might have succeeded if Cullis
had not got a hand back on the wheel and fought to
turn it the other way.

Simon lashed at him with one elbow, but it was too
late for that to be any good. The running board of

the other car slashed their front wing like a knife; and
there was a grating, tearing, shattering noise of tortured metal.

Simon was shot over the steering wheel by the impact. The car seemed to heave itself into the air, and
for one blinding, numbing second he seemed to hang
suspended in space. Then the road hit him a terrible
blow across the shoulder blades; there was a splinter-
ing clatter, another and more violent jar, and dead
silence. . . .

He did not know how long he lay there on his back
with his feet propped up somewhere in the air, bruised
and aching in every limb, and only wondering whether
he was really dead at last—and if not, why not. . . .
A colossal weight seemed to be pressing into his
chest. . . .

He opened one eye, and discerned brake and clutch
and accelerator pedals mysteriously suspended over
his head.

There was something else on his chest. He made
this out to be the front seat—and the body of a man.

He tried to raise one hand, and found that it moved
in a pool of something warm and sticky; and he wondered whether the blood was Cullis's or his own.

Then there was a thunder of knocking on the ship-
wrecked coachwork beside his ear, and a voice said,
rather foolishly:

"Are you all right in there?"

"Can't see how anyone can be alive in this mess,"

said another voice. "They must have been doing over fifty."

But the Saint had recognized the first voice, and a husky croak of a chuckle came from his lips.

"Dear old Claud Eustace," he said. "Always ten minutes too late!"

CHAPTER XIV

HOW SIMON TEMPLAR PUT ON HIS HAT

CHIEF INSPECTOR TEAL reverently unwrapped his fourth wafer of gum. Simon Templar had bought it specially for him, and Teal was doing himself proud.

"Though why you aren't dead," said Mr. Teal, "is more than anyone will ever know."

The Saint, with a bandaged head and nothing more, grinned cheerfully.

"You can't keep a good man down," he said.

"It was sheer luck you didn't get me down," said Teal. "And that would have been a good man lost to the C. I. D., though I says it myself. I shall never be able to make out why none of us was hurt. It may have been because we'd almost stopped when you hit us; but our car was spun round broadside to the road —off-side front wheel knocked off as if it had been cut with a knife, chassis tied in a knot, both axles bust, gear box all over the road, and a worse shaking for all of us than any of us want to have again."

"Will you be sending in the bill?" drawled the Saint.

They were at Upper Berkeley Mews, where they had repaired for a very late supper, but it was more like breakfast than anything else.

Then the story of Lord Essenden was told, and also the story of Waldstein, and the chief commissioner's verdict was given. He looked at the girl and smiled.

"I believe you," he said. "There's the Saint to back you up in the story of Essenden, and now that I know you a little better I'm not sure that I should question it even without that. As for the rest, outside of our four selves there is no one left alive who knows anything worth knowing. And I don't think any of us will ask for trouble. We've had enough of the Angels of Doom."

He looked across at Teal for confirmation, and Chief Inspector Teal nodded drowsily. He seemed to be on the point of falling asleep.

"And the 'Wanted for Murder' business?" asked the Saint.

"That can be forgotten. Fresh evidence has come to light, and the charge has been withdrawn. That can be arranged without any fuss. And if Miss Trelawney is going back to the States——"

"I want," said Chief Inspector Teal, with a sudden and startling loudness, "to wash my hands."

Three pairs of eyes revolved slowly in their sockets and centred on him with an intentness that would have shattered the nerve of a lesser man, but Chief Inspector Teal suffered his blushing honours without visible emotion.

And then the Saint laughed.

"But of course," he said. "There's a barrel of very good beer in the kitchen—you might try that. Duodecimo's out there blowing himself tight with Chianti, but Orace will move him on if you say the word. . . . Will you want any soap?"

"I think," said Sir Hamilton Dorn mildly, "that we shall be able to find what we want."

The Saint watched the door close behind them; and then he loafed back to the fireplace, lighted a cigarette, and stood there with his hands in his pockets.

"Only the epilogue is left," he said.

"And a joke to explain," said Jill Trelawney.

Simon regarded her with his cigarette in one corner of a smiling mouth and his eyebrows aslant—rather like a blue-eyed and boyish Mephistopheles. Suddenly she understood all his charm.

"Most of it's explained," he said. "I was pulled into the Secret Service to keep me good, but the job never meant as much to me as it might have once. And then, when I was on the very point of quitting, your father's case developed into the Angels of Doom. I remember the night when I was talking it over with Auntie Ethel, and I was shown a photograph of you. And I made myself a promise."

She stood up and came towards the fireplace.

"What was it?"

"That you were a girl I was going to kiss before I died. And I did it halfway through the story, which spoils the ending; but even now——"

And suddenly, with his quick light laugh, he swept her into his arms and captured her red lips.

In a little while she said: "Are you sure you haven't made a mistake?"

"No," said the Saint, "I've made a friend."

His arm lay lightly round her shoulders.

"I'm the fool who never grows old," he said. "But the manner of folly changes. Yesterday it was battle, murder, and sudden death; to-morrow—who knows? But while there's a boy you love waiting for you, and a song and a story for me—who cares? . . ."

One moment he held her eyes, and then he swung round and picked up a newspaper that lay on a side table. One swift glance down the page, and he was looking at the clock.

"The *Aquitania* sails in seven hours," he said. "I can get you to Southampton with hours to spare; and then I can work a pull with the company. I'll guarantee you a berth——"

He read his answer in her face, and flung open the door.

"Orace!" he shouted, and his man came running. "Some sandwiches—a flask—coffee in the thermos. At the double! Is the Hirondel full up?"

"Yessir."

"Good enough."

He went through into the garage, and in another moment the mighty car was roaring round to pull up snorting at the front door. . . . And the Saint returned, as Mr. Teal, roused by the commotion, emerged from the back of the hall.

"Going away?" asked Teal.

"Just for a drive. . . . Jill, you'd better have a leather coat—take this one. . . . That's the idea. . . . I'll take those things, Orace."

He saw the girl into the car, and came back to fetch another coat from the stand. Teal buttonholed him.

"Is this an elopement, Saint?"

"Now that's just what it isn't, Claud. . . . No, the Old Pentonvillains choker, Orace. . . . Anything I can do for you on the way, Claud Eustace?"

"If it *is* an elopement," said Teal lusciously, "you fixed it up quick enough."

Simon twisted the scarf round his neck and canted his most piratical hat at its most piratical angle over his right eye. And then he tapped the detective gently on the shoulder.

"Has it never occurred to you," he said, "that one day a story might be written in which the heroine didn't fall in love with the hero, and the hero didn't fall in love with the heroine—and they were both perfectly happy in spite of that? Because this is that story. I am the most superlative story-book hero that ever lived, but the rules were not made for me."

And he took down Teal's bowler from the rack, and clapped it rakishly on the detective's head, and pulled Teal's ear, and punched him in the stomach, and was gone; and an echo of Saintly laughter seemed still to hang in the little hall long after the clamour of the Hirondel had died away.

THE END